SOOT

Mickey Getty

Aperture Press

Paperback ISBN: 978-0-9910962-7-5
Library of Congress Control Number: 2014950025

This is a work of historical fiction. Some names, characters, places, and incidents have been used with artistic license; others are a product of the author's imagination and any resemblance to actual persons, living or dead, business establishments, events, or locales is entirely coincidental.

First edition, 2014.

Book designed by Stephen Wagner.
Cover photos by Lewis Hine. Courtesy of the United States Library of Congress, Prints & Photographs Division, National Child Labor Committee Collection.

To all the Bridies, past and present,
who struggle to gain their full and deep freedom
to become truly themselves.

Author's Note

When my family and I moved from South Florida to Southeastern Pennsylvania, I was intrigued with the rich anthracite history of the area. Visiting at Eckley Miners' Village, a restored 1845 mine patch town in Weatherly, PA, I learned about mining, the tools used, and what a Davy lamp looked like. I saw drawings that showed the intricate underground network of gangways and cross headings. Photographs of coal mines fueled my imagination.

One wall in the museum was devoted to women who lived in the mine patch town. She washed clothes on Monday, ironed on Tuesday, baked on Wednesday. Just wait one minute! There has to be more to these women who lived in abject poverty than this. What was her life like? What were her struggles? How did she feel about her life? Did she live in fear of a mine collapse burying the men in her life?

Bridie was born in my heart.

Soot is first and foremost a work of fiction, and it has been great fun to piggyback onto historical drama that took place more than one hundred years ago. Franklin Gowen was president of the Reading Railroad and owner of several coal mines. The question about whether his death was murder (many wanted revenge) or suicide had many tongues wagging. The way I have imagined him and his death is purely fiction.

Though Bridie and her family are fictional, they accurately portray life in a mine patch town. You wouldn't find Pottsville Number Six mine and town on any map.

All the folks who resided in *Soot's* version of the actual Wiggans Patch (the O'Donnells, the Carrolls, McAllisters, the borders, and the Pinkertons) and the massacre itself instigated by Gowen according to some are historical. Though Bridie wasn't really related to any of them.

The depiction of the events of Black Thursday in *Soot* really happened in Pottsville in June of 1877, with Sheriff J. Frank Werner and Father Daniel McDermott in attendance. Molly Maguires sought to change unfair and unsafe mining practices. Irish descendants still talk about the hangings on Black Thursday. People did climb onto roofs to watch so I put Bridie and her friends there so I could tell the story through their eyes. One source mentioned that the governor's secretary, Chester F. Farr, attended the Pottsville hangings with the message for the sheriff.

Minstrel Barney Kelly really existed. He did write and sing about the very real Locustdale mine tragedy but may not have done so in Wiggans Patch. Ed Foley, the wandering minstrel in the Saturday Night chapter, did have a hearty appetite for food and drink. The epigraphs and minstrel songs that begin many chapters date back more than one hundred years.

The Wormley Hotel in Washington, D.C. was run by James Thomas Wormley who was the first graduate from Howard University and received the Doctor of Pharmacy degree from the medical department. His father, James Wormley, a former slave, founded the Wormley Hotel that was famous for its turtle soup and Chesapeake Bay seafood.

Acknowledgments

Soot would not have been written in the same way if it weren't for fellow writers, friends, and neighbors. I would like to thank those who offered encouragement, support, feedback, multiple readings, suggestions, and listening. For Becky Masterman, Donna Searle McLay, Elizabeth Kann, Frank Mulligan, Clem Page, Marilyn Klimcho, Patrick Klimcho, Doug Arnold, Sue Lang, Liz Clark, Monica Yeager, Marcia Bell, Wayne Bell, the folks in the Pennsylvania Writing Project of West Chester University's writers group, and others inadvertently not mentioned, I am sincerely grateful for their opinions, patience, guidance, and honesty.

I am grateful for all those who wrote personal coal mining stories sharing their knowledge and lives and those of their parents and grand parents. They informed me and inspired me.

Many thanks to Loretta Murphy, singer, writer, performer and to Craig Czury, Berks County Poet Laureate for granting me permission to use their contemporary words as epigraphs. A big thank you goes to Deb Deysher, graphic artist, who designed my beautiful website.

For a space to imagine and write, I am whole-heartedly grateful for the GoggleWorks Center for the Arts and all its supporters.

I send sincere thanks to Aperture Press, an independent book publisher, and to Sharon Wells Wagner and Stephen Wagner, who have made *Soot* a reality. Thank you, Steve, for editing and especially for discovering the photograph that has become *Soot's* cover. It is Bridie to be sure.

Book One

1875 – 1880

ONE

She Ought
To Be Married

Oh, father dear I ofttimes hear you speak of Erin's Isle
Her lofty scenes, her valleys green, her mountain rude and wild
They say it is a princely place wherein the king might dwell
So why did you abandon it? The reason to me tell
Oh son, I loved my native land with energy and pride
Until a blight came on the crops, the sheep and cattle died
The rent and taxes were to pay I could not them redeem
And that's the cruel reason why I left old Skibbereen.

– Irish ballad "Skibbereen"

November 18, 1875
Bridie

Thursday, a rainy mending day, the kitchen table is piled with overalls, socks, underwear. I wash clothes for the bosses' wives on Monday. Iron on Tuesday, bake on Wednesday like my Mam taught me. Today I mend what needs mending. This is my job now, to earn money, whilst my father works in the Pottsville Coal Company mine all day. Da I call him. He's Danny to his butties, Mac or McAllister to the bosses. I'm, just Bridie.

'Tis just the two of us now that my Mam is dead. I grieve for her with every push and pull of the needle and thread but I can't think about her. I can't breathe when I do. Sympathy pains, says Mam Mary. Pains for my mother dead of the consumption. Too poor to go to hospital. She was killed. Murdered, not by a gun, not by any Molly Maguire assassin, but, like Da says, by those what own this mine and keep us beggars. Frank Gowen is his name, the owner, and I hate him.

My handkerchief is in my pocket but it is my doll that reminds me not to cry. Dolly, Mam made her for me out of rags, sits on the table with the mending. Black stitches sewn into sunshine yellow for her eyes, a patchwork of colors make her body so she doesn't need a dress. She looks at home on the pile of mending.

"You have your grandmother's special way of knowing, Bridie," Mam told me when she was sick, words coughed out, stuck between gasps for breath. "Dolly will remind you of that. She'll help you to be strong, to use your courage. Every time you're afraid, hold on to Dolly and remember how much I love you, Bridie girl."

I save my mending money, like Mam saved hers, tucked it away for me, she did. With every jab of the needle into my finger I remind myself that I, Bridie McAllister, nine years old, will leave this mine patch town and take my Da with me. That's what my Mam wanted for me. Da too. He says I could be a teacher like he was back in Ireland. That's why he makes me study every day. I'm good at sums but I hate spelling.

A big city, that's what I dream about, Dolly. A place where soot doesn't stain everything. Buildings so tall Mam said I'd get dizzy looking up at them. Pipe dreams, Da says. Only a miracle would get ye that dream, he says.

A real bed, too, under a roof that doesn't leak, in a room that is warm in winter. Outside there are streets that are swept every day. Streets I'll stroll alone with new shoes on my feet and not get muddy. And a bonnet on my head. I'll laugh and feel free and talk proper English. I'll take you with me, Dolly. We'll have coins to buy the bread and goods Mam said are stuffed into carts pulled by horses clip clopping on cobblestones just like in the magazines Mam loved to read. Hear that Dolly? Clip-clop, clip-clop of hooves... I jump up to see what's making the sound.

The mules snort as they stop in front of my house, the wagon wheels crunching on the dirt road. I race out of the house when I hear my Da's agonizing cries. Men shout about how to lift his body.

A wild gust of wind flings my hair into my face as an outburst of wet rains down, chilling me right to my gut. The rain has made dirty streaks that run along Da's gray face and around his bluish-white lips. His head is flopped back like a drenched rag. I think he's dead. Then I hear the last thing I will ever hear from him: a scream. I can't breathe. My chest is closed up and my feet won't move. I have lost him. I sink into a puddle.

"Aargh," my Da yells again, panting.

He's still alive. I would be glad to hear his voice again but for the agony in it. I get to my feet and go to him.

"Sweet Jaeesus." He sucks his breath in. "Don't let 'em... anyone cut me leg off, Bridie," he begs. "Sweet Jaeesus..."

Da's butty, Kelley, shoots me a look and shakes his head. "Dan, Dan. Here, drink this down." Kelley puts a bottle of whiskey to Da's lips. Da drinks, chokes, drinks more.

Four men hoist him from the wagon, Murphy and Gallagher on one side, Kelley and Quinn on the other, the rain pounding all of us. They are black with wet, muddy coal dust. The blood-soaked shirts wrapped around my Da's leg splat to the road. His leg is chewed up, great chunks of his upper leg torn off. The lower part is flattened, the flesh ground to pulp, looking more like a dead animal attacked by wild dogs than a leg. His foot, gone entirely. White bone sticks through like when my friend Maeve broke her arm when she fell out of the tree. She died of infection.

Murphy looks like he's holding back tears. Gallagher looks at me then looks away and then at John. They say nothing as they side step toward the door.

"Oh my God," I yell. I shut my mouth and clap my hands over it. "Oh God, he can't die." I yell through my hands.

Kelley tells me Da's leg got crushed by a roof fall while removing pillars in the mine. I know that's a job more dangerous than working with explosives. When the pillars come down, the roof's sure to follow, Da told me.

The men get him on the table in the kitchen, on top of the clothes. Dolly!

You'll get blood on all those clean clothes that don't belong to me, I think. My Dolly! My Da's gonna die. I don't want him to die. I don't give a damn about the clothes, the damn clothes. Still, I pull them out of the way. Dolly's not there.

"The only reason he didn't bleed to death, Bridie, was his leg was crushed flat. 'Tis gonna have to come off. Sean has gone to fetch the company doctor," says Kelley.

People rush all around me. Everything whirling. Kids crying. Voices saying something, somewhere. All I see is Da. I don't feel anything or see anything else but Da.

"No! No doctor," screams Da. "He'll cut me leg off without giving a second t'ought."

Then, Da is like he's sleeping, but he's not. Mary O'Tool is wrapping Da's leg with the clean clothes, me helping her wrap real tight, drenching everything in vinegar. My father waking, screaming with the pain of it, going out again. I fetch more vinegar and my Mam's medicine bag even though I see Miss Mary brought her own.

The men feed Da whiskey and hold him down when he wakes. Other women come; everyone's talking.

"Get more water."

"Poor girl, she's all alone now. Her Ma died a few weeks ago."

"He knew that roof weren't safe."

"More whiskey."

"Bridie?"

I don't know who's saying my name.

"He reported that roof, Mac did. Said timbers won't hold it."

"Get the children out of here."

"Don't use that vinegar."

"Bridie, it's me, Uncle James. Come here child."

"She's eleven, oughta be married."

"Stop giving him so much whiskey."

"She's not eleven yet, is she?"

"Uncle James?" I finally recognize him, James Carroll. He was here just a few weeks ago, after Mam died. "Uncle James, help my Da. He doesn't want his leg cut off."

"Here's the doctor!"

Dr. Rowbotham is mean looking, like we took him away from something important. He opens his bag, hardly looking at Da, puts his doctoring tools on the chair alongside the table—a chair Da made himself. I remember Da doing that, making the chair, because the doctor has saws and other things that look like my Da's tools for cutting and working with wood.

"He doesn't want his leg cut off," I cry, looking at the saws and thinking how bad it will hurt my Da.

He looks at me with great scorn, the doctor. "If we don't take the leg off, he'll die. Is that what you want?"

Uncle James pulls me close. "Isn't there anything you can do to save it?" he asks.

I have to tell them. It's my job to tell them what Da said. Ma's not here to do it. "You're just taking it off 'cause you don't want to be bothered with anything else. He needs his leg to work. He doesn't want to be a man with one leg," I scream between gulps and sobs. I tell the doctor this even though I know by the looks of the leg there is nothing else to be done. But I have to tell him what my Da said. I have to. He told me not to let them take his leg.

The doctor isn't listening. He arranges the tools. I hear one of the women from the patch talking to me in a soft voice, telling me to leave my Da to the doctor. Go into the other room.

"Take him to the new miners' hospital. Please, please take him there," I scream. "They can save his leg." I knock the saws off the chair, tug on the doctor trying to get him away from my Da. "Don't touch him," I scream hanging onto the table and Da's one good foot.

"Back, back," he says, as if he were talking to a mad dog. "They don't save legs there. No sense bringing him to the hospital; he'd be dead before he got there." He takes his jacket off, rolls up his sleeves.

Uncle James says, "C'mere, Bridie. Let the doctor do his work." Hands on my shoulders force me away. My Da opens his eyes, for an instant, and looks at me. I can tell he doesn't see me. They roll up in the back of his head, making his eyes look all white.

I look at Uncle James. He's betrayed me, betrayed Da.

Miss Mary startles me when she touches my face. I suck in my breath. "Thanks be to God you're here. Da'll be all right with you here." She gives me that look, too. It'll be all right, Lass, her eyes say. I love Miss Mary, like I love my Mam.

Mary O'Tool, my Mam Mary, she's an old woman, a healer like

my Mam was. She begins helping the doctor.

They put a cloth over Da's face and Miss Mary shakes some terrible-smelling medicine on it. The men hold my Da down, him screaming.

"This will put him to sleep. Now, go on with ye, Bridie love," says Miss Mary. The other woman tries to pull me out of the room.

I pray to my dead mother to help me remember what to do. "More vinegar on those bandages, Miss Mary," I cry. "Be sure to give him willow bark for fever," I scream. I'm pulled away, away from my Da, and I know I will never see him again. "Bitter yellow root for infection, please, please. That will save his leg. Mugwort too, and lovage."

Dolly! I see her on the floor, the doctor's foot on her arm.

~

Dolly has a new dress. Mam Mary rescued her. She helped me wash Dolly but we couldn't get her clean. But I still love her. I sewed her arm back on and made her an apron. She reminds me that my Mam thought I was special. She is all I have now.

I tuck her in my apron pocket because Uncle James is outside getting the mules ready. He is taking me to Wiggans Patch to live with some relatives. I've been there once for a baptism, another time for a wedding. I don't remember any of the aunts and uncles, or cousins either, but I don't care. I hardly know Uncle James even though he comes here to Pottsville town lots of times. He has meetings with the pub owner, Dan McMonagle. Uncle James owns a saloon in Tamaqua, Carroll's Saloon, so they talk business, Da said. What kind of business, I used to wonder. When he and Da talked sometimes, I'd hear their hushed voices complain about wages, bad air in the mines, and say words like revenge and bashing faces. But I don't care any more. I get put on the wagon and I feel like I'm no more than another sack to be sent to Wiggans Patch.

I don't say anything to him, Uncle James. He says something to me. I loved your Da, too, he tells me. That makes me like him. He's taller than Da, but talks like him and makes the same kind of smile Da did when he looked at me. We have the same color hair, Uncle James, Da and me—not really red, not really brown. Mine's all tangled. Mam Mary was after me to brush it, but I don't feel like it.

Mam Mary gives me a tight hug. "You'll be all right, my girl. You will. Both your Ma's and Da's people are there." I can't imagine ever being all right. She nods to Uncle James to start. I hadn't noticed him climb up onto the seat beside me.

"Was it Frank Gowen's mine?" I ask. "The one Da was taking down the pillars in?"

"'Twas. Why do you ask, child?"

"He killed my Da, then, and my Mam. I'll kill him if I ever see him."

These scenes played out in Bridie's mind almost daily. Sometimes in daydreams, but mostly in nightmares that ended in her screams.

TWO

Wiggans Patch

Forget not the O'Donnells, keep them close in your memory
For bigotry lives where reigns supremacy
Civil liberties lost, if we forget the cost
Of the price paid for freedom and democracy

> – *From "The Ballad of the O'Donnell House"*
> *by Loretta Murphy*

December 10, 1875

The singing made Bridie raw with grief. Her belly ached. Images of her Da's bloody leg and of her Mam spewing blood with every cough flashed before her eyes. At the same time something about the music and dancing made her remember her Da and Mam laughing and singing.

Any excuse to sing and drink was a good one, her father had always said, himself a fiddle player with a rich tenor voice. Daniel McAllister could belt out a song with gusto and Irish wit and would have at this party for the Widow O'Donnell, if he had not died.

"'The Start That Casey Got!' Sing that one," someone shouted.

"Yeah," yelled another. Barney Kelly picked up his fiddle and step-danced around the bar. The minstrel sang.

> "Sure Mike Casey got a job in a powder mill
> At a dollar and ten a day.
> And says he, 'By gob, dat's a very good job
> And the work is only play.'"

"Okay, Casey. You'll find out about play," jeered a man who laughed too loud. Everyone cheered, "Here's to Casey." The louder the singing the more people came into the saloon.

> "But he could not read,
> So he could not heed,
> The sign above the door,
> That smokin' on those premises
> is not allowed on any floor."

One fella with a pipe jigged in imitation of Casey. "Go on, with ye, Paddy," cheered the other revelers.

> "And if he had left his pipe at home,
> He'd have had his ould job still;
> But he walked right into the powder mill
> Smokin' his Henry Clay,
> An explosion occurred
> That was plainly heard
> One hundred miles away."

Even if Bridie couldn't get into the party spirit, happy faces were better than the keening of Da's funeral. The Wiggans Patch folks gathered in Carroll's Pub belted out the chorus:

"And he went away up far above the town,
But he didn't come down,
No he didn't come down,
No he didn't come down,
For men that travel like Casey did
Are seldom found,
Walkin' around."

Barney Kelly sang with a fair voice, though not as good as Da's. Uncle James Carroll, whose relatives lived in the house attached to the Widow O'Donnell's, paid the popular minstrel to come to Wiggans Patch, but beer and whiskey would have satisfied Kelly, who often sang at Carroll's saloon in Tamaqua. The same Uncle James, who at Mary O'Tool's urging brought Bridie to Wiggans Patch. "'Twill be better for her to get away from the bad memories," she'd said.

Fiddles ringing out the celebration of Widow's birthday provoked wild dancing and drinking. When Barney stepped up to Margaret O'Donnell, the dancing stopped. Said he, "You all heard about what happened at the Locust Dale mine but you ain't heard this song before 'cause I just thunk it up 'specially for your birthday, Ma'am." Barney belted down a shot, licked his finger, and placed it on his fiddle, hissing the sound of hot steam.

Applause nearly drowned out the singer as he began. "Sing it for us, Barney!"

"A new song!"

"Sing it out, lad!"

Glasses rose to cheer him on. Hoots and hollers and whistles gradually quieted. Bridie closed her eyes and imagined her Da singing.

"And if you will pay attention
To my sad and mournful tale,
Of the accident that happened
In the mines of Locust Dale.

"It was the eighteenth of November
In the year of seventy five
Four honest sons of labor
That day did lose their lives."

The minstrel's words faded in the upwelling of Bridie's anguish. November eighteenth, thought Bridie, the very day my Da died, a month ago. Bridie's eyes filled with tears at the thought of her father. Grief mingled with the image of his suffering and relief that the suffering ended.

"Daniel McAllister, a good man," folks had said. "God rest his soul." She hated the words that ran through her mind without invitation. People attached that saying to him, as if it were as much a part of him as the black stains under his fingernails. But she knew her father wouldn't rest knowing she was alone now, with no one but the people here in Wiggans Patch, who were family in some mysterious, tangled, Irish way. Who was uncle to whom back in the West of Ireland—or aunt, or cousin for that matter—she couldn't sort it out. But they had sent for her. It was Uncle James who arranged it, his wife being the Widow's niece, the Widow's daughter being married to a McAllister. Bridie had nowhere else to go.

Of her mother they'd said, "A hard working woman, she was. She has earned her rest." Bridie didn't understand that any better than she understood the ties that bound her to these people who were kind to her.

If God could do that, rest souls like her Da and Mam, why didn't he just fix it so they didn't die? "He took them to be in heaven with Him," people said to her. What a mean God he is, she thought. He should take me, too!

A laughing voice approached her, "Bridie, if you're not going to dance, come take this baby so I can," called her cousin, Ellen McAllister, Widow Margaret's daughter, who lived with her mother, her husband Charles and their baby, and four boarders—the household that scrunched closer to make room for one more: Bridie.

Maura Carroll danced past, shouting, "Bridie, Ellen, come join the fun. Let the grandmothers take the baby."

In the short time she'd been there, it was Ellen who found a way through Bridie's grief... Ellen and her baby—the way the boy smiled at her, grasped her finger as if wanting to hold her close.

Happy at the thought of holding the infant, Bridie said, "I'll bring him home and put him to bed for you, Ellen."

"His belly is full." Ellen patted her breast. "He's almost asleep now, Bridie. Put him in his cradle and rub his back. Sure'n he'll be dreaming of angels soon enough."

Bridie took the boy, glad to have something to do. She'd put the child to sleep before, when Ellen and Margaret had gone to church for a weekly evening novena. Usually, she'd wake in the morning, having fallen asleep on the floor beside him.

"Get him settled, then come back to the dancing, Bridie," said Ellen. "It's good for you to get to know the young people."

Bridie carried the infant up the stairs to the corner room at the back of the house. It was so dark she nearly tripped over Tom Murphy, one of the boarders. He slept on the floor, snoring off the beer he'd consumed. Tom, a good-looking man, much older than herself, had studied to become a miner. She thought of him when she overheard the women talking about finding her a husband. She's only ten, Ellen had said, but Margaret said 'twould soon be time.

Bridie sang the infant to sleep, then curled up on a mat and, despite the noise, escaped into sleep.

In the deep of the night, as all in the household slept, Bridie awakened to a loud bang that reverberated through the house— the front door slammed into the wall. Shouts and screams from downstairs followed. Loud footfalls from booted feet pounded through the downstairs rooms. Confused, she saw Ellen sit up in her bed and Charles hop into his britches. From downstairs, she heard Margaret cry out as if in pain.

"Where are they? The assassins," a gruff voice shouted, "We know the murderers of Uren and Sanger are here."

"Stay," Charles McAllister ordered his wife as he crept down the stairs.

Bridie grabbed the baby. She huddled in the dark windowless corner behind the cradle while Ellen listened at the top of the stairs. Tom still slept along the wall near the door.

Ellen kicked him. "Get up! Vigilantes! Get your gun." Tom raised his head. With unseeing eyes he looked around before his head flopped to the floor. She started down the stairs.

"Ellen! No! Stay here," Bridie whispered. But Ellen disappeared into the stairwell.

"We're here to bring justice to the murdering Mollies. Show yourselves."

A shot rang out and Bridie heard what she knew was Ellen's body tumbling down the stairs. She pressed herself deeper into the corner, swaying slightly through her own trembling to rock the wide-eyed baby. Don't cry, don't cry, she willed the boy.

Scuffling shoes, thudding on the wooden floor below, announced the arrival of more men through the front door. They stomped up the stairs. Loud, unfamiliar voices shouted. "Where are the murderers?"

"Here's one. James is his name. Hey! Look here," a man hollered to the other intruders. "Found James O'Donnell. You murdering bastard."

Moans and cries arose again from Margaret. "They're your sons, woman. Where are they," a man's voice demanded. A whimper, like the mewing of a cat, answered.

Bridie heard James's protest cut short by a blow that made him vomit. She wanted to shout out, "He's no Molly. He's a paying guest." But she knew there *were* Molly Maguires who lived in Wiggans Patch, too, right here in this house—her own kin. She could say nothing to help James Blair without endangering the baby and her two O'Donnell cousins, James and Charles. Where are they anyway? She wondered. Dead? Hiding?

"The noose! We'll hang him in his own house." After the sounds of brutal grunts and growls and thumps of fighting, the men dragged a silent Blair down the stairs.

She heard Aunt Margaret crying again, and then moaning between what sounded like a beating. "It's your sons we're after, woman. Where's the other one," shouted a husky voice that Bridie recognized as not coming from an Irishman.

A large bull of a man, armed, entered the room where Bridie hid, followed by three others, all with guns. They wore handkerchief masks and long oilskin coats. Bridie tried to make herself even smaller. She held the infant too tight so that he whimpered. She put her lips on the infant's cheek and breathed warm, comforting breaths. If it were not for Tom, they would surely have seen her. One of the vigilantes snatched Tom up and dragged him downstairs. "Here's another of them. Found him hiding upstairs like the coward he is."

She heard several men in the next room with Purcell, another boarder.

"Here. Rope. Tie him to the bedpost till we get finished with the two downstairs." They left the room. "Violence for violence, that's what I say," said one.

"Fighting fire with fire," said another. "We'll get the whole lot of them Molly Maguires, we will."

"Pinkertons," someone shouted.

They sound like Pinkertons, thought Bridie; though she'd only heard talk about them being hired by Frank Gowen to spy on the miners, she'd never spoken to one. Now it was quiet upstairs except for Purcell struggling to get loose. Bridie stayed still for a few minutes.

She could hear the men trying to get the noose around James Blair's neck. She didn't hear Margaret cry out again. Slowly she rose, thinking to free Purcell, when she heard a commotion in the backyard. Carefully avoiding the floor plank she knew creaked, she looked out the window, still holding the now sleeping infant. The moon was bright, which didn't help the two fleeing figures she recognized as her cousin James O'Donnell and James McAllister, Ellen's husband's brother. Closer to the house she saw a group huddled around a body being kicked and stomped on. A gunshot made the men step back. Bridie saw the man being kicked was her cousin Charles O'Donnell. A masked man in a long coat stood over him and fired his gun at Charles's head. He fired again, and again. She counted. Fifteen shots into his head. She could no longer see the two fleeing men.

Then it was over. The vigilantes left.

After a long time, Bridie put the baby into the cradle and untied Purcell. On the stairs, babe in arms again, she found Ellen dead and bloodied. The infant in Bridie's arms stirred, then wailed as if he knew he had lost his mother. Creeping into the kitchen warily, expecting a hard hand to grab her, she discovered Margaret in a heap on the floor, deathly still. Out back, Charles lay in a pool of blood, nothing left of his face, recognizable only by his boots.

Where did Purcell go? And Ellen's husband? Bridie wandered through the house in a daze, looking for them. She found James Blair lying on the floor beneath the noose dangling from the rafters. He was sobbing like a baby. She couldn't tease apart the ropes that bound his hands and feet. Bridie went back into the kitchen for a knife. Margaret moaned and tried to sit up, her eyes swollen and discolored, lower lip fat, the front of her dress bright red with blood. Thank God! She's alive.

THREE

Rescue

*Just think, James McKenna, the detective, has gained himself a
     name,
And in the detective agency has risen to great fame.
He said he came amongst our people in November 'seventy three
Which leaves many's the wife and babe to mourn and curse his
     memory.
He came amongst our people in a very quiet time
He was the foremost plotter of that atrocious crime.
He should be tried for murder, condemned he ought to be,
And along with his poor victims, die on the gallows tree.
That's not half of what he done as unto you I'll tell,
He plotted other murders and that you know full well.
Himself and Jimmy Kerrigan says they done it up in style,
While in Mauch Chunk they swore away the lives
of Campbell, Kelly and Doyle.*

– Irish song "Hugh McGeehan"

June 1877

A rough and tumble girl, haunted by too many ghosts for one so young, Bridie, even at thirteen, was small for her age, but always ready to take on any boy who looked for a fight. Scrawny, scruffy, and scrappy, she fit in with the boys more than the girls in the patch.

Soon after the massacre, James Carroll had brought her back to Pottsville to live with Mary O'Tool. The horrors of Wiggans Patch had left the child unable to speak or eat. Though she'd been mute by day, night time brought screams of terror. Mary became mother to Bridie. "A strange one you are," Mary had said. "Still a child in many ways with grown up burdens and resentments. You have the gift, Bridie, the healing touch, just like your Mam. Don't destroy it by hating Frank Gowen."

But back in Pottsville, with Wiggans Patch behind her, night terrors were rare these days.

The Tuesday morning before the hanging, Bridie went to the rectory at St. Patrick's Church where Father Daniel McDermott always had several chores for which he gave her a few coins from the poor box, if there were any, or from his pocket, and a blessing with holy water to drive away demons. Daniel, the same name as her father's. Sometimes he would forget the money, but Bridie always reminded him.

Bridie loved to walk into the center of Pottsville even in winter, except when the winds were strong. It was about a mile from the small company house where she and Mary lived. After her work at the rectory was done, she took home whatever newspapers the good Father remembered to save for her. Sometimes *The New York Times*, sometimes the *Philadelphia Inquirer*, but more often the *Pottsville Evening Chronicle*. Even the *Miner's Journal*, which surprised her, because the only time the Reverend Father went near the dirty mine was when there was an accident and miners were trapped or killed. She asked him once how he got his fingernails so clean. Her father's were black from the mines, no matter how much her mother had scrubbed them. Father McDermott said he had to keep his hands clean because he touched the Holy Eucharist every morning. Bridie was glad she wasn't a priest because her fingernails were always dirty.

She loved to read the papers, to see the pictures and illustrations, to read the stories and opinions. Bridie had an avid curiosity about the Molly Maguires. Oftentimes there were missing pages or rectangular holes where something interesting used to be. Father McDermott explained there were articles and advertisements not suitable for a young girl, that if she read them she would get ideas and have to go to confession. When Bridie brought great armloads of papers home her Mam Mary was delighted, too. The two plunged into them after supper. Mary explained things Bridie didn't understand. Bridie reported what she had overheard at the rectory, and at the sheriff's where she worked on Wednesdays.

The *Ladies' Home Journal* that Bridie brought home from the Werner house illustrated the latest fashion and home furnishings; both inspired wonder and envy. Sheriff Werner's wife paid Bridie to scrub the floors, and sometimes the privy, which she hated because of the stink, but it was a lot cleaner at its dirtiest than the privy her family had shared with half the patch. Mrs. Werner gave Bridie the magazines reluctantly, saying that she shouldn't let the pictures fill her head with fancy notions. It wasn't possible for an Irish girl to emulate the style and sophistication the magazines depicted, but she could benefit from the articles on cleanliness and hygiene. Bridie had to ask Mam Mary what some of those words meant.

Those days in June, before she became a woman while still feeling like a boy, were way too busy with the excitement of the coming Molly Maguire hangings for anyone to censor what she read. One of the men to be hanged was dear to her—James Carroll. The papers were full of news about the hangings, as were the two households she visited each week.

All the boarding houses were filled up, as was the hotel, so the Werner house had to be extra clean. Bridie worked extra days for the Werners, who had friends and relatives coming by train for the hanging. Two of these guests, being important people, which generally meant rich, had invitations to the hangings. Invitations—as if it were a fancy dress ball!

By train! It astounded Bridie that folks would come by train to see a hanging, like they were going to the theater to see some famous person on stage. She'd read that poor Thomas Munley's father, with no money for trains, would have to walk all night from Girardville to Pottsville to say his final goodbye to his son. It just didn't seem fair, she thought as she washed dinner plates. Well, there's a big surprise in store for those important people, thought Bridie. There'll be no hanging.

Each day that week, Bridie saw more and more armed policemen who both frightened her and piqued her curiosity. Soldiers, too. They paraded around Pottsville, showing citizens that law breakers, or anyone else who would attempt to free the prisoners, were no match for those who sought justice. Six Molly Maguires would be hanged for murder in Pottsville and no one could stop it, though all sorts of rumors about the bands of Mollies that would descend on Pottsville flew about like news pamphlets in the wind.

Bridie was hoping to see a Molly. She pictured a brawny, wild Irishman with long hair, sort of like a Viking, even though she remembered that her uncle James Carroll and her O'Donnell cousins didn't look like that—especially her last sight of Charles with his face blown away.

On her way to Werners' the day before the hanging, someone came up behind Bridie and shoved her so hard she almost fell over. Brian Dolan, her friend and the best fighter in the patch, two heads taller, with holes in his too-short pants, gave her another shove. "Wanna watch the hangings with me and the lads on Thursday?"

"I'm supposed to help the Werners with meals that day. They're having a big dinner. There won't be a hanging, Brian. You know that."

A soldier strode by, body erect in a stiff military manner, carrying a rifle with a bayonet glinting in the sunlight. Brian completely forgot about Bridie.

"Hey!" he said to the soldier. "Ever killed a man with that thing?"

"Stand at attention, son," the man with the bayonet commanded. "Why are you here? Boys your age are supposed to be working. You causing trouble?"

"N-n-no, no sir. No. N-n-no trouble." Brian stood tall, shoulders back. "No w-work today. Just walking me friend here to work, to the *sheriff's* house, to keep her safe, lest there be any Mollies about shooting up the place, sir. Come on, Bridie, you're too slow." He grabbed Bridie's arm and pulled her along. "She's late to the sheriff's wife. Sheriff J. Frank Werner," he said, as if the man was a personal friend. The soldier waved them on with a warning to stay off the streets. There could be troubles today.

"Why aren't you at work, Brian?" Bridie asked when they were far enough away from the soldier.

"Ah, we're taking off, some of us boys who don't like the idea of hanging innocent Irish for the fun of it."

"The good Father said that those who don't show up for work this week would lose their jobs. Brian. 'Tis your poor mother who will suffer if you and Tommy don't bring home wages. Did you think of that?" Outside of boarders' rent, fourteen-year-old Brian and his younger brother supported the family of seven since their father's death in a mine explosion a year ago.

"There's lots of men not going to work. They can't fire us all."

"With lots of men not going to the mine, there's sure to be a rescue, Brian."

The noise coming from the jailhouse grounds silenced them as they walked past the wall that enclosed the yard. The pounding of hammers and sawing of wood, the sounds of constructing the gallows, were enough to stop a number of passers-by and to draw curiosity seekers.

"I hear they are going to hang all six of them at the same time," said a man who wore a black bowler hat, a shirt with a stiff white collar, and clean shoes.

"A gallows for six is what I hear," answered another, just as finely dressed, leaning on a cane. "Saw sketches in the paper. First one of its kind, I hear."

"Death machines, they call them."

"Why drag it out with six separate hangings? Do them all at once, I say. More humane," said another.

"'Tis more like the Sheriff wants to show the power of the law. Scare the bejesus outta the Irish," said an unshaven man in a rumpled cloth jacket, a dusty gray cap, muddied boots, and a lilt in his voice.

"Maybe they'll start hanging boys who don't go to work when they should," said the man in the bowler hat, looking at Brian.

There was a loud *whumph* sound followed by a sharp banging clatter that made some in the gathering jump.

"What's that?" asked Brian in a pitch higher than his usual, swallowing hard.

"Sandbags. That's what they use to test the trap door," answered the man with the black hat. "The trap door slams against the gallows framework. Imagine what it does to the neck."

Bridie shuddered. "No, I don't think I want to watch the hangings, Brian." *James Carroll's a good man,* she thought. *Good men don't hang.*

"Here. See? Look at this pamphlet." The man with the cane pulled a rumpled paper from his pocket. "This sketch of the gallows shows nooses for six. Says right here the gallows was specially designed so the sheriff could prevent a long, ghastly affair by hanging all six murderers at once. He's thinking of the public welfare."

"If you ask me," said a man who'd just joined the growing crowd, "the whole of the Ancient Order of Hibernians should be hanged. They all had a finger in the murders of John P. Jones and Policeman Benjamin Yost, you know. They're all thieving murderers. Planning more murders, too, for Thursday, in retaliation for the hangings, if you want to know my opinion."

"Harrumph! Humane 'tis it?" said the man with the muddy boots as he walked away. "That Sheriff Werner has no love in his heart for the Irish."

"Like the paper says here," said the man with the black hat, slapping the back of his hand on the newspaper, "'The majesty of the law must be vindicated.' Them that are guilty, but not caught yet, will get the message. This hanging will put an end to talk of unions."

When Bridie arrived at the Werners' home, the housekeeper, Molly Mulligan, a rotund, ruddy-faced, gray-haired woman, was having a conversation with a man with a wooden leg who was delivering the groceries.

"The sheriff went to his office at dawn this morning," she was saying as Bridie walked into the kitchen unnoticed. She went right to work washing dishes so she could listen. "He has to make sure this whole horrible affair stays on schedule. He's worried the gallows might not be finished and tested today," said Mrs. Mulligan. "He has to arrange for special trains for the bodies and their families. The undertakers are coming to measure the prisoners for coffins."

How would that feel, thought Bridie with a shiver, to be measured for your coffin whilst alive? How could the sun possibly shine so bright on a day when living men would be measured for coffins? When James Carroll was measured for his coffin.

"Soldiers all over town. Catholic priests, too. Come from the prisoners' home towns, Port Carbon, Heckscherville, Minersville. Come to minister to the condemned men. I'll be glad when it's over. It's like every Irishman is a suspected murderer," said Sean, the grocery delivery man. "I hear there might be some pardons from Governor Hartranft. Thomas Duffy's sure to win a reprieve."

"Well, Sean, the gallows won't be cheated. Sadly, all appeals have been rejected, Sheriff says. Even the pardon board upheld the convictions. There's no hope left for us."

No hope left. The gallows won't be cheated. The words rang out in Bridie's mind, along with Brian's invitation to join them in watching the hangings.

'Tis wrong, she thought.

Wrong to watch something so hopeless, something that makes folks feel so bad.

But Mam Mary's sure there will be a rescue. That's what I want to see.

If there is no rescue, I wonder what a hanging would look like.

Would it sound different from the sandbags dropping?

Would we see their faces?

Eyes popping out?

Mouths drooling?

The hanged men, would they kick and struggle like rabbits in a snare? Or die instantly? She didn't want to see that, especially since one of them hanging was James Carroll, the man who'd been so kind to her.

No, probably not. Father McDermott said they'd die like Irishmen, facing their fate without tears or pleas for mercy.

That was the Irish way.

She saw Mrs. Mulligan's hand go to her apron pocket often and Bridie knew she was praying the rosary. Bridie heard her murmur, "Their hope is in the Lord. He's the Rescuer."

How could I go to watch such a horrible thing, Bridie thought, like it was a minstrel show? But how could I not go to cheer the Molly Maguires when they ride in to save their own and one of my own?

FOUR

Black Thursday

Come all ye true-born Irishmen, wherever you may be,
I hope you will pay attention and listen unto me,
Concerning ten brave Irishmen all in their youthful bloom,
Who died in Pennsylvania on the twenty-first of June.

Thomas Duffy and James Carroll as you can plainly see,
They were murdered by false perjurers all on the gallows tree.
Thomas Duffy on the brink of death did neither shake nor fear,
But he smiled upon his murderers although his end was near.

– "Thomas Duffy" by Martin Mulhall

June 1877

On Black Thursday, dark and cold for a June morning, Bridie and Brian scrambled up onto the roof of a house behind the jailhouse, expecting that they would be caught any minute. People had risen early to secure a spot on the hilltops to watch the hangings. Many had already gathered around the jailhouse hoping for a glimpse of grieving family members who were being allowed in early to see their loved ones, attend mass together, and receive Holy Communion. An altar from St. Patrick's had been moved into the jailhouse the day before. Some went to mass at the church to pray for the souls of the prisoners as if they'd already departed.

Hans, Gazsi, and Kevin didn't show up, probably couldn't escape their parents. The roof was slippery from a night rain and Bridie slid off once. When she hit the ground with a thud, skinning her knee, she thought, I'd better get out of here. Now. This isn't the right thing to do, she told herself as she struggled her way to the chimney where she could hold on.

They waited.

Bridie had expected to see Father McDermott arrive, but he didn't. Had he arrived earlier or had he stayed all night? He had long spoken out harshly against The Ancient Order of Hibernians and its members, condemning them and their evil deeds. He had offered no comfort or sympathy when the bishop excommunicated them, but every time she'd seen him returning from talking with the prisoners, he seemed more and more disturbed. The Tuesday before the hangings he'd been to see Thomas Duffy and James Carroll several times. She'd seen him on his knees, right there in his office, bent over, shoulders rounded, as if carrying a heavy sack, so deep in prayer he didn't hear what went on around him, didn't realize he was being observed. She wanted to ask him about James but was afraid to.

"I think we'd better be on the hill with the others, Brian," Bridie said. "We are going to get the dickens if we get caught here."

"Too late now; sun's coming up. Is that McDermott there? Who's that with him?"

"*Father* McDermott, Brian. He's a priest, remember? Yes. He's going to say Mass at seven for Roarity, Duffy, and my uncle James Carroll. That's James Roarity's wife he's with."

Brian looked at Bridie with astounded admiration. "Your uncle?

Carroll's your uncle?"

"Hush, you'll give us away," said Bridie, sorry she'd revealed her secret.

The wife of the condemned man was supported on both sides, practically carried, by her brother and one sister. The second sister walked behind, head bowed. Bridie had seen them at the rectory. The closer Mrs. Roarity got to the jail, the louder her wailing and sobbing grew.

"Father Gately is saying mass for Hugh McGeehan, Boyle, and Thomas Munley. I think it was his father who went in earlier, before daylight."

The sky clouded over. It rained a little, enough to make them wet and cold and keep the roof slippery. The jailhouse yard seemed quiet after a large group of people were let in. The important people: Chester F. Farr, the Governor's Secretary, and reporters. Bridie watched well-dressed men and women in big hats. They waited, some hugging themselves against the chill.

The crowd outside the yard was still, straining to hear the sounds coming from behind the fence. It looked like many of the people on the hills brought picnic baskets and blankets they wrapped around themselves instead of sitting on them. Some had food. Small children ran around. The sun rose steadily behind the clouds. Soldiers and policemen were alert for disorder. And the saloons had been closed by order of the sheriff.

The quiet was disturbed by pounding coming from the jailhouse door. "Let me in," screamed a woman. She banged the door with her fists. "I'm Thomas Duffy's sister come from New York City, come to say goodbye to me brother. Let me in." She wore a wide-brimmed hat, her hair wet underneath, the hem of her dress muddy. "I know I'm late," she cried. "The train was late. I've come a long way. He's my brother. For the love of God, let me in to say goodbye." She hammered the jailhouse door with her fists. Her cries echoed in the hilltops. "Have mercy," she pleaded. "He's me brother, for God's sake." Bridie couldn't see who came to the door. She heard voices arguing. Her shoulders slumped as she turned and walked away, after finally speaking with someone.

Bridie's stomach growled. Her mouth was parched with thirst. "Let's go, Brian. I can't sit here anymore. My bum is killing me and if it don't, me Mam Mary will."

"Go on with you then. I'm staying put."

Brian went behind the chimney and peed off the roof, laughing when he told her that his piss had been blown by the wind onto the siding. "Ah, well, the rain'll wash it off."

Bridie wished she could do the same as she climbed down, thinking she'd go home. Instead she headed for the bushes just as there was activity in the jailhouse yard. She did her business and scrambled up again, looking all over, searching the mountain for the rescuers.

The sheriff was first to come from the cells. Bridie felt important because she knew him, had put his clean underwear away. Then came two men, each with a priest. The priests were dressed in black cassocks, white surplices, and black stoles. They carried large crucifixes. Bridie was familiar with these vestments because she'd sometimes been asked to press the wrinkles out of them. She wasn't sure of the names of these prisoners until the sheriff mentioned them. James Boyle and Hugh McGeehan looked as if they'd had their Saturday bath with their hair washed and combed. They wore new suits and each held a rose which Boyle sniffed on the way to the gallows. Bridie wondered, why the rose? Did one of the wives bring them? Did it have something to do with the Blessed Mother? She looked toward the jailhouse for the other four men but the door was closed.

"Will you look at that!" said Brian. "McGeehan has new boots. What a waste to send new boots to the grave."

Bridie gave him a look of disgust. "He's going to need those boots to run when the Mollies come."

"Do you see any Mollies?" chided Brian.

The condemned men walked with their heads held high, as if they were going out for the evening. The procession mounted the gallows and the prisoners were positioned beside marks on the platform, nooses dangling beside them. They stood calmly as the priests said prayers, McGeehan playing with the noose, Boyle sniffing his rose. When the prayers were finished, each man put his rose in his lapel. Bridie was stunned that neither showed any sign of fear, while her own heart was racing and her stomach quivering, doubt of rescue mounting.

Sheriff Werner stepped forward and shook each man's hand and asked if he had anything he wanted to say. Each said no, they had nothing to say.

The sheriff's helpers quickly strapped the men's wrists and ankles. Werner himself put the nooses around each man's neck and a white hood over each man's head. Still not one flinch or cry of fear.

There was absolute silence for a moment, all eyes fixed on the noosed men. It was as if the world had sucked in its breath. No one moved or cried out. Bridie drew apart from Brian, from the roof, so that it seemed there was nothing left in the world but herself and two men with nooses and brilliant white hoods. Perfect stillness and the silence that follows a snowstorm settled over her. This is not real, she thought. I must be dreaming.

The loud crack of the trap door shattered the stillness and clattered against the mountain. The men dropped through, snapped to a stop, and twirled at the end of the rope, their feet just above the ground. There was a collective gasp as if the crowd were surprised by an unexpected event. McGeehan's body heaved twice, and then was still. When death had been confirmed, they were cut down and placed in coffins hidden behind screens.

The next two, James Carroll and James Roarity, each well-groomed and dressed impeccably, strode to the gallows in a procession with the sheriff and priests, heads high as if they were to be awarded medals.

Anxious, Bridie searched the distance and the crowd below. No signs of Mollies.

"Yes," Roarity said after the prayers, "I have a few words to say."

Bridie held her breath as he told everyone he had not given anyone ten dollars to kill Benjamin Yost, that he was innocent, that Duffy, Boyle, and McGeehan were innocent too, that he had never asked them or anyone to shoot any man, and that they should say so, too, when it came their turn. That their consciences were as clear as his own. He heaved great sighs and once appeared to have tears in his eyes.

Carroll had nothing to say. Bridie had seen Father McDermott talking to the newspaper men but wouldn't learn until the next day, reading the *Philadelphia Times*, that Carroll had prepared a written statement for Father McDermott to read to the reporters, saying Carroll was not involved in the murder of Jones and Yost. That it was James Kerrigan, the informer, who was the only one he had ever heard threaten Yost. After reading Carroll's statement, the priest paused for a moment, hesitant, and then continued, the paper said.

"I have been spiritual advisor to Thomas Duffy and James Carroll since they came here. I have heard their confessions and I have been their closest confidant. What I'm going to say now is what I feel I must say, and this is it: I know beyond all reasonable doubt, Duffy was not party to the murder of Benjamin Yost, and I think the remark will apply with equal force to James Carroll." But she didn't know any of this until the next day.

Bridie couldn't watch. She wanted to run. Yet she couldn't move; she was rigid with the realization that there would be no rescue. She closed her eyes, but her ears told her when the deed was done.

Thomas Duffy and Thomas Munley mounted the gallows, the last of the six. They were quickly strapped, hooded, and dropped. No sounds of shock from the audience who were by this time numb. Bridie couldn't move from the roof, couldn't breathe or speak. She got down somehow, pushed against the crowds of onlookers who were going in the opposite direction, toward the jailhouse yard, to get a closer look at the gallows.

She wandered about, finally arriving at home. Mam Mary sat her by the fire. She brought her warm soup and listened to Bridie when she was able to talk.

The next day, Brian told Bridie that he'd seen the gallows after she left. Hans and Gazsi came running by, excited with news of their day. They had seen the hangings in Mauch Chunk. The four prisoners were hanged at the same time, they said. As their bodies twisted and heaved and legs kicked, the chains on their hands and feet clanked and jangled. The hoods were taken off the dead men and everyone got to see what the noose did to them.

"They didn't die right away, did you know?" said Hans. "Seventeen minutes for Campbell. He took the longest for his heart to stop, Brian."

"Donahue struggled for a long time, legs kicking, hands trying to get to the rope that was strangling him. But there was only blood on his shirt. It was Kelly's face that showed it. His eyes bulged and his tongue stuck out," said Gazsi. "It was a real hanging."

"Doyle, did you see him, Gazsi? All the skin on his neck was ripped off. And his hair. Did you see that? Gone on one side of his head."

'Twas no wonder, Bridie thought, that the next day's papers said the Pottsville prisoners had cheapened their own executions by dying in such a cavalier way. 'Twas why some said afterward they'd been cheated of the horrors they expected and the condemned men deserved. They wanted a show like Hans and Gazsi saw. A real hanging.

Among the very important people who were permitted a close view of the hangings, the Governor's secretary Chester F. Farr, hand in pocket, had fingered the reprieve for Duffy that was written by the Governor, to be issued if one of the condemned men declared Duffy's innocence. Apparently he didn't think Roarity's words were explicit enough.

FIVE

Coílín's Company House

She among the untrodden ways
Beside the springs of Dove,
A Maid whom there were none to praise
And very few to love:
A violet by a mossy stone
Half hidden from the eye!
—Fair as a star, when only one
Is shining in the sky.

> *– From "She Dwelt among the Untrodden Ways"*
> *by William Wordsworth*

Winter 1878
Bridie

Coílín Mulhearn had a company house. He was looking for a wife. The priest joined us together a month after I buried my Mam Mary.

Even though I promised to obey, I didn't. I hid my father's books in pots and dishes, under clothes and towels. Coílín forbade me to read, but how would he know? Worked in the mine all day, he did. Out drinking all night. My Da, an intellectual, he called himself, before a famine drove him to America, to poverty of spirit as well as having nothing to show for his labors. The one thing he took pleasure in was reading aloud to me. As long as I had my books, I had my father with me. As long as I had my beans and herbs, I had both my mothers with me.

Hamlet in flames provided tinder for Coílín's stove, when he found it. But that was the only one he found. From the moment our vows were spoken, my place in his life was clear.

"The first ting ye are goin' ta do, girl," said Coílín when I moved into his house, "is get us a coupla boarders. Feed them, ye will, 'n wash their shitty britches. 'Tis me that'll collect the money, so."

"Yes, sir." He said I had to pay him the respect of calling him sir. Said he didn't think of me as a darlin' wife.

"Then, you'll take in more wash, ta pay for yer keep."

"Yes sir."

"I don't want no brats around here, but I guess I'll have ta put up with that. They'll t'ink I'm not a man, if th're no babies. And a man I'll be with ye, understand? Thirteen's a good age ta learn what wife really means." He grabbed me by the hair, dragged me to the bed, and took my virginity by force, again and again.

I used to think a girl should marry for love. There was no love between us. I thought that was my fault. Now, I think there is no such thing as love. I don't want to be anyone's wife.

There'd be no babies if I could help it. Some girls my age have already had two or three babies. By fifteen, they look old. My Mam didn't want that for me. Mam Mary taught me how to grind castor beans, press out the oil, and make a cream I put inside to keep a baby from starting. Didn't always work, very dangerous, too. I could be easily poisoned if the oil was not pure. But so what if I was poisoned?

If the priest found out I did this, I'd be excommunicated. Mam Mary didn't believe any man, even a priest, had that much power.

The beans do not grow here so she traded for them, with women from other parts. What couldn't grow here grew somewhere else. My own mother used it, determined not to bring another child into the cruel life in the mine patch. I used it too, but things don't always work the way you want them to. I learned other ways to survive the nights.

~

The door slams open.

I hope he's been with a whore. Then he'll have had his fill. Coílín falls before he gets to the table.

"Get away from me," he yells and grinds the lit end of his fag into the hand I try to help him with; I hear it sizzle. On his feet, swaying, he takes a swing at me, misses, and drops into the chair.

"Bread, woman." He never calls me by my name. "Bread with some of that honey you keep hidin' away. Can't you see I'm hungry?"

I fix his tea with a large dose of valerian, a little St-John's Wort, and, to disguise the taste, lots of honey, a luxury I've convinced him he deserves. He'll be asleep before he can get on top'a me.

"Here, have two cups, Coílín. It'll help that headache you have in the morning," I say, slapping honey on the last of the bread, hoping he won't want another tonight. Knowing I'm in for a beating in the morning—no bread for breakfast or to pack with lunch. I'd sneak out to borrow a slice but it's late and I did that last week. Tomorrow's baking day. I'll need to hide a loaf or two, if I've enough flour. I can buy some extra flour...

"Don't go running up no bill at the company store, if ye know what's good for ye."

It's as if he reads my mind.

"Ye're outta bread again, ain't ye?"

He lands a punch on my arm.

"I need to buy more flour, Coílín. You like to eat in the evening, you need it so's to keep up your strength. You work so hard. So, I'll just buy some extra flour for you. With three paying boarders now, we can buy a little extra flour."

"Ye'll buy no extra flour with me money, bitch." He laughs, licks his lips as if he's relishing the beating he'll give me.

He knows I need more flour, knows no money's mine. But I fool him. I keep back some washing money, saying the boss's wife is doing her own now, what with the mine work cut back. I trade herbs for fever and sickness for flour and beans. He knows nothing of this.

~

There is no grief in this house and no friends to view Coílín's body laid out in the front room when he dies—roof fall, bad air. Too bad.

Daniel is nearly two. We both have fresh bruises that tell why there are no tears. But grief is all I know six months later. Daniel and another lad, five, are buried in a culm slide. Take my eyes off him for a few seconds is all, to shoo off a snarling dog. The nippers play on that dirty pile of waste from the mine, especially when they're supposed to be pocketing scraps of coal for their mothers' stoves. Daniel must have thought it was too much fun to pass up with me looking the other way. By the time I dig him out, he is gone.

I want nothing more than to follow him. I think of the herbs that are poison with just a drop too much, or in certain combinations. I can't do it, cannot dishonor my dead Mams that way.

So I choose to live. Live dead until I have enough money to get out of this place—to live in a city where women wear big hats and have coins in their pockets.

SIX

Remembering Ridiculous Red Hair

Spring 1880
Bridie

"I never wanted to fall in love, like I did when I met you, Tim O'Doyle. Could it only have been six... seven years ago? "

"Uh huh," says Tim. He shrugs off the kiss I plant on his lips.

"It was on a Sunday. No work—only games to be played, songs to be sung, stories to be told. Everyone played, setting the dust flying. Not me. I hovered around the fringe. There was not a cloud in the sky and not a gray strand in the ridiculous red hair that sprang from your head." I tousle that still-full head of hair.

Tim looks up from the chair, hammer in hand, and grins. "Plenty gray now, to be sure."

"I didn't like you one bit."

"Just playing hard to get, ye were." Tim laughs a big belly laugh. "Not sure I can fix this chair, Bridie."

"Uh huh." I look at the chair but the memory clouds my vision. For having lost your wife and the baby she was trying to birth, not two months earlier, you were much too jovial, boyo. I thought, how dare he laugh in the face of grief?

Tim looks at me as if I'd said something quite unbelievable... like

I didn't like him.

"I like you now, but then, less than a year since I'd lost my own husband to the mine and a month since my small boy was killed in a culm slide. Parents dead, too."

"No smile found its way to your lips, 'tis true." His face looks like he's trying to say sorry. "'Twas just me way, girl. A man can't cry, can he?"

I nod like I understand but I don't. "You were playing that stupid ball game with the men and boys, running around with Sweeney like an idiot, laughing as if you hadn't a care in the world." I pull up a chair beside him. The herbs drying as they hang from the ceiling cast a soft fragrance. "You confused me, that's all. A man rumored to have killed with that pack of vigilantes, those ruffians the Molly Maguires, and there you were the very same man who swooped up your little daughter, tossed her in the air to her squeals of delight. You were both appalling and appealing. I loathed you and envied you—until you brought me that plate of food."

"Leave me, woman. Do ye want this chair fixed or not?" He gives me a pat on the knee. "I knew you were hungry. So young to be a widow living with folks too kind to turn you out."

"But trading me around like a communal guest. I scrubbed other women's floors for a few scraps of food. Too unsure of myself to ask for more. Bold, you were, to take my hand, to lead me to an empty place at a table. Kind to say not a word about my raw, lye-soap-cracked skin."

The words choke out. I feel so lucky to have him and at the same time wonder why he refuses to live in a city. Why can't he see life would be so much better for us?

"I know ye wanted ta keep yer girlish figure," Tim says "but Maureen McGonigal's stew was too good to miss on a nippy day. I piled the plate full. It was dripping." Tim puts his hammer down and sits on his haunches.

"I was hungry. I took the plate, grateful but not wanting to acknowledge it. I wanted to shout at you for seeing my need, for knowing my weakness, for collapsing my pride."

Tim pats his pockets, looking for a tool.

"You left me to eat alone. I had all I could do to keep from shoveling the stew in—two portions at least—and then I licked the plate after I'd finished sweeping it clean with the bread."

Maureen comes in without knocking. "I have some cider for ye." She looks concerned when she sees Tim kneeling on the floor, beside me and the broken chair. "Ye sayin' the rosary?" asks Maureen.

"'Tis that one that needs prayers," Tim says, pointing at me. "Talkin' about how she loathed me. That's what ye said, right Bridie?"

"That's how I feel about me Martin some days", says Maureen. "I have some cider for ye, after ye finish whatever ye're up to on that floor."

"What? You think Martin's needin' prayers?" asks Tim. "'Tis the chair, Maureen. We're fixin' it."

Maureen nods but gives me a look that all wives understand. I pour cider into mugs and give one to Tim. Maureen and I move out and sit on the front step to drink our cider. After Maureen leaves, I lean back on the doorjamb, remembering that day after the picnic:

When the ball game was over, Tim had come back with cake. The youngsters were playing their own game. Somewhere, there was fiddle playing and singing with cheers and clapping.

"There's talk that the clerk at the company store moved to the city. Bridie, ye could do that job, being one of the few ta read 'n write," said Tim.

That Bridie could read and write from the time she was a wee one was true. Her father had taught school in the west of Ireland—Galway—before the famine reduced him to a laborer. As he'd learned English in the mines, he taught her. Sums, too. Until he was killed by a fall of slate in the mine, it had been just the two of them. Took him three weeks to die with just Bridie to care for him, listening for her dead mother to whisper which herbs to use for the infection. Tell me what to do, mháthairín, she had pleaded.

"They'd never give me the job. Me? Irish and a woman?" she said, trying to dismiss him and the whole idea. She wondered how he knew so much of her business.

"What harm to ask?"

Tim left her there to think about it. Every now and then she looked for him in the tousle of men and boys tackling each other, chasing after the ball.

She couldn't find him amidst the squeals of playfulness and shouted disputes. Once, he caught her searching and he grinned, rubbed his stomach, and licked his lips. He had to remind Bridie of her shattered pride.

I smile at the memory. "As out-of-hand then as you have been since," I say aloud to no one.

That's why you brought me the plate, I thought. You were looking for a woman to wash your clothes and cook your food. And me a widow not looking for another man, I got my back up. I left after I'd eaten the cake, not wanting you to see my hunger satisfied.

"But there was no stopping your boldness, Tim," I say. The scent of cherry blossoms fills the air and merges with that same fragrance on which I slide deeper back in time.

A few days after the picnic, on the steps outside the company store, Tim, dressed in his best, came out with a pay envelope as Bridie went in.

With a jaunty bow Tim tipped his cap at her.

She nodded politely, tilted her chin, and walked on, saying to herself, no sir, I'll not look to another man for my keep. When she came out he was sitting on the step, growler empty of lunch but full of beer.

"Smell it? Apple pie, soon, for some lucky bloke. Did ye get the job?" He walked beside her.

"And what is it that makes you think I went for the job?" she said, thinking he was a bold one to ask... to sit here waiting for her, like they'd planned to meet.

"Your dress!" He laughed his big belly laugh.

"Sit," Tim patted the space beside him on the bench in front of the company store.

"As if I'd sit beside the likes of you, and your beer, for all to see the shame of it," she said. She walked off, not wanting to tell him she'd been turned down for the second time. But there he was beside her again. What was she to do but be civil?

"They'd let me wash their shitty drawers, but they'll not let me sell their goods or keep their books." She walked faster, hoping to leave him behind, but he quickened his pace.

Bridie's breath catches remembering what Tim said. She covers her face with her hands and laughs. It is still shocking even after these years together.

"Then marry me, Bridie," he said, just like that.

She felt as if she'd smacked into a tree. He said it as simple as that, as if he were asking about the price of bread. She couldn't believe her ears. She stumbled over a rock in the road. He grabbed her to keep her from falling. It was payday and the place was buzzing with folks. She hoped no one heard or saw his foolishness. Everyone went to the company store on payday.

Bridie shoved him. "Who do you think you are, Tim O'Doyle, making as if I were goods for sale." Beer sloshed out of his pail. "I'd never marry a drinker," she said, keeping the shout in her voice but the loudness out.

"I'm not a drinker, Bridie, just this wee bit on pay day. Don't marry me, then. Just help with me children so's I can get them away from that crabby Widow Murphy. I'll pay ye. I'll have me papers soon enough. A miner with papers makes good money."

His face lit up like he'd found a gold coin. It wasn't from the beer in him. It was then that Bridie noticed his beautiful lips.

He said if she were there, they could take in boarders. She'd cook their meals, do their wash. They'd pay her, not him. She could have a bed with the children.

"You would shame me? Sleep in the same house as you and not married? Now I know what you're after, O'Doyle, scoundrel that you are." Bridie was as impressed as she was shocked. What kind of man is this? Willing to pay her, to let boarders pay her? What kind of man to live with such a scandal for the good of his children, to help her help herself?

"I wouldn't touch ye, Bridie." He raised his hand as if taking an oath.

Funny thing is she had to laugh, more out of nerves than humor.

"I know how Cóilín treated ye, Bridie," he'd said. "I'd never touch a woman that way. Never touched me Máire Cáit that way,

God rest her soul."

He looked away then, but not before she saw his eyes fill up. A man who'd probably pulled the trigger on more than one poor soul when he fought for the union. Tears! "There'll be talk. I'll be not the only whore, but the most brazen one of the patch. Some think I cast the evil eye because I made the little Kielly girl better last year. Now I'll be a whoring witch." She laughed, a real laugh, because that was funny. It was his turn to be shocked.

Tim glanced sideways to see if anyone heard. Then he covered the side of his mouth with his hand and whispered, "Tis sacrilegious. And the priest," he said, his face stone serious, eyes laughing out loud. "The priest'd be knocking at the door every night looking to save us from damnation."

"I'd have to be going to confession every week and be on my knees with novenas," she said, getting caught up in his joking.

Bridie walked away from his improper ideas until the afternoon she saw the Widow Murphy taking the switch to his children.

"Hello," Bridie said, hoping to stop the beating. "And what mischief has happened here?"

The old woman continued lashing the youngest, Kathy. She was what—seven years-old? She curled in a ball, face in her arms, no sounds coming from her as if she were asleep. It was Patrick who was screaming, tugging, trying to pull the old woman off his little sister. Only eight and he defended his sister. The widow turned and slapped him hard in the face, then shoved him, knocking him down so she could whip him with the same switch.

Bridie moved fast and lifted the girl in her arms, soothing her with a low voice as she'd done with her own when his father had beaten him.

"That's enough." Bridie put her own body between the switch

and the boy. "Get up, Patrick, and go home. Go on with you. I'll carry your sister."

Then she noticed the lady across the road leaning on her broom. A few others came out to see what all the shouting was about. But none called over to help.

Everything changed that afternoon, I think as I stand and stretch. Tim cusses and the hammer bangs to the floor. When I'd go to his house every morning to get him and the boy off to the mine, I imagined being married to Tim though I kept refusing him.

True to his word, he paid me to cook and do his laundry. The two boarders paid me to do the same for them. Soon I could pay for my own board at O'Sullivan's and save some for a ticket. I was in such a hurry—a hurry to get on a train and go to a big city, Philadelphia or Washington, whichever train came first. Get away from coalmines, to find work as a charwoman if I couldn't get office or clerk work.

I kept you waiting for the better part of a year, I tell Tim in my mind. By the time I'd saved enough to set myself up in the city, I'd fallen in love with you and your children. I smile thinking about Tim's laugh. Tears stream along my cheeks flushed with emotion. Sometimes I wish I didn't love you so much. How could I ever live if I lost you?

Book Two

Winter 1887

SEVEN

Diphtheria Fever

January 1887

The wind howled around Bridie as she made her way down the crusty road—ice beneath a new snow, grayed by the black dust that was always in the air, even in the dead of winter. She breathed the foul air, shivering. She rushed along the slippery road, but the way seemed to stretch before her. Every moment counted. As she hurried, time slowed to a crawl. The wind sought to push her back home even as she leaned into it. At times like these, times when the obstacles seemed insurmountable, her determination strengthened rather than being thwarted. The need she sensed for her healing herbs rose above difficulties.

Will the child still breathe when I get there, she wondered. Yes. Somehow, she knew that this child would benefit. Sadly, that might not mean she would live. Hold on Bridie, she chided herself. No one has told you the child is a girl.

The chill bit her bones and she wished for more than the thick woolen shawl pulled over her head and face. Ice, encrusted on the hem of her dress, scratched against her ankles, making her aware of the numbness in her toes. Her skirt, swept by the wind, swirled about her legs, slowing her even more. She hiked her skirt up, lost control of the shawl. One end flung to the ground, causing her to stumble. Her ears burned in the wind.

I should have worn Tim's high boots. Trousers too, she thought, trying to rope in the shawl and untangle her skirts. A medicine bag filled with paper-wrapped packages of dried herbs remained safe under her arm.

She had shoes this winter, at least. A grateful mother had given them to her when Bridie had stayed all night with the mine boss's daughter, bathing her with cool water and forcing, drop-by-drop, infusions of wormwood and willow bark to quell the fever. She had used a poultice of mustard to ease the child's breathing. That was last winter. She'd had homemade boots then and the recovered child's mother had given her a few coins and the shoes she wore now. She hadn't discarded the footwear she'd fashioned last year—nothing could be wasted. She had resized them for her boy Johnny.

She'd had far to walk in those homemade boots, about a mile, because all the bosses lived at the far end of the patch, farthest from the noise and the choking dust of the breaker, next to the doctor's office and the church—the English church, the church of the masters. The doctor had been away that night and the boss knew Bridie was a healer. That was both a blessing and a curse, the familiarity with herbs that heal. A blessing because of the few coins from those who had them to give or some eggs or milk from those who didn't, or just the willingness to help when she herself had a need—like the time she and Tim built a summer kitchen. A curse because some folks looked sideways at her, walked away when she approached, suspicious, as if she'd hex them. Heal and curse—Bridie recognized within herself the ability.

Tonight's mission was critical.

Tim had protested her going out. "What is it yer doin', woman?

Goin' down to the likes of them, the Slavs. They're disgustin'. They eat like pigs. No wonder their wee ones are sick."

Tim had refused to allow the woman into the house when she came to the door. Made her stand out in the snow, sobbing and speaking a tongue he'd said wasn't civilized. Bridie brought her in, sat her down by the stove, hot still, but waning in the lateness of the evening and the nearness of bed-time-warmth from quilts and other bodies.

The woman, who she knew only as Yolanda, her last name unpronounceable, cradled her arms, rocking the emptiness there, coughing and gagging, pointing to the imaginary child. She stroked the little one's head, then quickly withdrew her hand and pretended to touch the stove, flinching at the touch. Bridie understood that her child had fever. Then Yolanda left hurriedly, gesturing and pleading with Bridie to follow.

"Ye defy me, Bridie," Tim had said as she went out the door, the bundle of what he called her magic weeds under her shawl. "And the honey," he protested, "yer takin' the fine honey. What'll I put in me tea?" Tim walked toward the stove then back, gesturing wildly. "He'll be takin' me job next. Ye know that don't ye? That's why all them foreigners have been brought here—to take our jobs. They work cheap and cause no trouble."

But angry as he was, he pulled the shawl higher on her head and closed the door quietly behind her. They'd been happy together. Bridie married for love, a deep affection that was beyond reason itself. Love for Tim and his two children.

He remembers, she thought. The night when their first child lay sick and Bridie, big with the next one, administered her homemade medicine. The company doctor didn't come to them, common laborers—too busy tending the superintendent's children, all sick with the whooping cough. Most died, including theirs.

This night, she didn't have to go that far; it just seemed that way, down the road a little to where they used to live. Double house, shared roof with a thin wall between, little more than shack with a high fence of pieced scrap lumber behind. She knocked, then walked in, not wanting to take the woman away from her ailing child. The husband greeted her.

"Hello," he said in a heavy accent. He spoke a little English, having learned it from working in the mines since summer.

Bridie could scarcely see into the small stifling-hot room that glowed with a faint orange light from the kerosene lamp in the front corner, near one of the beds. Yolanda stood with her back to the door. The room was stark in its frugality—ceiling beams, rough, unadorned walls stuffed in places with rags to keep rain and snow out. Cold wind seeped through the bare plank floor. Children, two or three, sharing each of the other two beds.

Yolanda, placed the small wrapped body she'd been rocking on a bed, turned with tears flowing down her cheeks, then stepped back away from the bed.

She's gone, Bridie thought, but then heard the rasp of a labored breath having too small a passageway for the great need that sucked it in. The child thrashed about, a little cocoon moving from side to side. Her mother reached to restrain her. Bridie approached and quickly unwrapped the child. The last layer was a rough wool blanket, underneath it, the girl who looked about six, hot and sweaty. Her hands, once freed, scratched at her skin which was covered with tiny red dots. Bridie wasn't sure if it was a rash or irritation from the crude blanket and the excessive heat.

"Open the door a little," Bridie said to the man. He did, but Yolanda rushed to close it.

"No! Miklos."

Bridie nodded yes, saying in word and pantomime, "The heat, it's making it hard to breathe."

The man translated for Yolanda, signing with his hands clutched to his throat that he, too, was finding his breathing strained from the heat.

Bridie wet rags in a bucket of water beside the bed and put them outdoors to cool for use on the girl's head and arms.

She examined the child. Every movement, every touch seemed to create a need for more air which the child struggled to draw in, her chest heaving. Her face pale with a bluish hue, her lips purple. Her skin hot with fever.

"I need to look in her mouth." Miklos appeared to explain to Yolanda, who then spoke the girl. Mari, she called her.

She refused to open her mouth. She thrashed weak arms and fists at Bridie, rasping a feeble protest, looking to her mother to help her escape this stranger.

A yellowish, blood-tinged fluid seeped from her nose and encrusted its edges. A yellowish-gray membrane coated the inside of her nostrils. Bridie knew from the fetid odor of the breath that the same membrane curdled in her throat.

"I can't see into the child's throat with her fighting," she said aloud. She prayed silently to the spirit she knew guided her—her mother maybe, but not the God of her church, a punishing vengeful being. Please, let me know what more to do: poultice for the chest, wormwood and willow for the fever, and honey for the throat. What else, she pleaded? What else?

"Water, hot water for the infusion," Bridie said to Miklos who pointed to the back of the room then translated for Yolanda. Cup, Bridie gestured. Not being understood, she wove her way between the beds to the stove he'd pointed to, feeling the frightened but curious eyes of the other children. There boiled a kettle of water. Yolanda rushed up behind her, saying something in a commanding tone to her husband that must have been "Don't leave her alone."

Together the women made a strong tea of skullcap and valerian for sedation—careful not too much for a child, added the herbs for fever, and sweetened with honey. In small sips, for she could only swallow the tiniest amount, they administered it to the child. When most of the tea had been consumed, they alternated tea with pure honey.

With the blankets removed and the rotation of cool compresses Mari quieted, then slept as the medicine began to take hold. They cleaned the crust from her nose to allow more air to get in. Her breathing was still noisy and labored and the women continued dropping honey into her mouth.

Bridie instructed the Miklos to take the children upstairs, though she knew there were boarders in the upper rooms. She explained it was necessary so that the other children wouldn't get the fever too, a small hope since they'd already been exposed. As sick as Mari was, Bridie knew that the next child to get it would be much sicker, that whatever caused the sickness seemed to get stronger as it passed from one to another.

By morning the child's breathing was less noisy and the fever not as high. Mari had slept in fits and starts throughout the night. Her mother curled beside her. Miklos maintained the vigil all night with Bridie, though his chin dropped to his chest several times.

Bridie's concentration never strayed from the child: willing her to heal, to breathe more freely, to live. Sometimes she thought it was the willing that healed as much as, or more than, the herbs. What happens? Bridie often asked herself. Do thoughts of an open passage, for air to flow through Mari's throat, cause it to open? Does the willing knead some mysterious place in the sick person? The soul? Was it possible to will someone to live? Could one will someone to die?

Miklos left for the mine before dawn. Bridie left at first light, but not before giving Yolanda mimed instructions and plenty of herbs. She told her to give the other children a tonic to strengthen against the sickness. Her son, Johnny, would bring the ingredients later. He'd get some, too, even though he hated the concoction and she'd have to bribe him with an extra piece of bread at supper. On the way home she made a mental list of the herbs she'd have to grow this spring and those she could harvest from the woods. She knew there would be a steady supply of fresh vegetables from Miklos and Yolanda, if their child lived, allowing more room in her garden for growing healing herbs.

EIGHT

Bridie Goes To The Mine

Hullabaloo Hurray Haroo
Oh happy day
To dig and toil for little pay
And never more see the light of day.

Go to town for beer and whiskey
Get on home a little frisky
Get away ye drunken bum
Me wife, the scrooge, she ain't no fun.

– "Miner's Ditty" by A.M. Getty

February 1887

The figure didn't attract any notice, though the person shuffling along felt as if everyone was staring. Packaged in ordinary dingy, coal-stained clothing, there was nothing ordinary about the wild shock of red hair stuffed under the cap, or the head it was on, or the bound breasts beneath the bulky jacket, or the long legs encased in rough coveralls. A gloved hand pulled the shabby wool muffler over the nose to the eyes, grateful for the disguise winter makes natural.

Tim O'Doyle, her husband, and his most trusted butty, Sweeney, walked in front of her, Colem O'Shaughnessy behind and Denny O'Reilly to her right. Still, Bridie worried. She adjusted her stride hoping to mimic the coal miner posture—a little bent at the knees, rounded at the shoulders. Her eyes shifted side to side as she walked toward the mine head, looking for signs of trouble, hoping to head it off.

The wind, fierce and cutting, seemed intent on blowing away any possible warmth or beauty from the imminent sunrise. In February, the dead of winter, the road to the mine, rutted with frozen ridges of mud, was too uneven for easy progress in boots too big. The breaker, a long sloping trough down which broken coal traveled, now deceptively silent, rose dark on the horizon, seducing its prey. Her breath made a mottle of murkiness in the air and a moist patch on the muffler, the edges of which crystallized with ice.

You're like every other laborer today, she told herself — glad for the pay, but not eager for the damp-darkness and danger. Why did I volunteer for this, anyway?

An extra day's pay, that's why. Jamie McGee's a good friend, still sick, unable to work, in danger of losing his job, that's why. From Donegal, too, his was family close to Tim's, my own husband, who pays Jamie for his labor. The mine boss told Tim, fire them that can't work. And don't bother coming yourself, if you don't have enough men in your crew, he'd said. Tim was already short several laborers. Bridie didn't know the only two other men who were able to work today, Campbell and Gibbons. Grateful not to be docked a day's pay, they were willing to go along with the scheme. Or, she wondered, had Tim threatened them?

Still, it was a ridiculous idea, her idea, strongly opposed by Tim. The very notion! Her posing as Jamie—wearing his cap and brown and white check jacket and muffler—the clothes charity from someone better-off, not meant for grime and coal dust. Not made to be crushed in a roof fall or infused with black damp gas. Warm, if not comfortable, too intimate, foreign with the scent of another body and cigarettes. Bridie fingered a rosary found in the pocket, probably put there by his wife Kate, who prays daily for her husband's safety.

"Fer God's sake," shouts a tall man. "'Tis a whipping you'll get from me if ye don't get off that culm bank before ye get buried in it." His sons continued their rough-housing on the mountain of scrap slate, coal, and slag. Seeing these young boys on their way to work in the mine triggered a tinge of fear for her son, Johnny.

What if there is a cave-in, an explosion? The beads roll between her fingers while pearls of sweat slide between her breasts. What if I am crippled or killed? Or worse, buried alive. In the pocket, she worries the cross, too big for the beads. Who will look after my Johnny-boy? He'll end up like other orphans: a beggar. He could work at the mine but where would he live? Who would take him in? There was always room in some corner for another body to sleep, but who could afford another mouth at the table? A breaker boy's wages are too small to be a paying boarder. He'd have to give it all over. How can he put enough by to be on his own?

As she watched the errant boys being dragged off the culm, she was more determined than ever that her own son, not much younger than these two, would go to school.

"Good morning to you, Jamie," someone hollered at her. She realized after a moment, he was calling to her. She waved, hardly noticing, deeply engrossed in her thoughts.

Can I take Jamie's whole pay, make his misfortune my good fortune? I'm not exactly taking his pay. It's that Tim won't have to pay him or me either since I'm his wife—but we benefit. I won't be able to load as much coal as he could. Jamie has many skills; I have none. It will be another day or two before he is well, strong enough to return to work. He has five wee ones to feed and no pay. Yet... I am saving his job.

Bridie wanted to push by Sweeney and Tim, to run ahead, to get to the face below where she'd be working. There she'd be safe from discovery. Too many bosses at the head of the mine, few below. Instead she forced herself to maintain a steady pace, waved in greeting as the men joked and shouted hellos.

"Hey there, Donnelly," Colem yelled, "Good to see you're back to work. Where's those boys of yours?"

"Home-a-bed," replied Donnelly. "I'm the only one on me feet today. Mary's down with the sickness, too, even the baby."

"Same with me," said Sweeney. "They're all sick."

"Mary's taking the baby to your place, Tim. See if Bridie can give him something for the fever."

Bridie cringed at the thought of not being there. She knew the baby would probably die with or without her help. The young ones die quickly. Two babies she had tried to help last week were gone this week. Herbs can bring down fever but not stop the damage done by illness. So many were sick. Tim was one of them, but he'd work dead if he could. That's what the mine boss expects. Contract miners were ordered to get rid of any worker who fails to report to work for more than two days, as if he were garbage.

"Plenty waiting to take your places," he'd said. "Some of them contract miners, too. But not lazy and drunk like you Micks."

An empty threat, Bridie thought, so greedy is the mine owner to keep up production. Gowen, who's buying up all the mines and railroads around, he's the greediest. So greedy, in fact, he cheats on the price he pays for coal, cheats on what he charges to transport it.

It's Gowen that keeps us living like pigs in slop while he's he builds a kingdom, living like royalty in a mansion. He can even pay a real doctor for his kids when they get sick, if they even get sick. His kids don't play in the sewage that spills out of the outhouses when it rains. Her teeth clenched and her hands knotted up into fists at the thought of Frank Gowen. Anger set off heart palpitations.

No, thought Bridie, no one, contract miner or not, will be taking Tim's job. More likely, Boss Heinz Mueller will expect the quota of coal cars to be loaded no matter how shorthanded they were. Tim's men were experienced, tested. Boss couldn't expect much from new men.

Still they'd embarked on this deception—she played Jamie today.

"Hey, you over there," shouted a rough voice. The shout, the thud and crunch of approaching footsteps, jarred Bridie from her thoughts. What is he doing here? Tim said inside Foreman Walsh would be in the mine office below, where it would be crowded with workers, easy to get by him unnoticed.

Walsh's hand clamped a tight grip on Bridie's shoulder and yanked her around. Fear slammed her gut. She coaxed herself to stay calm.

I'm caught, for sure, thought Bridie. Tim will lose his job.

She wanted to shout at Tim who didn't seem to notice what was happening. Her shoulder felt like it was about to be ripped off. She hoped Tim kept moving ahead. Boss Walsh was a cruel man, thought Bridie. If he had a whip, he'd use it on anyone Irish or Catholic. And Tim was both.

"It's McGee," Tim interjected, pulling at the boss's hand. "Sick, he's got no voice but he ain't no slacker; he's here today, to work."

"McGee, that you?"

Bridie's heart leapt. She nodded. Oh! How could I ever have

thought I could do this? Then she realized he didn't recognize the jacket. Sure, it's dirty and smudged like everyone else's, but the checks are still apparent. Doesn't he know Jamie from everyone else? Or does he see something else that gives me away? I'm too clean, should have rubbed more black dust into my fingernails, more over the freckles on my face. She was tall for a woman, broad in the shoulder, though not quite as tall as Jamie. Knots twisted her insides. She avoided eye contact with the supervisor. Her eyes were green with golden lashes, Jamie's brown. Would he even notice eyes if he hadn't identified the jacket as Jamie's? Who else wears a checked jacket? She shoved her hands in her pockets, wishing she'd kept on the gloves she'd found there. They were too big, uncomfortable, clotted with coal dust. Bridie feigned a gravelly, hoarse sound as if trying to speak then pushed the cap lower on her forehead, exposing her hand again. The mine boss tightened his grip. Bridie's shoulder seemed to shrink. She sweated beneath her clothes even as the cold wind cut through the jacket. He released her roughly, as she pulled her hand up into her sleeves as a turtle would withdraw into its shell. She wondered if she should cough or moan or something to show she, or *he*, was indeed sick.

"McGee? Must be. Who else would wear that stupid coat, like you was going to a damn picnic?" He looked directly in her face, what little was left showing. "Thought you were a stranger. Can't be too careful, what with them unions sending spies and all. Get going, move along."

No spy. Just a woman, thought Bridie. This was a serious offense—a woman in this place. 'Twas bad luck for a woman to enter a mine, they say, because a women can put a curse on the mine. Bad enough to be working in Satan's domain; why press your luck by letting women in, they say.

Some miners didn't want their wives to meet them on the road after work. If they did, those husbands, and other men, would go back to the mine and start all over so as not to jinx their luck. Many women won't walk the road to pick coal from the culm bank in the morning, until all the workers were in the mine. It's spies I need to worry about today, thought Bridie. Someone spying me, a woman in the mine.

Nothing had prepared her for the cage—a box-like, wheel-less cart, that would lower her hundreds of feet into the shaft. A thick, greasy-looking cable extended from the top of the thing which was completely open on two sides with little protection front and back. She knew she had to get into it, if she was to continue this ruse, but she found herself unable to move. A few extra coins and the tightly-knit bond of family-like friendship didn't seem as compelling now.

Tim nudged her forward. She stepped tentatively onto the wooden floor as if testing her footing on a rocky slope; the cage swayed. Tim pushed from behind. He mumbled something about men waiting. Bodies pressed in on all sides, arms extended downward, hands clutched tools and lunch pails. She felt as if the man behind was exploring her body with his. Bridie wondered if the man in front thought the same of her. She wished Tim was behind her instead of at her side. At least they weren't her heels at the edge of the rough plank floor, not her body held from slipping between the cage and the shaft wall only by a single chain loosely draped across the opening. The men jockeyed for position it seemed. Bridie tried to distract herself by wondering if they arranged themselves according to who gets off first, from what side. It was small comfort knowing she was safely in the center because she may be going deeper than the others on the edges.

A bell rang. The cage started its descent with a jerk, slowly at first. Wheels shrieked and timbers groaned as the cage dropped more rapidly past slimy moss-encrusted granite blocks at the mouth, then picked up more speed as it fell through soil walls held by a lattice of wooden strips. To quell the roil in her stomach, Bridie looked straight ahead at the back of Tim's head. He'd moved in front of her. Soon, the only light was provided by the fluttering flames on the miner's lamps.

The cage lurched to a halt with a suddenness that left Bridie breathless. Men who disembarked from both sides of the cage vanished quickly. In the shadowy lamp-light, Bridie saw tunnels extending from both sides of the cage and wheeled wagons waiting— for what? To be hoisted above? Delivered below? Before Bridie caught her breath the cage bucked and creaked then dropped to the next level. Here the cage emptied. Bridie felt lightheaded, like part of her remained above. Her stomach churned with nausea. On rubbery legs, she stepped into the darkness, feeling as if she were suddenly completely enclosed with no air. Pressure that squeezed and left no room for her lungs to inflate. No sound. A tomb. She smelled dank odors of rotting wood, wet earth, carbide gas, excrement, and others, harsh and unidentifiable to her. Despite a cold downdraft of air, it was difficult to breathe, taking longer to suck in a sufficient breath as the earth seemed to press against her efforts.

Pottsville Number 6 was a deep mine, straight down hundreds of feet below the surface with shafts, airways, and gangways reaching in all directions like tentacles on a strange underground creature. Air quality was unpredictable. The company supplied Davy lamps to the miners, assigning one to each man every day for safety, but in some mines, the practice became a way to check who worked and who didn't, who got paid and who did not. No miner would go into the mine without one. Some mines had canaries to do the job. If the bird died, the air was bad, a warning to evacuate. But a new law forced the mine owners to provide special lamps whose flame would change color or die out in the presence of bad air. If a man broke his lamp, the cost of replacement came out of his wages, as did the cost of the fuel.

They approached the office, a wooden shack built in an alcove carved out of rock, slimy with mold and coal dust. A pegboard hung on the wall outside the office listed the names of all the workers and the names of the faces being worked that day. Men gathered around it, hanging their numbered brass checks on the pegboard, a sign that they were working today and to where they were assigned. The fire boss gave instructions but Bridie was trying to remember his name.

Trying to blend in, she moved among the other men around the pegboard. Despite her clenched jaw and fists, and her acute sense of vigilance, she laughed at herself. *Other* men, she said to herself. You're thinking of yourself as one of the men. She found Tim's and Jamie's name quickly, but couldn't decipher the notations on the slate beside the pegboard.

Bridie had lived in the mine patch long enough to know a little about what to expect below. Women talked about mine scuttlebutt, repeating what their husbands told them. Tim had told her about the procedure at the office. Sweeney and Colem had spoken little this morning as they walked toward the mine, except to tell her to remain alert at all times and stay close. If she felt herself getting dull in her mind or numb in her body, be sure and tell Tim or one of them. Tim had talked about the different dangerous gasses, but though she knew them by name—firedamp killed Mike Boyle, afterdamp killed Paddy Ryan—she couldn't remember which was which, which was lighter than air and floated above, which was heavier and accumulated along the floor. She needed to know if she should drop to the floor for clean air or not. Some you could smell, some you couldn't, like white-damp, the most dangerous of all. One whiff of that and you're dead.

Before the shift began, the fire boss inspected all working areas, checking for gas, measuring fresh air, ensuring the ventilation system was working properly, testing the roof. He was responsible for the safety of everyone in the mine. Even so, Bridie had no confidence in him. Why should she? Every day there were reports of one or two miners killed or seriously injured, if not here then in nearby mines. Sometimes cave-ins or explosions involved the loss of many lives. These accidents won the attention of mine owners and operators and even the government, resulting, now and again, in new safety laws that were poorly enforced. But the daily loss of a few lives went unnoticed except for the inconvenience.

The fire boss noted, on the slate, the conditions in the working areas. Work began only when the slate was clean. If the presence of gas was noted, work was delayed until the air was cleared by the brattice man who manipulated the ventilating system. The fire boss lit the safety lamps and gave one to each miner. Here is where the difference between miner and laborer was clear to Bridie. Though many were called miners, the distinction rightfully belonged to only a few.

The miner, a man who served many years under the tutelage of experienced miners, studying all aspects of mining, passed an exam that certified him. Tim was a miner with papers. He hired his own crew and worked independently. In most mines the miner, not the laborer, was given the Davy lamp that would detect gasses which could suddenly fill an area that had been declared safe. Its flame flared up if small quantities of bad air passed through the gauze-like mesh: a signal to evacuate. Tim assumed the responsibility for the safety of his crew when he accepted the lamp and was required to turn it in at the end of the day. He had pilfered several lamps that he gave to Sweeney and Denny. Bridie got Jamie's.

The fire boss... Henry Schmidt! That's his name, Bridie remembered. Schmidt told Tim to watch the roof in the crossheading to Angela; the face Tim's crew was working today.

"You'll need to knock down some loose pieces of slate."

Knock down loose sections of the roof, Bridie thought with alarm. What's to keep the whole thing from falling if you're banging around up there?

Schmidt continued, "There's some firedamp about, not enough to keep you from working, but watch it."

Firedamp! For God's sake! He'll let us in with gasses about? Bridie's hand automatically covered her nose and mouth. A sense of dread filled her. This day will not end well. She dismissed that sense of doom, just the jitters, she thought.

"Bring lots of timber with you; you'll find the need for reinforcing."

All the reinforcing in the world isn't going to hold the massive weight of the earth up if it decides to let lose, she thought. Bridie's heart sank to her belly, inducing a wave of nausea.

They trudged a mile or more along a tunnel, single file or in pairs, tools chinking and lunch pails clinking to the rhythm of their strides. Rocks and coal crunched, and water splashed beneath their rubber boots. The lamp on her cap lit only the space immediately in front of her. At one point, when she'd fallen behind the others, Bridie crashed into the roof where it dipped so low she would have ducked had she'd seen it. It was just high enough for the mine buggies to get under.

The men carried large pieces of long, heavy timber that looked like tree trunks, but it was Bridie who stumbled, sometimes suddenly sinking in a water filled hole, sometimes tripping over rails that ran along the floor of the gangway. Twice the crew were forced to the edge, pressing themselves to the rib of the gangway, to allow passage of empty buggies pulled by mules driven by boys little older than Johnny, their small son. She'd fight him going to work when he rightly belonged in school, she thought. And Patrick, he shouldn't be working in a mine so far away. Bridie could feel the slick moldy moss slide beneath her jacket, setting her off balance. Disgusting.

Water trickled in the distance. Bridie could hear the fading rumble of the last buggy and threatening thuds that sounded like distant thunder. Probably explosions, she thought. The lamps on each person's cap flickered orange and yellow, casting ominous shadows. Occasionally the lamplight played on streaks of coal, making the rib of the gangway look as if it were bedecked with black jewels. Air sometimes howled through the shaft and ventilation system. No wonder folks thought the mines were haunted with spirits of killed miners, Bridie thought.

It seemed like they walked miles along the gangway. Even after they reached Angela, it was hours before the mining could begin. Tim and his men tested the roof in the gangway as they turned into the crossheading and along that avenue into the working face. They jabbed the roof with long drills. Bridie prodded overhead, timidly at first, but learned to be more forceful. She could hear the "ping" that meant the roof was safe. "Pong" indicated loose rock overhead and set everyone to work knocking it down.

When Bridie's bladder refused to be ignored any longer, she went to a small smelly area in the crossheading that served as the toilet. This was the only time Bridie was grateful for the dark. She unbuckled her belt, slid her pants down and squatted to do her business—like she sometimes did when walking in the woods with a friend.

Some timbers that formed a crude archway along the crossheading were buckled or rotted enough that they had to be replaced or reinforced. Bridie helped put these massive pieces of wood in place, passed tools, and got in the way more often than not, once falling on her backside into a pile of stinking mule dung. The real work could begin only after they made the area as secure as possible, but it was coal they got paid for—not safety.

Bridie's muscles screamed from overexertion. Her job was to toss the chunks of coal cut from the face into the mine car. Most she couldn't lift. She attempted to break up hunks too heavy for her. Her hands and fingers felt raw beneath the gloves and she was sure they were bleeding. When Tim hollered "fire in the hole," she could barely get her body to move along the crossheading to the gangway before the charge he'd set to loosen more coal exploded. The smell of black powder gave her a headache and despite the handkerchief tied over her mouth and nose, coal dust gritted against her tongue and teeth. At lunch time, too tired to eat, she curled up on the dirt floor and slept.

"Fire! Get down. Get down." Tim's shouts awakened her, confused, aware immediately of scorching heat.

"Don't breathe, Bridie. Don't breathe," shouted Tim.

Her eyelids felt glued shut; she forced them open a tiny slit. Tim dragged her to a clear patch of dirt where the others were already prone, face in the earth. At the far end of the crossheading, she could see a line of fire skittering along the roof, its flames blue with flicks of orange. The flame, halted as if by some invisible barrier, did not advance any further toward them. It was then she realized she'd heard a boom in her sleep but ignored it. The day had been filled with the thunderous sound of explosions. "Face in the dirt," Tim shouted and shoved her face-first into the earth.

Bridie thought she'd suffocate but found little edges of air in the dirt. She was aware of Tim's hand on her head, pushing her further into the damp earth. The *phwump* of the blaze informed her that the fire was still burning, though the heat seemed to lessen. She lay there waiting to be consumed, too stunned to even wonder about Johnny. She reached back to grasp Tim's hand so they could go together. She'd heard stories about fathers and sons lying dead in an embrace when rescue workers were able to reach them after an accident.

Sudden quiet filled the chamber. Bridie thought she was dead until Tim yanked her to her feet. "Run for your life. Get that jacket over your face. Don't breathe this air," he said, his voice becoming muffled as he did the same. Instantly the fatigue and pain she'd felt earlier vanished and she ran faster than she thought possible. When she stumbled, strong hands grabbed each arm before she went down. She was dragged along as she scrambled to regain her footing. Tim reached over and pulled her jacket farther up her face so she couldn't see as she hurtled along, completely out of control, propelled by others in search of clean air.

NINE

Witch She Is

The mine steals everyone I love.
It's taking me, too, piece by piece.

– Bridie O'Doyle

Fingers sifting through the silky flour looking for weevils, mind waiting for Johnny to return home from school. She anticipated his greeting and a warm hug, though he'd grown too old for that. Still, she could feel his skinny arms around her middle and see the love in his eyes. Sometimes those eyes merged with her dead son's and the grief in her heart doubled. What if...

How does a mother live with the loss of her babies? First Daniel, named for me Da; then what if Johnny, not quite nine... Tim? The mine steals everyone I love, she thought. It's taking me, too, piece by piece. Fear replaced grief, fear for the future. She felt herself turning hard, cold, but she knew, no matter what, nothing could stop her loving Tim.

Parasites, she thought, crushing the reddish-brown pests between her fingers. There was a certain satisfaction the crunching sensation gave her. She narrowed her eyes and lips as she crushed another. With each crackle of weevil shell she imagined Frank Gowen, god of the railroads, owner of the mines that took her loves away from her, being crushed by a hand more powerful than her own. Someday, she thought, something will hurt him and I hope I'm there to see his pain.

The sun began to dry the drenched earth. Wind blew the odor of the privy away to allow the sweet June scent of budding trees to waft in. Voices of women and children drifted in through the open window that framed the delicate lace of a new spider web. The breaker rumbled in the distance. Bridie closed the window so the coal dust would not stick to her dough. Water heated on the stove below a shelf that held jars of last year's herbs.

Baking pans and bowls, flour and yeast, mixing spoons and cups for scooping covered the long table in the kitchen. She combined the ingredients out of habit, by feel of the dough rather than by measurement. Twelve loaves of bread would emerge from the sticky mound on her white-dusted table. Bridie sprinkled more flour onto the dough. She plunged the heels of her hands into the dough and pushed it forward, curled her fingers around the rising far edge of the dough, folded it toward her, turned it, added flour, and kneaded it again.

After a few minutes Bridie fell into a soothing rhythm that slowed her breathing, relaxed her jaw and shoulders. She felt as if she were being rocked, like her mother had held her when she was about six, as they rocked in a squeaky chair. She felt the warmth of the embrace, the motion of her mother's breathing, the rough fiber of Ma's dress on her cheek, heard the soft tune she hummed. For a moment she let go of Daniel and her fears for her family, let her mind empty. By the time the bread was kneaded and shaped, Bridie was humming. *Oh, the days of the Kerry dancing/Oh, the ring of the piper's tune/Oh, for those hours of gladness/Gone, alas, like our youth, too soon!*

All the women in the patch shared the outdoor oven, which

could accommodate only twenty-four loaves, every Wednesday. They worked in shifts, in twos or threes, until all the women in the patch had an opportunity to bake. Bridie preferred to go first but they took turns with that, too. The women who readied the oven the night before and early morning were the first to bake. This day Bridie would be baking in the afternoon with Sheila, Brian's wife.

The aroma of baking bread filled the air and made Bridie's stomach rumble as she approached the oven with a spring in her step, a tune on her lips. *When the boys began to gather/in the glen of a summer's night/And the Kerry piper's tuning/Made us long with wild delight!* She could see the women gathered around the oven talking, little children running underfoot in the dirt, playing and yelling, dogs barking as they ran wildly, fetching sticks, chasing cats and kids. *Oh, to think of it/Oh, to dream of it/Fills my heart with...* A wild screech rang out.

Sheila flung her arms about. Though Bridie could hear her voice she was too far away to make out the words, but the anger was clear. Sheila had been snappish and fretful since Brian's accident. She groused at everyone and seldom smiled. She could be heard screaming at her children, and Brian too.

"Good afternoon to ye," said Bridie. She forced a smile on her face but inside was dreading another scene stirred up by Sheila. Things had changed for her since Brian had lost his arm. She took in three boarders to earn money, so she needed lots more bread for the week. No good word found its way to her lips, so full was she of bitter complaints about a live husband who couldn't work, who probably wouldn't work again except in the breaker for a breaker boy's wage. How were they to live with four little mouths to feed and not a one of them old enough to work?

Maureen and Yolanda came over to help Bridie carry her loaves.

Sheila, already placing hers in the oven, looked askance at Bridie then blessed herself, making the sign of the cross three times. She took her rosary out of her pocket and blessed the air around the oven, then kissed the crucifix. She removed the cork from a bottle of holy water the priest had given her and sprinkled it on Bridie, staying as far away as she could all the time mumbling tongue-tied-sounding words.

"For the love of God, woman, what are ye doing?" Bridie asked, brushing the water off her dress and one of her loaves.

"Making sure ye don't curse the oven, that's what. Or curse the bread so's we all get sick."

"Curse the bread, Sheila? Please. You know it was no curse that took Brian's leg and if it were, it wasn't mine. Don't forget, Tim was there. The roof fell on him, too," said Bridie. Now I know, she thought, why Sheila runs out the back door every time I go to see how Brian's leg is mending.

The heat from the oven scorched her already too-warm face. The other women backed away but watched as Bridie started to place her loaves in the oven.

"No," shrieked Sheila, a blotchy red rash rising from her chest to her neck. She pushed Bridie aside. "You're not going to put your bread in with mine. Haven't you already done enough damage?"

Bridie's eyebrows pushed her forehead into furrows. She shook her head as if the shaking could bring the right words to the surface.

Sheila glared at her, eyes narrowed, fists clenched, her red hair crazed by the wind, feet spread wide as if ready for battle. She held the crucifix up like a shield. "My Brian would have two good arms if 'tweren't for you, Bridie. I don't want you coming round to see him anymore. Stay away from him with your dirty leaves and wicked poultices." She was screaming, gasping between words.

"Would you rather a dead husband?" Yolanda said. "Brian

wouldn't have his life if it weren't for Bridie and Tim. He'd be still in there, choked by the white-damp."

"Or dead of infection. Don't ye forget 'twas Bridie who found it and got the company doctor to come." said Maureen. "What did the doctor say? That Bridie should keep on doing what she's doing. She saved his life, Sheila. Now that's enough, out of ye. We've the oven to tend, so it doesn't go cold."

Yolanda rolled her eyes. "Dirty leaves and wicked poultices, indeed!"

Bridie pressed her lips together. Her cheeks puffed a little as if she had a mouthful of something she could neither swallow nor spit out.

"Cursed the mine, she did." Sheila, hands on her hips, looked at each woman as if she were about to make a great revelation. Nodding her head up and down, she walked right up to Bridie. "Caused the accident, she did." Sheila glared at Bridie. "You think I don't know. I do. Brian told me what you did." The blotches, now a solid red that reached her cheeks, looked like intense sunburn. Sheila faced the group. "She went into the mine dressed like a man. Like Jamie."

Everyone knew a woman brought a curse to the mine if she entered it.

Bridie cringed. More than one hand went to a mouth in a look of surprise for some and horror for others. She could hear among the shocked murmurs: "'Tis true." "'Tis a curse, all right." "Ye can be sure o' that." "May Gawd have mercy on our souls."

Even Maureen and Yolanda looked stunned.

Bridie put her hand up, palm forward, as if to deflect the dirty looks that shot her way.

"Cursed Jamie's wife, too, didn't ye?" shouted Clair, pointing her finger at Bridie. "Why do ye think his baby was stillborn?"

Moisture formed above Bridie's pressed lips. The muscles in her belly tightened. It's Gowen, she thought. He's the one to blame for Brian's accident. The mine was in need of repairs

"It's them herbs she gives out to stop babies from coming. 'Tis against God's will, I say."

Like many women, Jamie's wife, Kate, didn't want more babies. Five were enough, she'd said. Bridie gave her concoction of herbs to put inside her body and another to drink. Sometimes the morning mix, as she called it, made women vomit and it didn't always work, but, Kate, at least, had a pregnancy-free year.

"That's me you're talking 'bout," said Kate standing behind the crowd with her loaves on a plank, ready to bake. "'Twas Jamie's job she was saving. If he'd missed another day's work, he'd of lost his job."

"Some would say 'twas indeed true that Bridie can curse with a look," said Kate. "Some of ye are suspicious of the herbal mixtures she uses to help those who've got the fever or the runs. That is until ye've need of them."

A few women, Irish and Slav, nodded their heads. The children looked up at their mothers. Even the dogs stopped barking.

"Dat's no magic she uses," said Yolanda. "Dat's like my granmudder and yours—poultices, purges, infusions, simples. Dem no magic potions."

"Just let one of ye get a boil that hurts," said Maureen. "Then, ye come running to Bridie. Who else around here will lance a boil and keep it from getting infected?"

"The doctor," said Sheila, hatred infusing each word. "We have the company doctor for that."

"Sure enough," said Kate. "An' by the time he gets here, you could lose your life."

"He'd be asking twenty-five cents for it, too," said Maureen.

"If dat can be healed, den Bridie vould do it and ask no money," said Yolanda.

"Those she's helped say she brings the luck with her," said Kate.

Sheila, who had been standing there swaying and moaning softly, made a sudden dash toward the oven. Before anyone could stop her, she shoved Bridie aside, seized two hot loaves from the oven and tossed them into the mud. "I told you I'll not have your bread in with mine." She reached for the third and fourth but dropped them as if she had only just noticed how hot they were. One fell to her feet, the other into the ash of the oven.

Sheila screamed in pain as she rubbed the still sticky hot dough from her scalded hands. "Me own bread," she screamed. "'Tis me own bread in the mud. She collapsed in a heap of shrieks and tears.

Maureen brought Sheila home. Bridie and Kate baked extra bread. Everyone gave something to help Sheila's family. Bridie slipped two doses of Laudanum in Kate's pocket.

"See that she takes one now, one later. She won't take it from me. Let me know if she needs more.

TEN

The Mule Boy

My sweetheart's the mule in the mines,
I drive her without reins or lines,
On the bumper I sit,
I chew and I spit,
All over my sweetheart's behind.

> – *Minstrel ballad "My Sweetheart's the Mule*
> *in the Mines"*

April 1887
Tim

Me Patrick was called to be a mule boy, of that I had no doubt. Known that since he was a wee lad. That's when he first spied mules friskin' about in the grass. 'Twas one of those cold, cold days with a clear, blue sunny sky and one or two white clouds. The animals had been brought up into the fresh air for the Easter holiday. One tired, old mule with half chewed up ears and covered with coal dust caught his attention. As soon as the fresh air hit the mule, he trembled a bit, and then went runnin' off to the far end of the field, brayin' and kickin' up his heels, nudgin' the other mules who were stunned by the sunlight. The old creature remembered the daylight. Mules have a good memory. They'd run in twos and threes, or a pack, zigzaggin' the field as if wild horses were chasin' them. Old Coalie—that's what Patrick called the beast—dropped to the ground and rolled over on his back and wriggled about, stirrin' up the smell of dry earth and new grass. Patrick was delighted.

"Da," he says, "They're having fun. Just like me and Martin Keough. Do they come out to play every day?"

He'd never seen a mule, never thought such a big animal might feel like just like he does when he is out playin' in the snow or runnin' through the new grass of spring with a butty and a ball.

"No, Patrick, they live in a stable below ground. Only come up when the mine is closed fer a holiday. Or a strike. When 'tis time to go back they'll dig their hooves in and lower their rump cause they don't wanna go."

Coalie came over to the fence where Patrick stood and nuzzled the boy. "Mules are smart, you know, Patrick. Smarter than some people. A mule driver needs to be at least as smart as the mule. Sure'n you know that animal thinks *it's* the master."

"Can I play with him, Da? Ride on his back. Like the pictures in Ma's book?"

"They were horses not mules, Lad. Mules are better on their feet, don't fall like horses do; more powerful too. They don't get sick like horses or tired neither. Those there mules are too rowdy to play with, me boy. Ye'd be trampled."

I pulled a quid of tobacco out of me pocket. Tore off a piece and held it out to the mule. Old Coalie's smeller quivered. He reached for the plug with his thick searching lips and drew it into his mouth. To Patrick's delight he stayed there as if waitin' fer more.

"Why's his ears like that, Da?"

"A mule holds his ears straight up to feel the roof of the gangway."

"What's a gangway?"

"'Tis a... ah... a tunnel in the mine. The roof gets low in some places. The mule's ears feel along the roof. When he feels the roof get lower, he drops his head so he won't bang it. Old Coalie's ears are worn off, that's all."

Patrick climbed up on the fence and soothed the dusty animal's ears. "Mules are not to be trusted, Lad. They can bite. Can take fingers off, even a hand. Best be careful."

"He won't bite me, Da. Old Coalie knows I like him."

'Twas true. I could tell right then. Patrick was meant to be a mule boy. Every strike or holiday, I'd give Patrick a bit of brown leaf for Old Coalie. They'd become fast friends. The old mule probably would have let the boy on his back if I'd allowed it.

Patrick, me first born. His mother, my dear Márie Cáit, God rest her soul, never wanted him called Pat or Paddy. He's named for a saint, she'd tell me. No one ever heard of Saint Paddy, she'd say, always gettin' after me if I called him Pat.

I stuffed me pipe fer a smoke, the beer in me tin mug at me feet on the floor of the porch. Bridie wept softly beside me, a letter in her hand, more in her lap. They and the fresh air her only comfort. We'd pulled two chairs from the kitchen even though 'twas still chilly, because the moon was full and new. We needed to be outside. There were too many folks inside, but the stink of beer and the rumble of voices and laughter drifted onto the porch.

"Remember when he went to the breaker, Tim? How he didn't want to go? He didn't understand why he couldn't be a mule boy straight away, why he had to be a breaker boy first."

Bridie, she loved that boy just like he was her own. Tears in me eyes forced me to turn away from her, couldn't let her see mine. She had enough of her own.

I could see Patrick, a tangle of red hair, freckles, elbows, and knees. Folks called him Little Tim, a small likeness of me, he was. I could picture him on his first day as breaker boy, in boots too big and so tall he could hardly bend his knees. He'd set out to prove he was man enough to be a mule driver. He had a way with those animals and they with him.

Bridie shuffled through the letters. "Oh, how I hated to send him away to work in another mine. And so far away."

"Would ye have deprived him of his dream, then, Bridie? No work was here in Number Six. Silver Creek Colliery put him to work as a mule driver, even with no experience."

"Sure he had experience. He spent every spare moment with mules. He'd go to the stables before the breaker started, feeding them, currycombing, helping to fit their harnesses so they wouldn't get sores or shoulder galls. He even slept in the stables once, remember? He had that note from the Number Six stableman, saying how Patrick was his patcher, a better helper than most."

Bridie found the letter she'd been looking for. "Let me read this one."

This was my first week as a mule driver. I was scared and happy too. I asked the stableman how I should do the job. He told me I should ask the mule. My mules name is Lizzy. Her last driver got killed because he did tricks and got crushed. Mam, I won't do that so don't worry. I led Lizzy over to the empty cars and watched what she would do. She went to the last car and looked around at me as if to say, Come boy! Hook me up to the car. Lizzy knows where to go and when to stop. She knows how much should be loaded into a car and won't pull one more hunk of coal. And quitting time she goes right for the cage. Won't work no more even if we're not done. Da, I always have tobacco for her. Mam the mule only knows cuss words so I hafta say words you don't like. That's how I hafta tell her what to do.

Patrick

PS Mam everyone calls me Paddy. I tell them my name is Patrick. They still call me Paddy.

I drew on my pipe and a cloud of smoke circled into the damp night air as if reaching for the light. "That's when I told him to always carry a container of water with him. Only way to get a mule goin' once he makes up his mind to lay down on the job. Pour it in his ear. Then ye'll see it jump up, boyo."

"Too much smoke in there," Maureen said. She sat on the porch steps, the screen door slapping behind her. "Can you read the letter? I was fixin' the food before."

Bridie read it again, her body heaving with soundless cries.

Dear Mam and Da. Here I am in Lizzys stable with two other mules. It's smoky but not too bad. This is the only scrap of paper I could find. This may be the last words you hear from me. I lay here next to Lizzy waiting to be rescued or for the gasses. She tried to find us a way out. There was none. What happened is there's a fire in the shaft. I couldn't get in the cage cause I knew there were some miners who didn't know about the fire. How could I get in the cage without warning them? Even though Lizzy didn't like it we went looking for those men. We catch the next cage up I told her. And we did tell them miners and ran quick back to the cage to pull the bell for a lift up. Too late. The cage was gone burned. So we started back to the men. There was smoke that burned my eyes couldn't see. Flames too. I had to bring Lizzy back to the stable. Had to pour water in her ear cause she wouldn't go another step just laid down. When I got to the miners they built a big wall around themselves. You know to keep the gas out. Da they wouldn't let me in. I yelled. I begged them. Let me in. I warned you. I missed my ride up to warn you. But they wouldn't. No. That would let the gasses in they said. I don't want to die. I don't want to die alone so I came back to Lizzy. I'm sorry for being bad sometimes. You are the best Mam and Da. I'm sorry to die.

Patrick

It may be no comfort, but those miners died, too.

Maureen held the letter to her heart. "Fourteen, only fourteen." She stooped over her legs as if she had a pain. "Who put that last part in?"

I shook my head, shrugging my shoulders. "'Twouldn't have happened that way if he were here," I said, swallowing my grief. "Or Sweeney there. They didn't know the boy."

ELEVEN

'Tis What We Do

March 1887

"I have lost two boys to the mine, Tim. Two. It's too soon after Patrick. You feel that loss, I know you do."

Bridie had fought with Tim about their Johnny working in the mine. Too young, too little she'd said. Bridie wanted Johnny to go to school, to run and play like a boy should. There has to be another way to get some extra money, she'd argued.

They needed the money desperately. Even when he was alive and working in a Scranton mine miles away, though not expected to send money, every time Patrick visited he'd brought coal or scraps of lumber, often harvesting herbs and roots he saw growing along the miles he walked. Without a boarder to pay rent, they couldn't make it.

His sister, thirteen-year-old Kathleen, worked for the superintendent's wife cleaning and washing laundry. She brought home coins and cast off clothing, leftover food that would have become pig slop.

Prices at the company store rose faster than Tim's earnings, gouging what little the miners were paid with exorbitant prices for goods that cost much less in the distant cities. Last spring, Sweeney and O'Malley borrowed a pair of company mules and a wagon. They brought some of the women to Scranton and Pottsville where shops offered cheaper prices. O'Malley lost his job when it was discovered his wife made curtains from fabric purchased outside the company store.

"I can clean, again, Tim. I did for years." said Bridie.

"No. I'll not have it, Bridie. You'll not be scrubbing someone else's floors."

"So, you'd rather send a wee boy to the breaker, is it?" The instant the words left her mouth, Bridie felt her retort was too harsh. But the truth is the truth, she thought. I meant what I said, but I could have said it softer. "Then we'll take in boarders again," she said, trying to keep the anger out of her voice. "We haven't had boarders for a long while. Kathleen and Johnny can sleep in the front room with us, then there'll be room for two or three boarders upstairs."

"I'll not have foreigners at me table, Bridie, or in my house. They're dirty and noisy."

No matter what suggestion she made, Tim's response was always the same. He dismissed it, accusing her of being too soft on the boy. In the end, Bridie took in laundry. That kept Johnny from the breaker for a time.

Lately they'd had the same argument every time Tim came home with his pay envelope, Bridie preparing super, Tim pacing.

"Com'ere. You have to see what those bastards have done. A man breaks his back all day and for what?" He ripped open the brown paper envelope. All that was inside was a slip of paper itemizing his expenses. "And I thought we'd be better off when I got me papers, that a miner with papers received the best wages. But here I am a jump-and-a-half in the rear of success and two jumps ahead of starvation. Look at this bobtail check, will you. Look here."

He shook the paper as if the motion would release coins like manna from heaven. "Rent deducted, supplies of blasting powder, tools deducted; pay for my helpers, helpers' rent—d'ya think I'm gonna get that back?—their powder, squibs, oil." He paced across the kitchen and back, flicking his finger at the paper. "Canned food and oil for us, more. Here, look at what you've spent, Bridie. It all adds up to more than the wages due me." He went down the list, itemizing their purchases at the company store, things they couldn't make or grow themselves. No finely milled soap for Bridie's face, no bows for Kathleen's braids, no coffee, no coal for the coming winter.

Bridie banged potatoes onto the kitchen table. One rolled off and thudded on the floor. Tim grabbed it.

"Isn't that reason enough for sending Johnny to school so he can learn a skill, get a better job?" she said, shaking her finger at Tim.

"And what kind of man do ye want him to be anyway. The *perfesser* kind?" Tim's voice reeked sarcasm, deliberately mispronouncing and drawing out the word. "A man who can't lift anything heavier than a book? A man who can't set a charge or heft a pick to cut coal from rock?'

Bridie scrubbed the potatoes so hard she wouldn't have to peel them. "A man can use his brain as well as his brawn, Tim O'Doyle. You want your son to never see the light of day? To be dragged lifeless from a mine for the sake of hefting a pick? My sainted father was a teacher. He provided well for his family until the famine came. Johnny could be a teacher or a bookkeeper; he's smart enough." Bridie let the potato drop into the bucket of water and turned to Tim, hands on hips. "He should be going to school."

"And what did your sainted father do when the famine hit? He became a sainted miner, is what. 'Tis the mining that will see Johnny through tough times, Bridie, not school books."

True, thought Bridie, retrieving the potato, resuming her furious scrubbing.

"Besides," Tim continued, "you taught Kathleen and Patrick

to read. Johnny's learning, too. He's already better at it than most around here."

"It's not the same, Tim. "There's more to school than reading and writing. Think of it as putting something by for the future, Johnny getting educated."

"I could say the same, Bridie. The plants you grow, think of them the same way. Putting something into now."

She couldn't have accepted money for the use of her gift, a blessed knowing from whatever entity existed above or for remedies given freely by the earth. That was not to be sold. How could she ask money from people as needy as herself? She did earn when she was called upon for her knowledge of herbs and roots for healing: bread, a ham, goat's milk, preserves, coal, wood, and the like, but rarely money. But it was only money that could satisfy the company store debt.

Tim stopped his pacing to face her, his eyes pleading with her to be reasonable.

"You want all the other boys to taunt him, calling him sissy for not working the breaker? What kind of a man will that make of him? Answer me that, Bridie."

A long, sharp knife appeared in Bridie's hand. She cut the potatoes so forcefully the crack of the knife hitting the wooden table top bounced off the walls.

"It's not being a sissy to use your God given brain, Timothy O'Doyle, and you know it." Thwack. A potato split and skidded across the table. "If *you* wouldn't be calling him a sissy yourself, he wouldn't feel like one. They just say things like that 'cause they're jealous, those boys. They'd rather be in school than on the breaker ten hours a day."

"'Tis what we do, Bridie. 'Tis what we do. It's been arranged."

TWELVE

Red Tips

There came to this country a short time ago,
A poor Irish widow from County Mayo.
She had but one son, his age it was eight,
And the boss gave him work picking slate.
The first day at the breaker the boys all did stare,
For poor little Mike was the youngest one there.
They asked him his age; he said I'm just eight.
So they nicknamed him Mickey Pick-Slate.

– "Mickey Pick-Slate"

1887

It was as if the world had died, the sudden silence of the breaker that fell over the mine patch at the end of the day—a hush as deafening as the rattle, bang, and clatter of the breaker, a looming monster that shook and sorted coal as it hurtled the stuff seven stories down iron chutes, breaking it into marketable sized pieces. Bridie had been waiting all day. Waiting for the shrill harshness of the whistle that controlled their lives and relieved the smothering blanket of quiet. Quitting time on Johnny's first day.

She leaped at the reverberation of the whistle through the chaos of her worry. Flinging her shawl around her shoulders, scant protection against the day's chill, she flew out the door, slipped into her shoes, and ran toward the coal mine, kicking up puffs of dry earth. Tears ran down her cheeks. Quitting time, she thought. Thank God!

Bridie searched ahead for any sign of him but she knew her son, Johnny, would be among the last of the boys to leave the breaker. This was his first day on the job: breaker boy at Number Six Coal mine. He turned eight this year.

The whistle blasted again, loud, demanding, relentless in its insistence. But those deep in the earth wouldn't hear it. Tim, her husband, would be late, staying until every last scrap of coal they'd forced from the seam had been loaded on the last car of the day—until all his men were out safely.

She shook her head at the custom of starting new boys at the very peak of the breaker so the experienced boys picked slate and slag the new ones missed. So high. Dangerous for a new boy—for any boy, my boy. He'd be the last one out.

A tune replayed itself in her mind, as it had all day, the way songs often do:

A poor simple woman at the breaker still waits
To take home her Mickey Pick-Slate.

That very morning, before the sun rose, men and boys issued from their coal dust covered, wood frame homes at the first sounding of the whistle, as if spellbound, like worker bees by the hum of the hive. Some stood on the porch and stuffed tobacco into their pipe bowls. A few called inside, hurrying sons who lagged behind or waved greetings to neighbors, calling, "How's she cuttin'?"

Together, father and son, friends and enemies, marched dark streets toward the breaker. Their steps aligned with each other's, momentarily blurring differences. They sang songs they'd made up, one trying to out-sing the other. Soft caps slouched under the weight of the teapot-shaped lamps attached to the fronts. Growler pails filled with cold potatoes and wedges of bread for lunch clattered at their sides.

Others slung sprags onto their shoulders, long pieces of wood they hoped would slow hurtling coal cars loaded with tons of coal. Men and boys with no legs were carried by those who had two, those with one leg hobbled along on makeshift crutches. They were the ones who misjudged the speed of the cars or incorrectly jabbed their sprag into the moving wheels. Those missing an arm had their supplies hung about their necks.

This afternoon the procession would reverse. The words to the chorus nagged at her:

A poor simple woman at the breaker still waits
To take home her Mickey Pick-Slate.

She could see in the distance the men begin to emerge onto the roadway. There! Up ahead. Was that him, the little one, piggy-backed on someone's shoulders, his head resting on the shoulder of the man carrying him? Injured? Please. No God, don't let him be injured. I've already lost two sons to the mines. She pulled her skirts up higher. Pushed ahead. Ran out of her two-sizes-too-big Salvation Army shoes. Feet bounded over stones, toes smashed into sharp rocks. Neither slowed nor hindered her straining to touch her child's face.

One day in the winter with seven below,
While poor little Mike was sifting the coal,

He tripped on a plank that was carelessly placed
And into the rolls he fell to his fate.
His body so mangled it's sad for to say,
The poor little fellow he soon passed away.
His mother demented still lingers and waits
For her little Mickey Pick-Slate.

For breakfast this morning she'd fixed porridge for him, just the way he liked it, when he liked it—brown sugar *and* honey *and* cinnamon—the extravagance did nothing to assuage her guilt or induce hunger. Five thirty in the morning, forced from warm blankets into dark cold—no wonder he'd had no appetite. She herself had been up for an hour, building the fire in the kitchen stove, sloshing ladles full of water from the big pails into the kettles to heat for tea and breakfast. She'd no desire for food yet. She plopped the porridge onto a piece of paper, wrapped it, and stuck it into his pocket. Maybe, maybe he'd get hungry before lunch.

Tim rose from the table. He had no trouble eating, no matter the time, a big boned man, well-muscled, not a scrap of fat to him. His rubber boots made a muted thud with each footfall as he crossed the wide, rough planks of the floor. He and the boy wore coveralls, Patrick's hand-me-downs clean but irreversibly stained from the black of the coal.

"Get over here, lad." The harshness of his voice seemed to hit Johnny as if it were a shove.

Tim lifted the boy onto a chair, tucked his too-long pants into the still untied hobnailed boots. "This'll be the time ye're glad they're too long, these pants. Glad of these high boots ye hate. The way you'll sit astride the chute, it's your legs that will slow the coal so's ye can pick out the slate and rock. Boots'll keep your legs from getting tore up.

You know ye'll be sitting on a board across a chute, don't you, lad?"

Johnny's blank look answered the question.

"Well, ye will. Coal will run down the chute, fast and hard sometimes. Loud, so ye can't hear nothin' else. Bony it's called, the slate and rock, anythin' that's not coal."

He tied Johnny's boots and returned him to the floor. "Keep them laced up tight, son." He looked up at Bridie. She dried her already dry hands on her apron, twisting it, untwisting, smoothing it out over her dress, then drying and twisting again, eyes glistening with moisture.

Johnny nodded. He'd heard this before but today it sounded different, real but not real.

Tim wrapped a handkerchief loosely around the boy's neck, knotting it in the back. "Pull it up, like this," he demonstrated, pulling his own up over his nose, his eyes peering over dingy, grayed-red cloth. "It'll keep ye from breathing too much of that dust, keep it off yer t'roat. Don't take it off, mind ye, lest you want the black lung. Shake it out at lunch, too. Get the mornin's dust off it. Your cap, too— pull it down, like this."

The child looked up at his dad, then away, his eyes shiny.

Tim sneaked a plug of chewing tobacco into the pocket holding the cold porridge. "Stick this in your cheek," he whispered. "Don't taste too good at first but it'll keep ye spitting that black soot 'stead of swallowin' it."

Tim looked around to see if Bridie was looking. "Stuff costs, so most of the time I suck on a lump of coal. And sit still, ye hear?"

Johnny's head lowered, his eyes cast down, staring at the tips of his boots. He nodded.

"Ye know how high that breaker is?"

Johnny shook his head, no, then nodded, yes.

"Seven stories. Ye've seen it. You've seen the coal cars being hauled to the top."

Johnny nodded.

"Coal gets dumped into grinders at the top, to break it up before it goes down the chutes."

"Ye'll be on the very top. New boys go on the top."

Johnny was still.

"Not so bad being on top, son. Lower down, the bony is slimy from spit and tobacco juice from the lads above," Tim laughed.

Johnny made a face as if he'd tasted something rotten.

Tim knelt and lifted his son's chin, looking him straight in the eye. "Big ones and wee ones have fallen from it, Johnny boy, wiggling and fooling. Getting dared to spit on the Picker Boss should he go below. Ye gotta sit still." He stood and gave Johnny a rough smack on the back. "Ye're a man now. Let's go and do a man's work." They put on their coats, Johnny not even objecting, this time, to the one he had to wear.

"The other boys say only sissies go to school," said the child-man.

"Bringing home the bread—that's what men do, son."

Off they went without so much as a goodbye. Bridie held herself back from snatching her son and running.

Up ahead, was it her Johnny? Yes! She recognized his coat, the red one, blackened now by coal dust. He hated his sister's old coat. I'll never make you wear that thing again, she promised him silently in her heart. It's not a girl's coat, she whispered. It had belonged to the fancy-dressed son of the colliery operator, a child who would never sit atop a breaker.

Alive, you must be alive or the whistle would have blown before quitting time. A mid-day sounding, apart from the lunch whistle, brought terror to the hearts of all. It signaled an accident or worse. She could see both legs wrapped around the person carrying him, Sweeney. She could see now it was Sweeney, God bless him, and one wee arm holding on to the front of the man's jacket.

"He's sleeping, Bridie. Exhausted. He'll get used to it," Sweeney called to her.

She stopped running. "'Tis indeed a poor demented mother I am, Sweeney," she said when they approached. "Out of my mind with worry. Ten hours for an eight-year-old. 'Tis too much. For the love of God, 'tis too much."

"One kid there was six—first day, too. Tim'll be along, just making sure everyone's up."

Sweeney carried the boy all the way home. Johnny didn't wake when Sweeney placed him in the front room. Bridie gently removed the hideous red jacket, his shirt, pants, shoes, and socks that had been darned and darned again. All released puffs of soot and built little hills and clots of coal dust.

The child still slept. His mother dipped a rag into one of the large pots of water that was always on the stove this time of the day and wiped the boy's face and hands, turning soot to mud. The tips of his fingers were raw and bleeding, his nails ground to stubs from picking bony from the coal on its way to coal cars below.

There was a long raw-red welt on the back of his hand and Bridie wondered if he'd fallen asleep on the job. Or maybe Picker Boss had struck him with a switch for daydreaming. Johnny was too scared and too new to have misbehaved. He stirred when she cleaned his fingers and slathered them with goose grease. She'd wash that off later when she bathed him, because they would toughen quicker if left exposed to the air. She wondered if Tim had remembered to tell him pissing on his fingers would make his skin tougher.

Bridie looked at his little face, still smudged with black, still sound asleep after his first day as a breaker boy. She prayed to a God she couldn't risk not believing in. She lifted her eyes to the sky beyond the window of this small room that was the gathering place for fun and food, rest and love. Keep him safe, was all she could manage to ask. She shook his clothes over the porch railing, then hung them behind the stove to dry for the next day's work. Johnny rolled over on the braided rug and continued to sleep near the warmth of the stove.

Tim came along soon, his growler dripping with beer from the Irish pub where he stopped some evenings. He walked a long distance for that small pleasure, passing the Slavs' pub on the way there and back. Bridie thought that was silly. Beer is beer. Irish beer or Polski piwo—what's the difference? Why not stop at the Polish pub, especially in the winter? They could little afford it anyway. But she held her tongue, grateful that he didn't spend every evening there to drink up what little money they had, running up another bill. She wouldn't deny him that small pleasure after spending the long day in the dark, hoping the air wouldn't suddenly turn and the timbers wouldn't creak or the rats run wildly for the mine head. This time of the year he never saw the light of day until Sunday.

"I should hate you, Tim O'Doyle, risking our son's life but I'm too relieved, grateful that he's home safe."

Tim's head hitched sideways toward the sleeping boy. "How's he?"

"He fell asleep on Sweeney's shoulders. The boy didn't wake when I undressed him. God bless that man. You know he carried Johnny all the way home?"

"He's a good man," Tim nodded. "I sent him up early to look after the boy. Don't baby him, Bridie. Let him undress himself. He's a breaker boy now. He's not your baby anymore." He took a long pull on his beer, now in a tin mug. "But ye can baby me all ye like," his grin reached across his round, ruddy face toward the cap he'd pushed back onto the top of his head. Red-gray curls fell rakishly on his forehead. Both had red hair—his more toward orange, hers more auburn. He was a tall man, over six feet, but Bridie was tall too, for a woman, coming to his shoulder.

Bridie had already taken his coat and unbuttoned his vest. "Get out on the porch with you, boyo. I've no time for sweeping again." She shoved him out the door.

"What? Aye, it's too cold. Ye wanting the neighbors seeing me in me underwear? Haven't you a decent bone in your body, woman?" He pulled her close to him.

"And what is it *you're* wanting the neighbors to see? It's more than your underwear," she said when she took off his trousers, wet and heavy with dirt. She shook the dust of the mines off of them. He jerked her close again and kissed her on the mouth when she tried to tuck his shirt into the front of the long johns he wore even in the summer. "Cover that thing up," she giggled and left him standing on the front porch alone.

Eddy Roarity swaggered down the road, one foot crossing over the other, nearly tripping himself, singing slurred words to his own tune. His wife, a woman bigger than some men, flew out onto the stoop of the house across from where Tim stood, her fists beating at the air.

"And where did you get money for drink? You're already on the tick at the pub."

The man fell up the steps.

She grabbed the back of his shirt and raised him to his feet. "Take those boots off before you come in the house and don't be expecting no supper this night. How'd you expect me to feed the kids, you off drinking the baking money? 'Tis you who won't eat tonight. I had to take in two new boarders; they'll be the ones to eat."

She jerked her thumb toward a large wood pail. "There's the tub, and some water," she said, pointing. "You can wash yourself; the cold water'll sober you up." She slammed the door, leaving him weaving, bent over his boots, fumbling with the laces. He fell on his side and didn't move.

"Eddy's at it again, on another tear." Tim came in and stripped off his underwear and hung it behind the stove to dry. "At least today he was sober at work." He stepped into the too-small, oval, tin tub that Bridie had filled with hot water. "Hot, hot. Are ye trying to scald me?"

Bridie added cold water.

"He was wanting to buy everyone a pint." Tim squatted in the tub, his knees up around his chin, his butt sitting on the rim. "Good, good, not too much cold." He slid the rest of the way into the tub, his knees like protruding knobs, his legs too long to straighten, the tub too narrow for crossing them. "Ah. The best part of the day. None of us'd drink beer he bought, you know, not counting him as friend. He works drunk sometimes, putting the rest of us at risk." He looked at his wife. She never minded bathing him, "Knowing, too, the huge knockdown he takes on his wages."

Bridie had poured warm water over Tim's head. She lathered his hair with her special herb soap. "And am I to understand that you, Tim O'Doyle, never knockdown your pay, keeping your own spending money?"

"Only for what you see, me love—the few pints I bring home and the one or two I drink at McMonagle's." He grabbed the soap from her and washed his face, blowing into the stream of rinse water as it splashed on his face. He reached up and hooked his hand around her neck, lowering her lips to his.

"Shh. Stop now," Bridie pushed away, nodding her head toward the boy on the rug, keeping her softened eyes on Tim.

"Sure'n he's asleep, Bridie," his wet hands unbuttoning her dress, pushing aside the layers of cloth underneath.

His wet-warm hand felt hot on her chilled breast. Her soap-slippery hand, departed from the usual routine, slid below the water and her mouth opened to him. She kissed the brown mole on his neck. He smelled like a man who'd worked hard, sweat sour tasting on his neck, pungent in his armpits. His smell always excited her. She carefully washed the black from his ears, the left one larger than the other. Her breasts, now loosed from their confines, brushed his face as she reached up with one hand, maneuvering the wash rag around the back of his neck to his shoulders, keeping her other hand on him below. She worked her way to his chest with her free hand, giving special attention to his raised nipples and to the powder burn scars. She tickled his ribs with her tongue, feeling for the deep scar carved in his flesh by a bullet, a reminder of his days as a Mollie Maguire. As she brought both hands together under the water, he arched his back and discharged a deep groan. By the end of the bath she and the floor were as wet as he. They both hummed a tune to an old Gaelic melody.

They awakened Johnny and both bathed him in the still warm, though quite black, water. He fit in the tub, able to sit cross-legged. They listened but Johnny told them only a little about his day. Neither pressed the exhausted boy for details. "Did'ya look in my pocket? A proud expression crossed his face. There Bridie found four pieces of coal.

"You know it's wrong to steal, Johnny-boy. God knows we need it, but it is wrong. What'll happen if you get caught? Did you think of that?" Bridie put the coal in a bin beside the stove.

"'Twasn't stealing, Mum. They slipped into my pocket accidentally, coming down the chute so fast they jumped up, hit me then slid into my pocket. After all that, I figured 'twas mine to keep. All the boys do it."

"That's no reason for you to do something wrong. Everyone else doing it doesn't make it right," said Bridie.

"I won't be going to the culm banks any more, now I'm working. Is that stealing too, mum, taking coal from the culm bank?"

Bridie knew it was. The refuse belonged to the company. With the little one working, she would be getting up extra early, to take her squeaky wagon to the culm bank and scrounge through the rubble for chunks of coal. Everyone did it. Sometimes the guards looked the other way. Sometimes they didn't, and wagons and wheelbarrows would get smashed. The fines were steep, in addition to having to pay for the stolen coal, often getting charged for more than was taken. The trick was to get there between shifts. For Bridie that would mean three or four in the morning some days or around midnight on other days. She wasn't willing, like some of the other women, to take the chance of getting caught in the daytime.

As Bridie closed her eyes that night, sleep evaded her. She wondered what her small son had endured. Did he feel like one of the men as he went off to the mine? How scared was he? Terrified? Did he eat his porridge? He didn't eat lunch. What was his day like? Bridie imagined the worst.

THIRTEEN

Black Water Baptism

I'm a little collier lad,
Hardworking all the day,
From early morn till late at night
No time have I to play.
Down in the bowels of the earth
Where no bright sun rays shine,
You'll find me busy at my work,
A white slave of the mine.

– Minstrel ballad

March, 1887
Johnny

I was dreaming of clouds shaped like elephants and giraffes, like I seed, uh saw, in the picture book Ma has. High in the sky, floating, like me big brother, Pat, does in the swimming hole. Then I was riding on the elephant in the clouds, flying with a whole lot of elephants. *Faster, faster,* I yelled, laughing and jumping up and down like me feet was in stirrups, swinging a switch.

Suddenly, I was falling. Falling from the breaker. Falling down to the ground. Falling so fast I couldn't breathe. Tumbling. Head down. Head up. So fast I couldn't yell. Grabbing at the air, trying to get hold of something. Falling so far down I saw myself go deep into a mine shaft.

"Time for work, Johnny. Wake up."

Falling. Da's voice. I reached out to grab hold of him but still fell.

"Johnny." He shook me and broke me fall. There was his face. I was in me bed, not falling. I grabbed at his sleeve; he pulled away. So happy to be safe, I jumped out of bed and hugged him. He pulled me hands away, not liking hugs.

"Happy to be going to work, I see. Get dressed now. Put that wool vest on, too, like I showed ye last night. Socks. Heavy ones so's ye don't get blisters from them boots. Socks'll make them fit better."

"Tim. Johnny. Breakfast."

I wouldn't tell him I was scared, I wasn't no sissy, so I rolled up all me clothes and ran down to the kitchen where it was warm. Ma stoked the coal stove for heat for us working men. She plopped porridge into our bowls. Ma said eat, you need a full belly on your first day. Couldn't eat. Me Da was scared. I could tell 'cause he tied me boots. He never did that before. And giving me tobacco to chew. If Ma saw that she'd be whipping the both of us. His face looked as if all the things he was telling me were scaring him, too. Can't remember what he said, only his scared face.

We got outside and said hello to everyone else walking to the mine. Once the singing started, I forgot about being scared. I thought it could be great fun up in the breaker. I saw friends, too, on their way to the mine—older boys, but we'd played ball together. One of them, Kevin, he liked me baseball. Asked Ma how she made it. String, she said, wrapped around a rubber ball and covered with electric tape. He let me play with him after that, 'cause Ma made one for him. String she saved, but how did she buy the rubber ball? Where did she get the tape? We didn't have money for buying.

And Martin. He was a breaker boy, too, walking to work. I caught up with him. Martin-Joseph O'Boyle, his mum called him. Get home right now or you'll get no supper, Martin-Joseph O'Boyle. Martin was me size, or rather me age but bigger than me. One winter we made a sled together out of scraps while the bigger boys were at work. We'd had a great time of it, sledding down the culm banks. Till the quitting whistle blew. Then the bigger boys who were not big enough for going to the pub, they took the sled away from us. Martin always found it for us the next day.

Yes, working in the breaker is going to be fun. I heard the bigger boys tell about football games they played at lunch time. Playing jokes on the other boys, that was fun they had, sometimes. They talked about playing jokes on the boss when he was mean.

Small for his age, that's what me Da said yesterday when he signed the age blank. That's what he told me to say if anyone was bold enough to ask. I'm twelve, I was to say, but I'm small for me age, the runt of the litter. That's what the law was, so if I didn't want to work I could say the truth, I'm eight. But then I'd get trounced by Da and we wouldn't get me week's wages. Sixty three cents. That's a lot of money. I'd get to keep some for candy, Da said. So I'm the runt with candy in me pocket. Breaker boy. Runt slate picker with sweets.

The Picker Boss, he never smiled. When he talked to me, it felt like he was yelling at me for doing something wrong. Stroh was his name and he shoved me toward the gears and stuff at the top of the huge room. I remember Da said the breaker was seven stories high. Seemed a lot higher looking down.

"Look here." Stroh pointed to a track coming up through an opening. "Look down dere. Soon, coal cars'll come up from da pit, all the vay up dat track. Coal gets dumped in da grinder. Got dat? Know what da grinder does?"

"Yes, Sir."

"See here, Runt? Dis here is da grinder. Got dat? See da teeth on it? Iron, and dey'll grind up runts like you. Stay outta dere. Keep away from da machinery. Got dat?"

"Yes, Sir," I said, like Da told me to. Call him sir, Da said, and don't be sassy. I wondered if any boys got grinded in it or if he was just trying to scare me.

"After da grinder, da pieces of coal goes to dis here place with all different size holes in it. Den down da chutes. Big chunks here. Small chunks dere. Got dat?"

"Uh-huh. I mean yes, Sir."

"You pick out da bony. Know what's bony?"

"Yes, sir. Anything that's not coal."

"A runt, but smart. Know what coal looks like?"

Everyone knows that. Coal is black and shiny but here everything's black. "Yes, Sir, I do."

"See dis?" He stuck his leg out. It was a wooden peg. "You want one of dese tings? Legs an' arms get cut off real easy." That's when I saw the whip stuffed in his belt.

Boys sat on boards across the chutes. Stroh went hopping across the boards like he had two real feet. With his peg leg, he kicked a boy who was laughing. "No laughing. No talking." The boy shut up fast. "Don't just stand dere, Runt. Get over here. Sit dere for today."

I kinda fell onto the board over a chute. It was like a bench. It made a cracking noise. I looked around me. I was the top boy on this chute. There were five or six down behind me.

"Pay attention to da run, Runt. Fall in and you'll end up under a pile of coal. Maybe even dead. Coal can cut you up pretty bad. Sharp as a knife some. Don't want no bloody coal."

Me belly rumbled. I wished I ate me porridge.

"See dat dere chute? Dat's for da bony."

Someone musta turned the gears on 'cause all of a sudden there was so much noise I couldn't hear Stroh. He was still talking, pointing, making faces. I couldn't hear anything. I raised and lowered me head. "Yes, Sir," I said, moving me whole body so he'd hear me.

He grabbed me collar. "Got dat?" he yelled in me ear. "Pick out da bony. Don't miss any."

I was too scared to answer. I looked out at the track. Coal cars that looked like small, toy trains started up. The whole breaker shook and swayed. I thought it would come apart, tumble down in a pile of sticks. It was so noisy I couldn't remember anything the Picker Boss said or that Da said. I felt like I couldn't breathe. Yesterday, playing kick the rock was a dream, not real.

The coal started coming down. Big thick clouds of dust came down, too. I forgot what to do till I got a peg leg jabbed in me back. Coughing, I pulled the handkerchief over me face. I got the switch across me hand for that. After a few minutes, me fingers were bleeding. I started crying 'cause I got blood on the coal. Probably missed bony, too. Bloody and tired when the quitting whistle blew, I kept falling down on the road home. Sweeney carried me.

Then on the second day I knew it wasn't going to be fun at all 'cause of me friend Martin, the same Martin-Joseph-O'Boyle I went sledding with last winter. Yesterday, we'd climbed the steep, shaky steps to the top of the breaker. He said he was scared every day when he climbed these steps, along the high wall. I looked out the dirty windows 'cause I didn't want to see his scared face and saw the ground instead. Martin said he sometimes heard ghosts of the boys who died in the breaker. Boys died in the breaker? It must be true what old Stroh said. That was scarier than Martin's face.

Where was he today? I had to climb the wobbly steps without me best friend. When I got to the top, there he was, sitting several rows from the top 'cause he wasn't new anymore.

He yelled out, "Look, there's Johnny." And he laughed like crazy. I think we're going to have fun for sure, he's me butty.

"Look at him," said Martin, pointing his finger at me. "He's wearing a girl's coat."

Everyone was looking at me and me red coat.

"Red coat, red coat." Everyone started to laugh. "Sissy, sissy. Momma's boy. We don't want no little girls in here."

No one bothered about me coat yesterday, the boss having his whip. No jokes the first day.

The Picker Boss laughed, too. He shoved me onto a plank laid across the empty chutes. "Sit here, Runt. Dis is your place every day till I tell you to move. Got it?"

Boys filled in the seats, each to his own place. They put their feet into the chutes. I wanted to look around but I was too ashamed to let anyone see me cry. So I kept me eyes on me feet till the machinery was turned on and the first car came. The coal came toward me. Black dust puffed up and hid me. Gritty coal dust came through me handkerchief into me mouth. The noise was so loud it was hard to think. All the mean things Martin and the others said skittered down the chute with the coal.

I forgot to worry about lunch time. I wished for a back rest to lean on but there was none—not allowed, the boss told me yesterday, don't even think about nailing one on. How'd he know I was thinking that I'd ask me Da if he had a scrap I could use?

By the time the lunch whistle blew, I was too tired to care. Me fingers was cracked and bleeding. They hurt so bad I couldn't eat lunch. Me back pained so bad, I didn't want to play, even if I'd been wanted. So tired I couldn't fight back when three big boys yanked me red coat off. They stripped me naked and slopped me with axle grease. They threw me and the coat in the black water pool along the culm bank. It was Martin who pulled me out, both of us black from the water.

"Water comes from the breaker," Martin said. "Don't tell. They'll kill you if you're a snitch."

He dragged me back to work. I was wet and naked, black and stinking. I hopped on one foot, then the other, trying to get into me soaked clothes.

"Best get back on time, said Martin. Lest the boss kick in yer ribs again, like yesterday, er worse."

We left the red coat floating there like a dead fish. If Ma wanted me to wear it, she'd have to come get it.

Martin said me fingers would toughen up in a few weeks. His did. There was some kind of sulfur muck, he said. It's on the coal. It gets into the cuts from sharp rocks and slate. Makes your fingers black and sore. I did toughen up. Already on me second day I was making up me own song about how the Picker Boss could go pick his ass.

Ma'd be mad if I came home with no coat. 'Twas the only one to fit me. I'd have no coat unless there was one in the Salvation Army bin at the church. When I went to get the coat out of the water, it wasn't red any more.

The third day, when I reached for me lunch, I found me growler nailed to the floor. Me lunch inside black and gritty. Everyone laughed hysterically at the joke. I laughed, too, so I was told to come play tag when the breaker shut down for lunch.

Blessed quiet. Da says that all the time. Now I know why. Fresh air. That was the best part about lunch. Martin warned me to stay away from the big boys' football game or I'd be the ball. We traded lunches, he liked me potato sandwich and I wanted his beet sandwich 'cause I'd never had one before. I gave him half of me green apple and he gave me half of his cabbage. Both were mushy. We were friends again. He taught me the finger signs the boys used to talk when the boss wasn't looking.

Book Three

Spring 1888

FOURTEEN

Saturday Night

Let me hear those tales of recess
That only little folks can tell,
Cuddled up upon the green grass
Close beside the old town well.
The man in the moon had charge of the light plant,
Our cottage walls were not of bricks;
Young and old enjoyed the night camp
On the green at Number Six.

– Minstrel ballad

April 1888

A dance floor—large sheets of iron borrowed from the Number Six colliery—was set up on the new green grass next to the community pump. The Slavs had taken it over with their polkas and fiddlers. Shouts, hand clapping, and foot stomping on the metal sounding board added to the music and incited the dancers. Skirts swirled and flew up. Boys, young and old, tried to snatch a glimpse of what was underneath. Bystanders stamped feet and slapped thighs to quicken the beat. Breathless, the dancers kept up, faster, faster, faster until they fell in exhaustion, laughing and gasping. One lone survivor raised his hands in victory. Cheers ascended into the starry night.

Silhouetted against the moonlit sky the colliery buildings, the culm banks, and the now quiet breaker were ignored. Peals of laughter floated in the air along with coal dust and the smell of brimstone. The shanty-like homes stood empty; everyone was out on the green, young and old alike. Squirrel and rabbit roasting on an open fire filled the air with an aroma that foretold of full bellies. Potatoes and guylás, beans and soups, bread and cakes filled tables brought from kitchens. Johnny dragged chairs out of his house. He joined the other boys and girls who piled last year's dead twigs and branches on the bonfire. The hardships of the day, wrapped in games and gaiety, drifted away as if on wisps of smoke from the fire.

Maureen McGonigal, Sharon Garrighan, and Bridie had taken off their aprons and put on their Sunday shoes for dancing but instead they huddled close, laughing at a book, *American Woman's Home*. Kathleen had taken it from the burning trash pile at the superintendent's home where she did cleaning and laundry.

"Would you want such a thing in your house, Maureen?" asked Bridie, pointing to an illustration.

"I'd rather have some of the other fancy stuff in the pictures. Which American woman is this about? Not mine patch women!"

"An earth-closet? Look, even directions for building your own," said Sharon, kneading the sides of her forehead.

Yolanda joined the group. "Bridie, dat ting, how it work? Where go da... you know... Where go da...?"

"Says you sit on it, and do your business, and all the shite and piss goes into a bucket below that's filled with dirt. Then you use it in your garden for fertilizer," said Bridie, who was the only one able to read.

Sharon laughed. "Would swallow you whole, that ting. I don't like the idea of having it in the house. Ours are outside, 'tis better."

"Better, yes," said Bridie, "only if the company would clean the privies or give us the lime to do it ourselves." Bridie wondered if the earth-closet would stink like the privies.

Maureen shook her head and scrunched her nose. "I'll not eat potatoes that have grown beneath Martin's shite, no thank you." The women howled with laughter.

The Minstrel Foley jumped onto the dance floor, turning it into his stage. He sang a few songs while folks filled mugs with beer and plates with food. Eddy Roarity staggered by, stumbling over the uneven ground and singing a Gaelic song. His rendition was more slurred mumbling than singing.

"I've read there's what's called water-closets. You do your business in a bowl, pull a chain that opens a tank of water above, and everything is washed away somewhere. The hotel in Washington, DC has that in their rooms," said Bridie. "Wouldn't you like to stay in a hotel?"

"No buckets to empty, no privies to clean," said Sharon, rubbing her eyes. "Sure'n what will they tink of next?"

"I've something for you, Sharon." Bridie pulled a wrinkled clipping from the *Miner's Journal*. "Says here in this ad that this medicine, Vegetine, will cure your headaches and constipation, piles, scrofulous humor tumors, dyspepsia, faintness at stomach, female weakness," Bridie looked up and smiled. "Probably a laxative," she laughed. "There's more: general debility, catarrh... What's that? Ulcers and cold sores, pimples and humors on face. Just what you..."

"Look! Miklos is the only dancer left standing. Again! Those Slavs have the strangest dances."

"Off the dance floor with ye, Miklos. Let an Irishman show them what real dancing is." Friends and neighbors applauded and hollered as Tim skipped onto the iron slab, sloshing beer on himself, and darkening a mahogany splatter on the rust-colored slab.

Sweeney, not to be outdone, grabbed the minstrel's fiddle and bounced the bow across the strings. "I challenge ye, Tim, for I'm a better dancer than ye, any day."

Foley, good-natured as he was, snatched his fiddle from Sweeney. "Not me fiddle, son, not me fiddle."

"Colem, are ye up to it, lad?" Tim and Sweeney shouted at the same time.

Colem claimed a place between Tim and Sweeney. Denny and Jamie joined them, too, jumping and dancing around Sweeney and Tim.

"You're in fer it now, you are Tim," said Colem. "Who'll be judge?"

"Ya, dat'll be me," said Yolanda, laughing. "Dat's goot. Me Slav judge de Irish dance. Yah!"

"And me," said Maureen.

"'Tis three we need now," said Sweeney, "in case of a draw. It can't be ye, Bridie."

"We know ye'll vote fer Tim, no matter what," said Colem.

Everyone looked at Colem's wife, Megan O'Shaughnessy, who was sitting off by herself with the usual sour look on her face.

Sweeney's wife Hanna stepped forward, hand up as if asking permission to speak.

"'Tis right, he is," said Sweeney, "No wives for judges." He shook his head at Hanna."

"Then it's me," said Mave McGeehan, whose husband tended the bonfire. "I'll be your third judge, then, if you'll let me play me banjo later." She bounded onto the dance floor, ferociously plucking her banjo in time with Foley's fiddle.

"No," said Miklos. "Der's only Slaves what should judge Irish."

He held his mug of beer up as if toasting Tim. "Neci, dis a job for youse."

Neci three-stepped his way toward Miklos and Yolanda. "Yah," he said laughing. He still had his polka costume on as did Yolanda.

The Slavs' pride in their heritage was as strong as the Irish's. Their ceremonial costumes would not be sacrificed even in the face of prejudice or starvation. There was often tension.

"Then I'll be playing me banjo anyway," insisted Mave.

Ed Foley jigged on the iron floor and positioned himself on the front-right corner, fiddle under his chin, bow traveling across strings as fast as a bee's wings. The big-boned, heavy-set, shabbily-dressed man would not be upstaged by anyone. He was the most popular minstrel in the county and especially loved in this patch.

Though he walked from patch town to patch town, county to county, whenever he neared Pottsville he always stopped at Number Six. Often he carried herbs, roots, or other medicine, like Laudanum being traded to Bridie, who sent back with Foley something her trader couldn't grow in her area of the county.

Foley ate and drank extravagantly. Though he mostly appeared at wakes and weddings, christenings and balls, and parties of all kinds, his very arrival was the occasion for this shindig.

The three men jigged to the beat of the minstrel's bow. Tim stepped forward. Sweeney, Colem, and the others shambled back to give their friend room.

"As awkward as ye are, Tim, ye'll need lots of room," chortled Sweeney.

"Ah, go on wit ye, then. Let a master show ye how 'tis done." He performed a strange combination of a jig and, step dancing, with *help-there's-a-wild-dog-after-the-seat-of-me-pants* moves mixed in. Sometimes he held his arms straight down at his sides, only to suddenly shout and throw them up or out, the iron sheet a sound board for his stomping feet. He hurled and twirled his body about, nearly careening into the fiddler, who stamped his right foot to keep the beat. The redder Tim's face became, the more trails of sweat appeared, the slower he danced, and the faster Foley fiddled. Tim turned to face Sweeney, then sidled to the back as his friend came forward.

Sweeney was an accomplished step dancer, so controlled and graceful, you'd never guess he was a coal miner except for the black stains on his hands. He reached out toward his wife and nodded his head. She joined him and brought their three children into it as well, two boys and a girl, all square-shouldered and straight-backed as their feet sped through the steps. The crowd roared with approval.

Colem was up next. By this time the audience, dancing on the grass, was clapping their hands to the pounding of his feet.

At a distance a girl shouted "Ring" and then once again. All the young folks turned toward the edge of the green near the woods and away from their parents. A growing ring of girls and boys holding hands laughed and circled until they named Kathleen "it."

She walked slowly around the outside of the circle, sizing up the boys, looking them over carefully. The first choice was important. She acted as if she was unsure which boy she'd choose. The girls giggled. They all knew who she'd pick. The boys looked more sober-faced, as if afraid they'd be picked, or afraid they wouldn't.

Bridie observed from afar. "She always picks Sean Slattery first," she said to Maureen.

"Aye, she does indeed. She has an eye for the boy, she does. Many a husband's been chosen during a ring game. The first pick is usually the last, too."

"Kathleen! A husband! Get on with you, Maureen."

Around and around Kathleen skipped, picking up speed till she tapped Sean on the shoulder and sprinted off with him chasing her. She ran around the circle as fast as she could in her bare feet. Sean could outrun her easily but he didn't until she slowed some. The players in the ring jumped and cheered, it seemed, in time to the fiddling and stomping.

Kathleen allowed herself to be caught. She turned to face Sean, put her hands up, palms out. He touched her palms with his, forming a barrier over which they both leaned for a light kiss, little more than a peck.

A shout went up, "Sean's 'it'."

"You can't pick Kathleen."

He didn't.

The merriment continued until everyone had kissed everyone else at least once. On the last round, Kathleen tapped Sean, but this time skipped slowly away. This time the barrier was breached with a serious kiss. Sean tousled Kathleen's hair and pulled her into a hard embrace, to show who was in charge. Their friends clapped and cheered the couple, who walked off by themselves.

Maureen raised her eyebrows and nudged Bridie and nodded her head in the direction of Kathleen and Sean.

"Kathleen," called Bridie, "Come help with the food, will you?"

Maureen raised her eyebrows again and laughed as she wiped spilled soup from the food table, while she conferred with Mave and Bridie about the dancers. It was an easy decision for them, but they were not the judges.

"The winner! Who's the winner?" Tim shouted, chest out, thumbs in his suspenders.

Ed Foley scraped out a dramatic tune on his fiddle.

"The winner is..."

"Now, don't you think we need a song first?" asked Maureen.

"No!"

"No song!"

"Who's the winner?"

"Sweeney's da vinner and Sweeney and Hanna dey second vinners," proclaimed Miklos."

"Am I third place, then?" asked Tim.

"No turd place dis time, Tim," said Yolanda.

Old Man Mulligan attracted a group over near the bonfire. No party would be complete without one of his stories. "Johnny, me lad," said Mulligan. "You first, boy. Tell your breaker boy story."

Johnny pulled away, but just a little, shaking his head, smiling at the same time. He had practiced it with Bridie. He was glad she wouldn't be listening now.

"'Tis a grand story you made there, Laddie. Let's hear it, then." The old man's proud smile deepened a road map of lines on his wizened face.

Johnny pulled himself up to his full eight-year-old height. Tim always told him to stand tall, that he's of Irish blood. He nodded. "Long ago in Number Six mine, there was a wee lad name of Seamus O'Malley."

"How long ago, Johnny?" asked the old man.

"Long, long ago, before the moon was full grown."

"Is it a ghost story, Johnny? A ghost story like the ones I tell?" They'd practiced this.

"Don' know. See what you think. Seamus worked as a breaker boy. He shook with fear climbing to the top of the breaker but he did it every day because his Mam and Da needed his puny salary. Mam told him she prayed the rosary to keep him safe. Angels, she said, would keep him from falling into the breaker whenever he'd go up the stairs or sorted coal."

Johnny got a blank look in his eyes. "The picker boss..." whispered Mulligan.

"Oh." Johnny nodded. "The picker boss whipped the boys with a switch till they bled. The Welshman kicked them with his heavy boots so they couldn't hardly walk. He never touched Seamus. His Mam said that was the angels protecting him, so Shamus began to feel safe. Though he'd been warned about the danger of falling into the breaker and getting ground up, he'd dance on his bench over the chute when the picker boss wasn't looking. He had great fun making all the other boys laugh at his queer faces.

"One day, he fell into the chute of fast-moving, sharp coal and slate. The other breaker boys looked on in horror. Seamus became more and more bloody as his arms and legs were pulled under the coal and tossed up, and pulled under again. The picker boss jumped from bench to bench trying to grab the boy, but he couldn't get hold of him."

Johnny looked over at Mulligan, who made a swooshing sound.

"Suddenly, there was a swoosh of wind and the sound of singing. Seamus flew up from the coal chute and onto his bench at the top of the breaker. His body wasn't bloody, his shirt wasn't tore, no cuts or sores. He sat there smiling. By that time the breaker had been stopped. Everyone, boys and boss alike, were stunned to silence.

"A blood curdling scream tore through the breaker. The picker boss, on his knees, screeched and hollered, "Mercy, Mercy", holding his hands and arms in front of his face while an unseen something beat him bloody with his own switch.

"Later, the folks of Number Six mine patch couldn't agree about what had happened. Some said it was the ghost of the breaker boy they call Mickey Pick-Slate. Some say Seamus was saved by the Little

People who'd come from Ireland. Others said it were all the ghosts of all the boys who had been beaten by that picker boss.

"Seamus's Mam said 'twas the angels from heaven, sent by the Blessed Virgin Mary, what saved her boy. The end."

Johnny beamed with pride and looked around for applause.

"The angels for sure," said Bridie, who'd crept into the group of listeners.

FIFTEEN

Roof Fall

April 1888
Tim

Gently, with his fingertips, Tim feels blood, caked on his head, dry on his face, etched in lines across his brow and under his nose. He walks down the road, stopping now and then to stare, not seeing anything except the tumble of his own thoughts. His right hand, fingers rubbed raw, is wrapped in his handkerchief. Bloodied gloves hang from his pocket.

He looks at his left hand. Ain't had bloody fingers like this since I was workin' as a breaker boy in the mine in Ireland, he thinks. 'Twas a long time ago, that.

A vivid image of his dead father's face emerges from that memory. Me Da, Tim shook his head. Ah, there never breathed a more rugged man, hardened by the toil of life, but never lost his sense of humor. A coal miner like me. He worked right here in the mine fields of Schuylkill County. Some of the green hills in the spring reminded us of Donegal. He'd always intended to return to Ireland so he could visit me ma's grave. 'Twas birthin' me what caused her death.

Tim stops, seized by a wave of grief.

Other folks maneuver around him. A boy, kicking a ball, sidled up to him. "Gotta fag?" he says.

"Be gone wit'ye, lad, before I tell your mother. Stunt yer growth, smokin' will." The boy scuttles away, kicking up dust and rocks along with the ball, as if unconcerned by the threat.

I know what me father woulda done today, thinks Tim, walking again. Someone would get bashed. He remembers how he'd accompanied his father on those kinds of jobs when they were part of the Molly Maguires.

Tim had been inducted into the Ancient Order of Hibernians at age nineteen. Members of that order formed a separate secret society: The Molly Maguires. Some called us ruffians, recalled Tim. 'Twas not so. We used the only weapons we owned to fight against unfairness: our fists and guns.

Some think the Molly Maguires are dead, but I know different, he nodded, fists clenched, a wry grin on his dirty face making his teeth look whiter than they really were. They still extract retribution from those that won't listen. And 'tis retribution I'll have for today's happenin'.

He looks up and realizes he is home.

~

Bridie is beside herself when she sees me limp into the house. "You're hurt. What happened? Here, let me get a look at that head, then."

She rushes around, gettin' me lunch pail, takin' me jacket off, fillin' a bowl with water. "Let me see your head. Gawd, look at your hands."

I hate ta see her upset, fussin' over me with vinegar and those weird leaves of hers.

"Leave me be, woman. Me feet are on the ground, not under it."

"Sit."

I sit, feelin' a bit outside meself. "I tell you, I reported that roof ta Schmidt and ta the inside foreman, Walsh. Reported it many times. Timbers, they'd say. More supports and cross beams. Eejits! No amount of timber's gonna hold that section if it decides ta go. Me gut tells me so, I say."

"C'mere, hold still so's I can see how bad 'tis."

We are in the kitchen, me fidgetin' in the chair, her dippin' a rag in the bowl. Me head in a fog.

"There's just somethin' about the way the timbers creak and buckle. Great hunks of slate come down every day. And we seem ta be takin' in water. Not so much so you worry about it but 'twas regular. The water smells bad, too, like it come through a pocket of bad air."

"I have to cut your hair around that gash, Tim. Will you sit still, for Gawd's sake! How can I take care of it if you keep getting up and wandering around? What happened?"

"I'm tryin' ta tell ye, Bridie." But I can't tell her the worst, not yet. I didn't wanna say it out loud 'cause then it might be real, not just a dream floatin' about the fog. "We been workin' Angelica for months, pushin' the face back. We'd opened a nice size chamber with a rich, wide seam. Every day fillin' more car loads than the quota. Each time we fired a shot we was thinkin' of the extra pay we'd get, not payin' attention, maybe, to the warnin' signs."

"You thinking you missed the warnings?"

"I don't know. Lookin' back... emm... I think maybe we did. We heard the crossheadin' workin' like mad, but the rock is always noisy, more some days than others. You get used ta hearin' it. Timbers creak. More today? I don't know."

I raise a hand to comb me fingers through me hair, to help me think. Bridie smacks it away.

"You're always looking out for your men, Tim. You do right

by them."

"When we'd blasted so much coal there weren't room fer no more, we worked on loadin'. No blastin', so... emm... t'ings got quiet, except fer the sounds of us jokin' and the coal bangin' into the buggies.

My voice catches in me t'roat.

"You know how Sweeney's always kiddin' me, Bridie? He was in rare form today. I can still hear him. 'Hey, Tim,' Sweeney said, 'can ye hoist that rock there? Bet ye can't. Bet ye a pint ye can't.' Sweeney, he's a bull of a man, Bridie. The rock he'd be talkin' about were bigger than two men could lift."

"You're keen to take him up on a challenge, boyo," says Bridie. "'Bet you a quart,' you probably said."

"'Twas all in good fun."

"He's a good lad. I love him for carrying Johnny home that day. He's got a good heart, Gawd love'm."

I take a breath and nod to give me a minute.

"He teased Denny, too, askin' him if he'd be tellin' his wife how much he's really makin' diggin' down there and how much he'd be leavin' at McMonagle's gin mill. You know, Denny isn't much of a drinker, Bridie. 'Tis just Sweeney bein' a smart ass.

"Sweeney pestered Schmidt, the fire boss, too. 'You're in me will only if I die above ground, Henry. If I go to me reward below, you'll be owin' me family money, man.'"

"He's dreaming. Widows get nothing but the company store bills," says Bridie

"This one timber lets out a groan... emm... splinters, and buckles." I can't go on with the story. "Any beer?" I ask, wipin' me face with me shirt. I know there isn't, just need to think about beer for a minute.

"No." Bridie fills a cup with water, hands it to me.

"Then a tremendous rumble. Rocks and grit fall on us. The rats run. Took us a second or two to take it all in before we grab tools and hightail it for the shaft, still not realizin' how bad 'twas. Can't go as fast as we want, the roof hangs so low. We kinda duck-waddle along, me knees screamin' wit' pain. Sometimes I can see Denny and Colem and the rest of them ahead of me. But mostly, too much dust and grit fallin' to see beyond me own nose. Sweeney is behind me, havin' gone back fer blastin' powder, squibs, 'n stuff. I imagined him yellin' fer me ta get a move on, ta get the lead outa me drawers, though I really can't hear him, the rock bein' so noisy.

Bridie is silent, cleaning me wounds with her hands but her mind musta been livin' the story.

"Big hunks of slate fall in front of me, big, like bigger than you could get your arms around. Don't take much to fill up that low tunnel. Nothin' but rock all around. I try ta push through the small openin' left of the tunnel but the roof let loose another load. I am squattin' in water, the space only big enough to take two or three steps in any direction, the crew on the other side of the rock in front of me. Or under it. Sweeney somewhere behind me.

Bridie doesn't speak. She stops messin' wit me head.

"The air seems all right. I'm still breathing it. No smell of gas. I dig into the rock fall in front of me till I think of Sweeney. He'd be diggin' too. I start pullin' rock away behind. I dig away from where I think he'd be. Get him out. Together we'd make our way to the shaft. Soon, there's no room for the rock I pull away. I turn around and work on the shaft side. Hopin' to break through. I pile the rock in such a way so's to mark which direction the shaft is, and which is Sweeney's side 'cause once I'd got twisted 'round and lost me bearings.

'Tis dark as a grave 'cept for the lamp on me cap. How long will that stay lit? How long will the air last? Should I just sit still, save me breath, 'steada tryin' ta dig out? Give the men time ta get ta me? Time.

I don't know how much time'd gone by.

I hold me cup out for more water.

"So I decide ta sit there, rest. I'm not exactly sittin'. I make a seat outta rock, ta get me butt outta the water. Seated, I fold me arms on me knees and rest me head on them, so low is the roof. I sit and wait, the breathin' gettin' harder, water tricklin' in, coverin' more of me feet. I sit there thinkin' about Sweeney, wonderin' if he is all right. I hear nothin' from him." I put me hand to me ear. Ejet! "See? I'm listening still. Thinkin' about you, Bridie. Knowin' how grieved you'd be if I don't get out. I worry about you worryin'.'"

I look at her, at the pain in her eyes. "Not about you bein' able ta take care of yourself. I know you'd probably move outta the patch. Go ta the city. Take some shitty job cleanin' up after rich people. Kathleen and Johnny'd go with ya.

Thinkin' of Johnny up above me, in the breaker, does he know what happened? Is he upset? I'm wonderin' did they blow the whistle for us. Were all the women and old men standin' around the mine head waitin' fer us ta come out? Is anyone tryin' ta get ta us, Sweeney and me?

Bridie is pulverizin' a mixture, 'tis mugwort and pennyroyal, she says, graspin' the pestle so's her knuckles are white, grindin' her teeth and clenchin' her jaw. "No. No whistle, Tim. I didn't know there was an accident 'till you showed up bleeding. Johnny's still on the breaker. They didn't close the mine." She slams the pestle on the table and spreads the poultice on me head.

"They shoulda listened about that roof, Tim," she says. "'Tisn't right that you get buried alive so's Gowen'..." She can hardly say the name, she hates him so much... "So that vile Frank Gowen can get richer while we lose our boys and men. We're trapped in this patch. Nothing we can do about it."

There is somethin' I'm goin' to do but I can't tell her what. She'd

not like me bashin' folks, even if I promised there'd be no shootin'.
She's said, many times: No guns, no beatin's, no Mollies.

"I am wishin' I had somethin' I can make me mark on, you know.
I heard of men leavin' letters for their families, letters that was found
with their dead bodies. I have nothin' to write on. Maybe I can scratch
me name on a rock, I'm thinkin'. If I get outta here, I'm gonna make
sure Johnny keeps learnin', maybe go ta school at night like some of
the other boys.

Bridie sits in front of me, forehead crunched, eyes flashin', teary
as if she were imaginin' readin' such a letter. She snaps. "Go to school
so's he can get a better job." Her eyes shot me a look. "Not so he can
write a better letter if he gets trapped in the mine, Tim. That means
quitting the breaker. You wouldn't want this to happen to him." She
bangs the pestle on the table.

"'Tis what a man does, Bridie, work in the mine. Still, maybe he
should go to school for a year. Then go back to the breaker."

"Next week, then."

"In two months' time. By then, we'll be back to workin' every day."

"Two months, then. Now finish tellin' me what happened."

"Well, I hear somethin'. Diggin'. I was never so glad of anythin'
as I am ta hear that. They're comin' after me, I think, so I get up and
started movin' rock as best I can, shoutin', hopin' they can hear me.
I'd been jowlin', rappin' three times on the rock, meanin' I'm alive,
then once meanin' there's only one... but gettin' no response. When
they finally break through, I say I'm not leavin' till we get Sweeney.

"'Tweren't much of a cave-in, they say. Everyone got out except
me and Sweeney. We dig till we see... um...see... a hand... mmm...
Just a hand."

Bridie's cryin' now, keenin' softly, as she listens to me.

"Clawin' at rock. Pullin' hunks away as fast as I can. Shoutin' like a crazy man. "Sweeney! Sweeney! We're here, boyo! Were comin' to getcha. You're goin' ta owe me a pint for this. No a quart... emm... Then we," I let out a big breath, "see him." I swallow hard. Me face wet now for the tellin'.

"Eyes swollen in his blackened face like they was bein' squeezed out of his head. A ton of roof restin' on his body. His head and shoulders and the bloody stump of what is left of his arm, 'tis the only part of him I can see."

I try to gulp down the sobs.

"But 'tis his eyes." I wipe me hand hard over me mouth, like that could change the words comin' out of it. "'Tis Sweeney, me best butty's eyes, that haunt me. They was open, as if he was lookin' to me for help. But he was gone. Still, I claw at the rock that half buried him, hopin' if I could release him, the breath would rush into him, that his eyes would see me tryin' to get him out."

I hear meself keen, low and soft. "That's what he'd do fer me."

Bridie's weepin' loudly, bendin' forward, her arms wrapped around her belly like she was hurtin'. I pull her close ta me.

"Now I'm askin' meself, what is it a union is goin' ta do fer us? I report a bad roof and it goes nowhere. Sweeney dies 'cause of it. There's some that think the union fellers are in cahoots with the coal owners and operators. There's some that think the Molly Maguires shouldn't have gone underground. At least we were heard, at least there was somethin' we could do ta make ourselves heard."

Bridie's shakin' her head.

Coffin notices! That's what I'm thinkin'. That's what we need to do again, let the operators and superintendents, even some of the bosses, let them know they'll be restin' cozy in coffins if they don't make t'ings better fer us who work underground. No killin' this time, just notices ta remind them justice can look like revenge.

SIXTEEN

The Spirits Speak

April 1888

Folks came from near and distant collieries and mine patches—men, women, and children. Sweeney was well liked, but even if that were not so, there would have been a crowd of mourners. Loss of even one miner due to a mining accident was felt deeply by all. Folks came with sympathy, loaves of bread, and jars of preserves to stock the widow's cupboard, hand-me-downs, a rare pair of shoes. The hat in the corner had had to be replaced with a pail, so generous were they. Visitors paid their respects, some kneeling, praying, silent. Others talked to Sweeney as if they expected his customary boisterous retort.

Sweeney rested in the front room of his company house. His pine box, tightly packed with ice, festooned with fragrant-dried herbs— wormwood, feverfew, lavender, rosemary, anise, hyssop—perched on two chairs against the wall. He lay there with his hand on his chest. At the moment Tim was alone with his friend, the only sound the drip-dripping in the pail below the box.

The box was a bit short so that Sweeney's shoes didn't quit fit. He was barefoot in his box but that was okay. Hanna, Sweeney's wife, had pulled the simple blue cloth lining over his toes up to the frayed ends of his pants. Tucked his shoes in alongside him. Then the men placed a board over the end of the box. On it Tim placed a tin cup and a jug of home brew, Sweeney's favorite.

"This'll stay right here," Tim whispered. "No one's to touch it till afterwards, then we'll drink to ye, Sweeney.

"I'll be back, butty," Tim said as he patted the clasped hands. "I'm goin' ta see if I'm needed ta fetch more beer."

While quiet prevailed in the front room, laughter and fiddling filled the back room where they ate, drank, played games, and sang songs. Daniel McMonagle, owner of the Irish pub, was generous with the beer and whiskey and food.

A plateful of beans and pickled beets in one hand and a mug of beer in the other, Tim joked with Denny. "Did ye hear the one about the greenhorn who fell down the pit shaft?"

"No," said Denny dutifully.

"Pit boss says, 'Have ye broken anything?'"

"'No,' says the greenhorn, 'there's not much ta break down here.'"

Tim's belly shook with laughter. Denny rolled his eyes and turned to leave.

"Wait. Wait. How do you confuse a Welsh coal miner?"

Denny shook his head.

"You show him two shovels and ask him to take his pick."

"Ye gotta do better than that Tim," complained Denny. "Here's one and it's no joke: Eddy Roarity!"

"That one! I hear him comin' home some nights. Sure'n he lives closer to me than I'd like."

"Well, he'd been out on a payday toot and plannin' on sleepin' it off, the next day being Saturday. He comes staggerin' home at five in the mornin'. Carefully opens the door. Creeps into the house, over to the bed. He manages to avoid the loudest of the floor boards. Bangs into the broom but catches it before it crashes to the floor. He starts to undress when his wife wakes up.

"'My, but ye're up early on a Saturday.'

"'Aye,' says he, and quick pulls on his pants and heads for the kitchen.

"'Good,' says she. 'I've a load of chores for ye.'"

Tim laughed his big belly-laugh. So did Colem O'Shaughnessy who'd been listening. "I have one," he said.

Before he could begin, the old woman who'd been paying her respects to Sweeney ran into the back room, her hands covering her mouth and her eyes bulging.

"Mary, what ails ye, ma'am," asked Tim.

She shook her head, removed one hand from her mouth to point at the box.

"'Tis, all right, Mary. Tell me."

"I heard..."

"'Tis just the ice meltin', Mary."

She murmured something. Tim leaned closer, shaking his head. "Ye'll have ta speak up, if I'm to hear ye."

"He spoke."

"Who?"

Mary pointed to the coffin.

"Ah, we all are missin' him something fierce. Me, I come in here just to joke with me butty. I can hear him smart-mouthing me back. Come on, have a wee nip in your tea, Mary."

"No, I heard him with me own ears."

"I'm sure you did, Mary."

"'Tis true, Tim. I believe you, Mary," said Ned, a Donegal man from Silver Creek Colliery. "Spirits do speak. Sweeney's spirit will be roaming the gangways and faces of old Number Six. Mark my words, he'll be helping you get the job done, Tim."

"Did I ever tell ye about the time I was workin' an old colliery up north of here?"

A few youngsters sat on the floor to listen. One called out, "C'mere, Michael. A ghost story!"

"That mine was fulla ghosts of dead miners, most of them good natured." Ned continued. His voice lowered, he shot a menacing glance at each child. "Hear them during a lull in the mining, we could. Bang, and knock, and crash about, they did, to let ye know they were there. Tommy-knockers, we'd call them."

"I'm not a mind to hear about spirits," Mary complained. "'Tis a shot of whisky I need now."

"I've seen them with me own eyes, Mary, just like you heard Sweeney with your own ears. Lights flickerin' off in a distance, shadows gettin' bigger and closer and closer, then suddenly the light goin' out and a breeze blowin' up right there deep down 'neath the surface where no wind blows."

A fiddle played out back and some of the women sang old Irish songs. Kids joined in and the dogs howled along. Spring tried to warm up the air, the ground still wet from morning showers. Crocuses were the only flowers to break through the still-cold earth.

"Some of them ghosts had only one arm or no legs. One almost headless but for one skinny neck cord that kept it from falling off altogether. It'd flop onto his shoulder then back up onto his neck."

One little girl started to cry and ran calling for her mother.

Ned continued undaunted by the frightened child. "On this particular day, me butty Martin and me had noticed Leo O'Reilly loaded his cart faster than we did and he worked alone. His butty, Ryan, had been killed months ago. Martin said Ryan's ghost was helpin'. I said that was bunk. There was no ghost helpin' nobody. We decided to test this. Martin and me, we went to visit Leo. He was workin' the Lady Queen of Heaven face, not far from us. We kept him busy talking, jokin', sippin' from a flask we'd brought for the occasion."

"Tim, Denny," called Bridie. She made her way through the back door into the kitchen. "Will ye start a fire, Tim?" she asked. "It's a bit nippy out. We can roast those potatoes, too."

"Sure, give me a minute." Tim eyed Denny, who nodded. They'd heard this story before but enjoyed it every time.

"We passed the afternoon thus, sippin' and talkin'. 'You'll see,' I say to Martin when we leave, 'there's no ghost, and Leo's car will be as empty as ours.'

"Out in the gangway, lo'n behold, there was O'Reilly's car, loaded to the top with coal. From that day, swear on me mother's grave, I believed in ghosts."

"Sure'n there's one right in the front room," said Mamie Roarity. A burly woman, she showed no fear. "I heard him. Sweeney. Told me to quit beating Eddie up, he did." Everyone laughed, except her. She went right to the whiskey table and belted down two shots like they were water.

Tim, Denny, and Colem built a tremendous bonfire and banked it carefully to contain it. They speared potatoes on sturdy sticks for the older kids to roast in the fire. He came around the side of the house and spied two boys laughing so hard they held their sides. At the same moment, there were screams inside.

"What are ye lads up to?" demanded Tim. The boys were so startled they had no time to run before Tim collared them and whipped them around to face him. "Johnny!"

In the house, the screaming stopped and the fiddling grew louder. Old Man Mulligan's voice droned on in another story. Women's laughter and children's squeals of delight filled the gaps. The older children began the ring game.

"Tell me what mischief are ye up to, boy," Tim asked, still holding each boy by the arm, one his son, Johnny, the other, Martin Joseph O'Boyle. They jerked their head toward the side wall where Tim saw a wooden tube hanging from the crawl space under the side of Sweeney's house. On the end of the pipe hung a hose with a funnel.

"The other end is behind the coffin," said the larger boy, a nine-year-old. No further explanation was needed.

"Scarin' poor old women, 'tis it?"

"No, sir. Yes, sir."

Tim saw Henry Schmidt, the fire boss, coming down the road. Though he had fiercely denied having anything to do with it, it gave Tim great satisfaction to see Schmidt's blackened eyes and the sling around his arm.

Tim sprawled on the ground. "Johnny, quick, get to the road, watch Schmidt. Let Martin know when he gets close. Martin, tell me when Schmidt goes into the front room with Sweeney. Hurry, now."

Schmidt felt relieved the front room had no other visitors. With any luck, he'd pay his respects, give the widow the pay envelope, and leave before Tim O'Doyle saw him. He wouldn't be here at all except that the mine owner insisted both he and foreman Walsh pay a visit. Walsh was nowhere in sight. By rights, it was Walsh who should be giving the envelope, but he, Schmidt, got stuck with the job.

Schmidt knelt down and bowed his head as if in prayer.

"Schmidt, you damn phony. Me soul won't rest with the likes of your prayer. You owe me family money, man! Pay up or ye arm will be broken." Tim intoned the words in an eerie rendering of Sweeney's voice, made even spookier as it traveled through the tube.

Schmidt leaped from the kneeler, dropped his pipe and the pay envelope, and ran out the way he'd come in.

Johnny and Martin ran to Tim, the three laughing so hard tears streamed down their reddened faces. "Da, Da, Mr. Barney from the company store is comin'."

"Get Denny and Colem and the rest of them. Tell them ta get in the front room fast and sit quietly in the chairs. Quick now. Tell them I said so, Johnny. Tell them I said don't ask questions, just do it. Martin, go down the road and see if ye can slow Barney down."

The room was quiet when Barney entered, except for the murmuring of clothing and chairs on wood. He removed his cap and clasped it to his chest. He nodded solemnly at Sweeney's widow, Hanna, and a few others before moving to the coffin. He knelt.

As if from the spirit world, a voice called, "Barney! Swine! Hypocrite! You plucked me poor, cheatin' me, overchargin' me. You'll not have another easy day for the rest of your life, you slimy rat."

Barney jumped up so violently he knocked the kneeler over, nearly upsetting the coffin. He backed away from the coffin, arms crossed in front of him, as if protecting himself from the flames of hell. He ran out screaming.

It was such a good trick that Johnny and Martin weren't punished. All the mourners laughed and said Sweeney's was the best wake in a long time. Mourners entertained themselves until dawn with retellings of the Spirit Who Spoke.

After Sweeney's funeral mass, after he was buried, the men gathered to drink a toast to their butty: "There lies Sweeney, once the coal king's slave, but now he's passed. Thanks be to God. He's free at last."

SEVENTEEN

Hold Onto The Joy

I inherited the voices and attitudes of the men and women who
were shut down and abandoned.
A tremendous anger... a tremendous silence.

— *From "Gouged Earth / Gouged People"*
by Craig Czury

May 1888

Spring arose from a lollygagging winter, and in the Pottsville Number Six mine patch May demanded to be noticed by tugging at a sparse remnant of Bridie with lightheartedness, a whisper of silk in a thorny patch. The sun warmed even if the breeze chilled. Crocuses and daffodils flaunted their delight to have survived. Trees sprouted tiny green buds. The air was scented with the earthy fragrance of new growth that seemed unexpected in a thicket of grief.

"Spring comes every year, but it is always a grand surprise," Bridie said. "Today is a day suitable only for a picnic. We'll celebrate your last week on the breaker, Johnny. Don't be thinking you'll spend your days playing, Johnny-boyo; next week you start school."

"I'm playing ball with me friends today, Ma. I don't want to go on no picnic." Johnny stamped his foot.

"With *my* friends, Johnny, not me friends. I don't want to go on *any* picnic. Kathleen, slice some bread, would you now? We'll bring it with us. Johnny, fetch the basket and help Kathleen smear jam on the bread. Last jar, but soon there'll be more strawberries to put up."

Johnny widened his stance. He crossed his arms in front of his chest, elbows up, fists balled, chin lowered.

"Go on with you now, you fresh article. You'll be wanting to eat soon's we get there. "

"Ah, shite. First church, now a picnic."

"Two months on the breaker, and it is swearing at your mother you're doing now. Don't let your father hear the like of that, lad. It's the switch he'll be taking to you."

Tim burst into the house juggling three sweet potatoes. "Bridie, look here! What the neighbors gave me. We can roast 'em today. Build us a fire for our picnic. Bring some honey for 'em. We've got plenty of that since you cured the Slavs' kids. And grand honey 'tis." He gave the sweet potatoes to Bridie as if they were diamonds upon a satin pillow. She made a face at the withered skin and roots that sprang forth.

"Fine to have bee keepers in the neighborhood. Not such bad folks, after all," he said as he dipped his finger in the honey pot.

Bridie smacked his hand.

"If the roof falls again," Tim teased, "Ye'll be sorry ye denied me."

Since the outbreak of diphtheria, Yolanda and Miklos had become friends, close enough to trade certain food and clothing items, Johnny being the right size to wear their son's outgrown pants. Bridie made strengthening tonic for them all; Tim was never short of honey for his tea.

"They're coming with us, Miklos and Yolanda. Miklos will be

bringin' some of the beer Yolanda makes. Not as good as Irish beer, mind ye, but passable. Mmm." Tim's eyes widened and a satisfied smile overtook his face as if he lingered, for just a moment, over a frothy brew. "Johnny, think of it! That's three lads, and their father, and ye and me. We'll have a grand ball game. The girls can play too."

"Not me," said Kathleen, "you boys are too rough for me."

"Bring your boyfriend, Kathleen, the bean. Then you can do more kissin'," teased Johnny.

Kathleen's face turned crimson. "Shut your hole, you stupid article," she yelled.

"And who is this ye been kissin', Kathleen Mary?" Tim asked, not grinning his usual grin.

"Sean, Sean, he's a bit too long," sang Johnny.

"That's the one ye were dancing with last night, is it? One of the Slattery boys is he?

"The very same bean pole," said Johnny.

"Ah, he *is* a tall drink of water," said Tim. "Everybody sings and dances on Saturday night, but what cause have ye to go kissin' him? Ye are too young for that stuff, Lass. Ye know you'll have to go to confession, now don't ye?"

"It was a game. Everyone was doing it." Kathleen stamped her foot and made a face at Johnny.

"Now, leave the poor girl alone, the both of you," Bridie said. "Tell me that you weren't thinking about girls when you were the same age, Timothy."

"Ah, 'tis different for boys, Bridie."

"Why do I have to go to church anyway? You and Da don't go," piped in Johnny.

"'Tis a mouth ye have on ye now, lad. That's why ye need to go. There's good things to be learned, such as *Honor your Mother and*

Father. Especially your father," said Tim. "You'd better start honoring right quick by helpin' your mother pack up for the picnic. Fresh air in the countryside, miles away from the breaker. It'll do ye good to get away from those older boys fer the day, especially that Dougherty boy. He has a mouth on him! What's his name? Brian?"

Bridie felt disappointed that Yolanda and her family would come, annoyed with Tim for asking them. She liked Yolanda, but today she'd been looking forward to being alone—well, not alone exactly. She knew Tim and Johnny would play ball, even if it were only the two of them. She and Kathleen would go off looking for herbs that might have pushed through the earth, noting places they would return to for harvesting. She'd be alone with Kathleen, who was taking an interest in the healing herbs, but a greater interest in the Slattery boy. Maybe she and Kathleen would talk about that boy. Bridie noticed they often separated from their group of friends and went off by themselves.

She stepped out into her garden. New tips of green had pushed through the soil next to the daffodils which were surrounded by flattened, brittle, whitish remnants of fall plants. Bridie wondered at the butterfly that flitted past: black lace against a pale yellow. Are you lost, little butterfly? It's too early for you. She remembered a picture in a magazine she'd seen long ago. Butterflies pinned against a white board, all iridescent blue with black accents. The butterflies in her memory changed: they had her face now. Bridie nodded. I have been pinned into my life, held fast. I see the same ahead for Kathleen.

Bridie would have liked to tell Kathleen that as all women she had the wellspring of great power, of life itself. Yet, as certain as life itself, there was a predictable death involved in bringing forth life, death to girlhood. That she, Kathleen, should not be in such a hurry. That she should look around, see how women in this patch lived. That she should grab hold of the power within her, release it slowly, so that the fullness of her own life would be protected.

How do you say things like this to your daughter, Bridie wondered. The woman is supposed to give her life to her husband and children, but somehow it seems to me that it's a sin to neglect your own life.

Bridie needed to feel that wellspring of life within herself. For her that meant to feel part of the earth, part of the new growth of spring, to feel the sun on her skin and the breeze in her face. She'd looked forward to being alone with herself, if only for a few minutes; to get her hands in the soil; to smell flowers that smelled new even if they weren't yet sweet; to touch tender green leaves; to feel the roughness of tree trunks on the palms of her hands. But now, she'd have to wade through the tangle of peculiar words and inadequate gestures with Yolanda, the language of another tongue, while the language of a ball game among men was universal.

They sang as they walked about two miles up a slight grade to a spot overlooking the valley. Yolanda taught everyone Hungarian words. *Jó reggelt!* "Good morning." *Jó napot!* "Good afternoon."

Tim belted out a fine, if a little off key, tune.

"The green Hills of Erin are dear unto the view
The green hills of Erin, though old, are ever new..."

When they arrived at their picnic place overlooking the valley, Bridie spread a cloth under the sunny side of a large maple tree. The men built a fire circle. The boys laughed and raced each other, scurried off to find wood for the fire; the boy who gathered the most won the right to be captain of one team and choose first player for his side. The women unpacked the food: beans; boiled eggs; bread and jelly; Yolanda's fragrant potato, carrot, and onion gulyá. Bridie wondered what their picnic would have been like if they owned this land and the black treasure beneath it. Surely there would be meat and coffee and sweets.

While the men and boys hollered over which team got the extra player and whether or not they should play the men against the boys, the girls went for a walk. The women tended the fire, roasted potatoes, and kept the ants out of the food. Kathleen and Magrit walked stealthily back, being unusually quiet, trying to shush the boys. Yolanda's youngest girls lagged behind.

"C'mere. Look what we found," Kathleen whispered. "Come look. Shh, be quiet. Don't scare them."

She brought the older women to a large evergreen bush. A bird slashed out of the bush, nearly crashing into the group, squawking and fluttering as if it were about to attack. Instinctively the women raised their arms to protect their faces. The girls were nonplused.

"Here, on this side," said Kathleen. "Slow, now."

"See, there are four," Magrit said, translating to Hungarian for her mother.

"It is a robin's nest," Bridie said slowly for Yolanda. "Rah-bin, Rah-bin. Brrr-duh." They admired the tiny blue eggs while the mother robin scolded them from afar. Yolanda didn't offer the Hungarian word for bird, as Bridie helped her with pronunciation.

Both women had fourteen-year-old daughters and, despite the difference in language, the subject of marriage came up while the girls were off looking for herbs and roots. Bridie was not eager for Kathleen to marry. Yolanda said she looked at Slavic boys as potential husbands for her daughter. When the girls returned with some interesting looking leaves and gnarled roots, Yolanda's daughter, overhearing her mother, unleashed a torrent of sharp words. Bridie and Kathleen understood only the anger in their voices as they argued.

"How old you are when get married?" Yolanda's daughter asked

Bridie. Magrit spoke her new language more easily than her mother.

"I was just a girl, Magrit, same age as you. No, a little younger."

"That's me point altogether, Ma," said Kathleen. "I've been trying to tell you." Determination resounded in her voice. "I'm old enough to get married. Just because it wasn't a happy time for you until you met Da doesn't mean it will be the same for me."

"Get married, is not I like dat. Boys, dey nice, but make too much babies. I not like dat," says Magrit.

Yolanda rolled her eyes upward and raised both arms, shaking them to heaven. "Aye, aye, aye!" she yelled, pointing her finger at Magrit, scolding her loudly in Hungarian.

"Now is not the time to talk about this, Kathleen," Bridie said while she fussed with the food and poked the fire.

"That's what you always say when I want to talk about it. Sean and I want to get married."

Bridie didn't respond.

Yolanda seemed to understand the need to change the subject and started speaking in Hungarian. She mimed hunting, pointing to the slingshot hanging from Johnny's pocket. "Now dat it spring, we'll have meat for the gulyá," Magrit translated. "Squirrel, rabbit, and maybe deer too... how you say? Keep strong for the winter... smoke? Not same smoke as dis." Magrit mimed bringing a cigarette to her lips. Yolanda told Bridie how she cooked squirrel with tomatoes and carrots and lots of fresh basil. Bridie told her how her mother made Irish soda bread.

Tomorrow is another day, Bridie thought. Tim will be at work deep in the earth; Johnny will be high in the breaker. She fought to keep those thoughts away, to hold onto the joy of this Sunday. She kept the fire going, heated the food, patched skinned knees and elbows, tried to please Kathleen who seemed out of sorts, served food, responded to Tim's teasing the way he liked her to, and helped Yolanda with her English. The women laughed at each other's attempts at a new language. She put aside her need to get her hands in the earth.

Kathleen and Magrit separated themselves and seemed to be having a serious conversation until a huge wood bee drove them from their perch on a fallen tree trunk. The lads shrieked and bellyached at the play of the game; the birds sang; the sun shone, and the air was clean. All the while, the earth around them shimmered with change.

EIGHTEEN

The Black Maria

May 1888

Monday morning—too dark to wake after a day in the sun. Tim and Johnny dressed for the mine. Johnny ate breakfast, having learned that he got too hungry if he didn't. No more brown sugar *and* honey *and* cinnamon in his porridge. That treat was reserved for Sunday, unless they were fortunate to have eggs and meat. Bridie watched from the front porch as her men walked toward the mine head greeting others. Johnny laughed and joked with Sweeney's son, Billy, who joined them a few houses down. Shame assailed her as she brushed aside a feeling of gratitude that whispered, *thank God it's Billy who has no father.*

The work at the mine shut down some days in order to drive up the price of coal. Bride took in laundry to earn money so Johnny could quit the breaker. And to buy flour and kerosene.

It's worth the work, Bridie thought. This is Johnny's last week on the breaker. I'd scrub my fingers raw for him to go to school.

Bridie waited in line at the community pump for water to carry home, two huge wooden buckets at a time, two more trips to have enough for the day's washing, two more trips for rinsing. As water heated on her stove, she trudged along the rutted road for more than a mile to the top of the patch. First stop the fire boss's house, then the superintendent's. The crude wheel barrow threatened to tip out the laundry she lugged home to wash in a great wood tub in the yard.

The rhythm of washing lulled Bridie away from the sting of lye soap and the ever present worry about Tim and Johnny. She always half listened for the shrill alarm of the breaker whistle at an odd time in the shift announcing an accident. Overalls rumbled over the wash board. Dip and splash into the water, a stiff brush swooshed over rough fabric, splash and dip. Rumble, splash, dip, swoosh, into the rinse water, squeeze and fling over the line.

They don't get clean even with all the scrubbing, Bridie thought. She looked at the air as if it were something solid. Bridie turned away from the breaker and gazed out over the land, at first not seeing, but then slowly becoming aware of the soft rolling hills close by, the distant mountains, the brilliance of not-quite-white shirts flapping in the breeze, shabby houses, crude privies, the earth with greening grass studded with yellow flowers, new tender shoots, everything coated with a film from the mine fires, soot that held fast the fine particles of coal dust as if it were glue—everything, everyone sullied.

What was this place like a hundred years ago, before the riches of coal were discovered? Clean, fresh air and green meadows? Farms with roaming cattle, sheep, big farm houses, or small huts? Crops, children playing at work in the fields? Were there now hidden cities below the earth, below the coal? Did they become the coal? Will we, Bridie wondered.

Not so many years ago, she remembered, when she was a girl in the Shenandoah patch, the contents of the seven outhouses shared by thirty families flowed into the streets when it rained. The coal company cleaned the privies once a month, but they always seemed to be too full. Those privies were just outside their back door. That was the first thing they smelled when the breaker whistle awakened them. Today, Bridie and Tim shared an outhouse with only one other family. Still the stink was too much to bear on most days. A good strong rain still washed the excrement out.

Kathleen returned from cleaning the mine owner's house carrying another huge load of laundry. They talked about Sean Slattery; that is, Bridie talked, trying to persuade her daughter to wait another year.

"We love each other, Mum."

They sorted the new load.

"Look at Maura. Your age. Two babies. Another one inside her. She looks like an old woman."

"We'll need more water for these sheets."

"This is serious, Kathleen."

"It'll be different for Sean and me. We love each other," she said, grabbing the buckets.

"Love is not enough," Bridie called after her. "Maura was in love, too, remember? Couldn't wait to get married."

Kathleen sighed, rolled her eyes, and headed to the pump.

Bridie gave up. She remembered how much she loved Tim. And it *was* different from her first marriage. We still love each other, she thought. But I had to give up my dream. I decided to stay. I couldn't have both. I was Kathleen's age—but older, much older.

"Will ye look at these," she said when Kathleen returned with the water. Bridie held up the superintendent's wife's underwear: pink cotton, trimmed with lace. "Fa-a-ncyy," she said. Bridie strutted about, holding the garment up to her waist, throwing her hips side-to-side.

"These are fine drawers, but I'd think Frank Gowen's wife's, Mrs. Coal-Mine-Railroad-Queen herself, wears undergarments much fancier than these. Wouldn't you say so, Kathleen?"

"She probably shops at Wanamaker's. Corsets with lace. Flannel in winter."

"You can be sure Mr. Franklin B. Gowen himself has never worn underpants like ours." Bridie shuffled through a pile of wet clothes.

"Get a load of mine, will ye, now? Mine are laced too." Bridie held up a pair of her own undies that she'd made from a flour sack, twine laced through the hem at the waist.

Kathleen splashed rinse water on her mother and the two laughed as they wrung by hand some of the lighter weight clothing.

They brought heavy overalls and dresses to the shared wringer near the pump and put their baskets in line waiting to use it. A cloud hid the sun, making the breeze feel chilly.

The place was a hub of activity and gossip, where women gathered waiting to use the wringer. Children chased each other playing tag. "You're it." "I got you. You're it." Dogs ran after the children, adding barking to the squealing laughter. Hellos and well-wishes from women who had formed a closed circle around the wringer greeted Bridie and Kathleen. Yolanda and her daughter, Magrit, stood off by themselves while the younger Hungarian children played nearby in the dirt.

"Hey there, Maureen." Bridie greeted her neighbor with a hug before she moved her basket to the wringer. "Sharon, are you feeling better? Has that new mixture helped your headaches?" asked Bridie. Sharon was deep in conversation and didn't appear to hear. Bridie walked over to Yolanda, gave her a big hug, and had a greeting for each of Yolanda's children, calling them by name. "Ferenc and Gazsi!" She tousled the boys' hair. "Juliska, and little Mari, are you making castles?" She asked after Imre, the oldest boy, who worked the breaker with Johnny. Kathleen was already talking to Magrit. Bridie drew Yolanda into the larger circle of women.

"...his face bashed in and nose broken, too," said Sharon.

"They found him in the woods a couple of miles away from his house," Maggie said. "A coffin notice stuffed in his mouth."

"'Twas the Molly Maguires," said an old woman whose knobby fingers mended a pair of overalls, nodding her head as she spoke,

"Arm broken, too. He's in the Ashland Hospital."

"Who," asked Bridie?

"Foreman Walsh."

"Schmidt, too. He was beaten, but not in the hospital."

Bridie's mouth dropped open, stunned to learn this so many weeks after Sweeney's death. I wonder what Tim knows about it, she asked herself.

The breeze picked up and a distant rumble of thunder made everyone take notice.

"I hope it doesn't rain," several women said at once.

"Well, I'm surprised *you* didn't know, Bridie," whispered Maureen. "Some say 'twas Tim what did it."

"Shh! don't be spreading that around. Tim did no such thing. He promised me."

"Too late for that, Bridie. And no one is sad about him doin' it. We all loved Sweeney."

Some women laughed at a pair of giant sized overalls that wouldn't go easily into the wringer. "How in the world could someone this size possibly work in the mine?" one asked. "He'd get stuck there, for sure."

Bridie helped Maureen wring her clothes and fold them into the baskets. Maureen returned the favor.

A buggy rattled down the road to the clippity-clop of two mules' hoofs. The sound drew the women's attention away from the wringing. The buggy itself, a flat bed with shallow sides on wagon wheels, was unremarkable but instantly recognized.

"Gawd have mercy!" cried Bridie. "The Black Maria!"

Small boys ran alongside the crude carriage yelling, "Where're ye stopping? Is it me Da?" Front doors swung open. Women emerged to stand on front porches or stoops. Maureen pulled rosary beads from her pocket, moaning in a low voice the prayer to Mary, the Mother of God. Women dropped wet laundry on the dirt and ran toward the slowly-moving buggy.

Bridie knew every mind had but one thought: Please don't stop in front of my house.

As the buggy proceeded down the road, past one house then the next, the relief of some of the women could be seen in the lowering of shoulders and releasing of breath. Past Maureen's, past Sharon's. Then the makeshift hearse stopped.

"No! No," screamed Bridie and Kathleen simultaneously. Bridie ran down the road, her skirts pulled up to allow for speed. The driver... just stopping there... getting his bearings... finding the right house. Sure 'n it couldn't be Tim or Johnny. I'd know. I'd know in my heart if 'twere.

"Not my house!" Kathleen screamed behind her.

There he was, lying on the flat bed of the buggy, blood on his face, soaked into his shirt and pants, his small body tossing, moaning. Bridie clambered into the buggy, knelt in a pool of blood.

"Help me! Help me!" she pleaded while she struggled, frantic to remove the rope belt her son wore. "Did no one think to try to cut the bleeding?"

Maureen climbed in, too. She ripped off her apron, offered the tie. Bridie fumbled with Johnny's left arm, a frenetic searching through mangled flesh and fiber for substance around which to tie it.

Bridie mumbled incoherently.

Maureen leaned over Johnny, held his head in her lap. Blood soaked her dress. "God Almighty, have mercy on us poor sinners.

Mary, Mother of God, help us," she prayed. The rosary, dripping red, dangled from her wrist.

"Bleedin' had stopped when they put him in, Ma'am, Mrs. O'Doyle." said the driver He didn't move from the weathered, rough board that he sat on. "I thought he was dead, Ma'am. I was told he was gone, to bring him home."

The driver, a frail looking old man, his face lined with deep crevices, leathery and tattooed with black from years of working in the coal mine, held his body hunched over so far that he looked about to fall forward. His rough hands, nails outlined with black, held the reins to steady the mules that seemed to want to keep moving. Their ears flapped and twitched. They stamped, shaking off flies, blowing and snorting, tails swishing. The pungency of fresh dung mixed with the smell of blood.

Johnny moaned. Opened his eyes. Turned toward Bridie without recognition. He tried to sit up. Reached out with his bloody arm. He toppled over.

Bridie stood; the crude wagon wobbled. "Bring him to the hospital in Ashland. Now, for the love of Gawd," she demanded of the driver. She wiped her son's blood from her hands onto her apron.

"The ride's a rough one, Ma'am. Takes too long. He'll be dead by the time he gets there. That's why boss said bring him here, Ma'am."

Johnny's moans lost urgency and strength. Bridie knelt beside him. Stroked his face. She saw his white face and blue lips. His skin was cold and moist.

Bridie traded places with Maureen, who climbed out of the wagon and scrambled up to the driver's seat. She seized the reins before the driver realized what was happening.

"Now, *I'm* taking over for the boss. To the hospital we're going. You hear that, you heartless article? What would you be doing if 'twas your son dying here?" She shouted orders to her daughter, told her to take the little ones home and to look out for them until she got back.

"We're going with or without ye driving, old man," she said to the driver. "And ye'll show us the way."

"Hey! Hey!" Imre shouted as he ran down the road toward the buggy. He waved both arms as if he were holding signal flags. Magrit and Yolanda ran to him, half dragged him to Bridie. Crying, he fell to his knees, breathless. Words spilled out like bad air from a blowhole.

Magrit translated.

"Dey work de breaker. Imre, Johnny, other boys... dey send da signals... like signs wid hands. Dey play like dat. Imre no know what happen. Johnny's hand... stuck in da... coal chute dat pull him in. Arm get cutted by a piece of... metal? Is dat how you say?" She spoke Hungarian to Imre.

"Ya. Metal. Sharp. Johnny pull arm out. Blood dat, uh... squirt all over. Squirt. Squirt. Squirt." Imre pumped his fist into the air each time he said squirt. "Boss say him dead. Imre t'inks Johnny looking living. Dat's why him run here. Say Johnny *not* dead. Boss wrong."

Johnny didn't respond to his friend's voice. He didn't move. He didn't groan or cry out in pain. His face had turned ashen. His open eyes stared at the sky; he didn't blink.

"Maureen, let's go," Bridie shouted.

"Giddap! Get on with you, now." Maureen slapped the mules with the reins. The driver protested, but she turned the buggy toward Ashland anyway.

As the Black Maria ricocheted between ruts and holes in the road, Johnny's body bounced so violently it left the bed of the buggy several times. Each time blood oozed from the stump of his arm. Bridie knew he was dead, but took several miles before she could bring herself to admit it.

A wail shattered the moment. So intense, that rain clouds seemed to form. It became a howl, then faded to a moan. Maureen pulled back sharply on the reins. The buggy stopped.

"He's gone," said Bridie, her voice rough, hardly a whisper. "Turn around. Take him home."

"No," said Maureen. "We'll get him to the hospital. You'll see. He's going to be all right."

This must be what hell is like, thought Bridie. Her blotchy red face was wet, tears dripped from her chin, and snot ran from her nose. One hand clutched the other as if holding on to something unseen. I'm in hell for not going to church, but making Johnny go. In hell because I lust after Tim, but make sure no babies are formed. Hell because I didn't insist Johnny not work in the breaker. Why? Why? Is the truth that I didn't want to take in more laundry? I'm in hell for hating Frank Gowen and all the mine owners and operators who make sure this place is hell. This, being here with my dead son, is hell.

NINETEEN

A Voice Soft Like A Whisper

May 1888
Johnny

I hear a voice calling.

"Johnny."

Me. That's me name. Who is calling?

"Johnny."

I open me eyes and see a bright light, brighter than the sun 'cept it doesn't hurt me eyes.

"Johnny," says the voice, soft like a whisper... In me head, not me ears.

There's music too, far away. I see an angel. Light twinkles around her face. That's all I can see, her face. No wings or anything, but I know she's an angel. She sings to me real quiet, like Ma used to. She touches me arm and when she does, the pain there goes away. I wonder where I am, where's me Ma, but I ain't scared or nothin'.

I remember. I was on the breaker. The breaker boss caught me once making signs to Brian Dougherty. Let's eat lunch, then get up a ball game, he signed. I was telling him, Yes, I want to play. The boss's switch whacked my back so hard I almost fell in the chute. I didn't see him back there. A mean piece of work he is, the boss. When he went down to whack Brian, I stood up, shaking me rear end and making faces at his back and signs for words my Ma wouldn't like. The other boys laughed. The boss turned around.

"Shut your hole and get to work, you stupid Mick." He started up to the top, toward me, to have another go at me with the switch. Below, Brian started making faces and the same signs. I tried to keep me face straight, hold it stiff, but I had a hard time to keep from laughing. Then everyone laughed and boss don't know who to hit first. There were too many boys. Five or six, one behind the other going down the chute. Lots of chutes across. All of us laughing at him. I laugh so hard I lost my balance, reached out. Something grabbed hold of my arm and pulled me in.

I don't know how I got here with this angel all lit up. 'Tis no dream. I'm not going to wake up.

Book Four

Summer 1888

TWENTY

Close Call

A soft green flannel shirt, faded blue overalls, and a frayed gray cap hung from a nail in the splintery wall boards. For weeks they had hung, flat and unoccupied beside an empty bed. Johnny's church clothes, they were to have been his school clothes, sleeves and pants too short, but not coal stained. Bridie wouldn't let anyone touch them. Every day she took the clothes off the nail. She caressed the shirt with her hands, nestled her nose in it to smell the little boy smell, imagined his body inside the shirt, sitting in a classroom—an excellent student. Fingers fondled the cap as if they tousled a head of hair; hands pressed the overalls.

A homemade ball sat on top of the bed, near his pillow. It was the pillow that smelled most like Johnny. Bridie fluffed the pillow, buried her face in it, then fluffed it again. On the floor, between the bed and the wall, rocks formed a small mountain—Johnny's rock collection. Beside the rocks, two Y-shaped twigs rested side by side, replacements for his slingshot. His boots waited next to the slingshot.

The water for laundry heated on the stove but Bridie sat on her son's bed, his clothes in her lap. She made no move to sort the laundry or set up wash tubs.

Tim worked miles below the surface of the earth, a labyrinth of passageways, gangways, and crossheadings between him and the pit bottom, between him and the grief the green flannel shirt induced. The darkness felt right, almost comforting. Only black rock in the narrow beam of his lamp and explosives waiting on the floor. Tim lay on his side, sharp rock and coal pieces cutting into his shirt. The coal auger, held at an awkward slant, powered by Tim's fury, chewed into the rock as he opened a ten-foot-long hole into the working face. Muscles strained and relaxed, bulged with effort, and became flaccid—Tim's whole body transferred might to arms and shoulders that rotated the auger. *Face*, what a strange thing to call the immediate area being cut, he used to think. But not today. Today, the only face that came to mind was Johnny's—and that face Tim pushed away.

The hole finally deep enough, he placed black powder in it, not too much, not too little. Squib next. The squib he held in his hand was familiar, but he examined it intensely as if seeing it for the first time. The cost of it had been deducted from his pay.

I could make me own squibs, he thought. Some miners do, filling rye straws with powder. The store-bought squib is more reliable than any I could make, and waterproof too, he thought. Yet, makin' me own might have saved some money. For what? So that Johnny wouldn't have to work on the breaker? Johnny was a boy, he argued with himself. Boys work on the breaker. Were there other ways I could have saved? Do I need beer after work? No, but the cost of a pint now and then doesn't put food on the table.

The laundry, he thought. It made me feel like a man to tell Bridie no more washing other peoples' clothes. What was the reason for that? Was I thinkin' Johnny would end up at the washtub if he didn't work on the breaker? Washtub's no place for a boy!

Squib in. Detonator cap on one end of the fuse. Push it into an explosive cartridge, then into the hole. Tim shouted the warnings, but as Tim was about to light the fuse he smelled smoke.

"Smell that, Tim?" asked Denny.

"Smoke? Don't see it," said Colem.

"Let's get the powder put away," Tim said. "Go. See what you can see."

He knew Colem's progress would be slow as he ran to the gangway, dodged low roofs, squeezed through narrow passages, splashed through water, and stumbled on lose rock underfoot there and back.

"Smoke!" Colem shouted when he returned. "Can be seen drifting from the direction of the main gangway, Tim. Headed this way. We'd better get outta here, now, before it reaches the pit bottom. There's a big fire somewhere."

An alarming noise, like a hundred tiny hooves heard at a distance, became apparent and grew louder by the second. Within moments of identifying that noise a thunderous sound cracked close by, followed by a chorus of squealing and red flashing eyes skittering along the floor of the tunnel, looking like hundreds of moving jewels.

"Hurry. Get outta here. The rats are running over me feet."

As they rushed into the main gangway, which was wide in this section, a boy leading two mules shouted the alarm. "Fire! Fire! Hay's burning 'n I can't stop it. Fire!" Smoke seemed to follow him.

Just then another earsplitting crack, closer now, traveled overhead. The roof unleashed huge rocks, stones, and crossbeams. When it crashed to the floor of the gangway, a plume of dust rose. A curtain of particles descended with the fall. Tim squeezed his eyes shut, pulled his jacket and shirt over his head which he then covered with his arms and hands. Still he coughed with each breath, spitting dust and grit.

Mules screeched their agony. The boy sputtered and hollered, "Me leg! Me leg! Help me! I can't get it out." Dust clouded the darkness. Keeping his nose and mouth covered, Tim turned toward the sound, feeling his way forward with his hands, arms, and feet.

"Colem? Denny?" called Tim.

"Aye, trying to get to me feet," said Colem, his voice weak.

"I'm here," said Denny. "You all right, Colem?"

"Took a hit to the head, I did. I'm ok."

The boy shouted, "I can't move. Help me. Get me mules."

After Tim relit Colem's lamp, the men searched for the boy using the narrow beams of the lamps on their caps, little rays of hope playing along the debris. The dust was thick as a morning's fog. Tim found him.

"Colem, help me with the boy. Denny, pit bottom. Go for help. Ring to bring the cage down, quickly man, quickly. This roof's gonna drop some more." Tim and Colem heaved away rocks to get to the boy.

"Help! Come quick! Help is needed!" Tim shouted to anyone who might hear.

Other miners and laborers, having seen the smoke and heard the fall, passed by on their way to the cage to take them up top. Some stopped to help. The squealing sounded distant now, as the rats got out, but the cracking of rock continued—close—quiet—then loud—then quiet again, heard only between the mules' anguished brays.

"Colem, use the drill to jimmy that rock from the boy." Tim hoped the boy was lying on coal debris that stayed in the mine floor, small pieces of coal, dust, gravely stuff. "May be soft with gob under him, you'll be able to wiggle him out. You there, Helmut, get the auger. Help Colem lift that rock. Carefully lads, quickly, that roof is working. You," Tim said, directing his beam of light to a short fellow holding an axe, "grab the boy by the shoulders. Pull when the rock is lifted.

And you," he tells a Welshman whose name he couldn't remember, "I need something to bandage the leg. Your shirt. No, the leg of your long johns will be cleaner. And your belt, take it off. We may need it. I'll check the mules."

Thick smoke mixed with coal dust. The lamp on his cap did not penetrate the dust and dark which threw the light back at him. Tim located the mules by the sound of their agonizing cries and a jab from a thrashing hoof. The animal was suffering. If I had a gun I'd shoot the poor thing, he thought. He discovered that only one mule was making all the noise. The other animal was nowhere in sight, completely buried.

Another deafening crack traveled overhead. Rock thundered onto the gangway floor. Timbers fell. The tunnel quaked with the force. Tim was tossed onto the rib of the gangway. He pulled his arms across his face to shield himself from the shower of dust that rained down. He waited for the deluge to stop, not sure if he was dead or alive. When he felt the downpour subside, he wiped his face and eyes with the inside of his undershirt. When he opened his eyes again he saw only darkness. His light had been extinguished.

"Gawd Almighty!" shouted Denny. "Tim! Colem! Anybody there? Anybody?"

Tim saw the tiny light on Denny's cap, grateful to know his eyes were still working. "Here, Denny. Over here. Over here," he repeated again and again until Denny located him and lit his lamp with the flame from his own.

"Hey, Colem. Helmut. Anyone!" Tim and Denny shouted. No answer.

When the dust cleared, Tim searched the littered gangway, barely passable now. The mules were silent. He couldn't find the lad. The only thing to be seen of the short fellow was his axe beside a pile of rock.

"Colem," shouted Denny. "Colem!" Denny bumped into Helmut.

Helmut had brought himself to his feet but seemed unable to speak. Denny lit Helmut's lamp and cleared grit from his nostrils. The deep wells of Helmut's eyes were caked with dust and grit that Denny removed with his fingers.

"Hold still," he said. "Let me clear your eyes. Have to do it the old way. Nothing clean here." He licked the eyelids clean as best he could. Then he opened Helmut's eye and, with his tongue, he wiped the eyeball, spitting the gritty paste out. He repeated this several times, with each eye, until finally Helmut could open his eyes and see. He just stared at Denny, then looked around, an expression of disbelief on his blackened face. That's when he noticed Colem, just inches from him. He nudged Denny and pointed his lamp in Colem's direction.

"Tim, Colem's here," Denny shouted. Colem lay on his side, still and soundless, his leg at a strange angle, sandwiched between two huge rocks. Tim saw Colem's body, the chest rising and falling shallowly. The position of the rocks allowed them to approach Colem from only one side. The mound of rocks leaned on a timber, which was bulging. Any more pressure on the timber could cause it to buckle or give way completely. Tim listened to the roof. Still working.

Tim, startled from his assessment by a moan, searched through the darkness with his headlamp. The Welshman. Yancy, he remembered the man's name. He laid flat on his back naked from the waist down, clutching his long johns in his hand, his overalls in a pile beside him. He began to move, first his head, which was bleeding, then his arms and legs. He rose up on one elbow, brushed the grit off his face, spit, and said, "What the hell? Where're my pants?" He appeared not to notice the roof fall. He shook his head and tried to stand, first getting to his knees. He reached out to find something to steady himself. Tim helped him up, too hastily, so that the man moaned again and retched. Then, as if the retching had cleared his head, he asked, "How many men are down?"

"'Tis ye, Denny, Helmut, and me standing. Colem's breathing but his leg is trapped. We gotta get that rock off him. We still need them long johns. Get over there and see what you can do to help. I'm still looking for the boy. Mules must be dead, don't hear 'em. We need more timber to support the roof. Could drop any minute. Need more men for that. Help! Help needed here!" Tim shouted.

Tim turned his head side to side, pointing his face to direct the light. "Laddie," he called, "mule boy. Make a sound if ye can hear me." No sign of the boy or the mules. Tim heard the roof working, crackling sounds rolling through the stone, and the grunts from the men trying to lift the rock from Colem.

"This rock ain't budging, Tim. We're gonna have to crack it with the picks. We got two here. Do you have one?"

"No time for that. This roof's coming down. This time it'll bury us all."

As if responding to Tim, the roof cracked and dropped dust and small rocks. Tim grabbed the short man's axe and opened his mouth to give orders. Unable to make any sound, Tim picked up a chunk of coal and popped it into his mouth to get his juices going to relieve the dryness.

"Denny, on me say so, you get Colem's shoulders and pull. Helmut, you get ready to lift his good leg when I tell you."

"What are you gonna do, Tim?"

Tim just shook his head; words were not possible. The roof cracked again, more dust showers.

"Yancy, you get that belt ready to tie around his upper leg."

Yancy pulled up his overalls. He looked dumbfounded at first, then apparently understood. Horrified, he said, "No belt. Will me shirt do?"

"Do it." Tim positioned himself squarely over Colem, raised the axe, then slowly lowered it, as if gouging an arc in the dusty air.

Denny yelled, "No!"

The roof gave a loud crack.

Tears rolled down Tim's blackened face, his heart pounding. He tried to think of Colem's leg as a timber he was splitting; one skilled swing would split timber. Tim raised the axe and swiftly brought it down exactly along the imaginary groove, with all the force he could muster, striking Colem's leg just above the rock and below the knee. One mighty blow split the bone with a loud, splintering crack that competed with the roof sounds.

"Pull, Denny," he shouted. "Tie it off, now, Yancy."

Moments after the men squat-walked under the low roof through the crossheading carrying Colem's body, the roof gave way again, burying the man, boy, and his two mules beyond anyone's ability to retrieve the bodies for a proper burial.

The people of the patch mourned the loss of their fellows. The operators mourned the loss of the mules, for another pair would have to be purchased; the loss of people cost nothing.

Bridie, after hearing Tim's account of the day, put the green shirt, the overalls, Johnny's pillow, and belongings in a box. That night, she comforted Tim with her body.

TWENTY-ONE

Defend A Wife

Summer 1888
Tim

Tim sat on a rough, wooden bench outside his house. Not his house, the company's house. I'll never own me own house, he thought, but pushed it away, replacing it with an acute awareness of the sensation of the evening air: a touch of cool on his face, the smell of a night-blooming plant, clean open space, freshness, endless sky. It felt like freedom.

He should have been content. He'd had his fill of supper, and honey for his tea, though Bridie didn't sip hers with him as she usually did. Even on a warm summer night, the air was cooler outside than in the kitchen. But she stayed there busy with... with what? He didn't know. There was even some beer left; he'd saved it to drink while he smoked his cigar. A cigar, given to him by one of the mine owners along with a promise—no, not exactly a promise, more like a hint than a promise—a hint of additional work. Given in exchange, Tim suspected, for hope of a good word when the mine inspector came by. Tim made no such promise.

He blew out a long stream of smoke that drifted away on the evening's soft breeze that wandered through the kitchen. He hoped the aroma would tempt Bridie to join him. She'd been known to share a cigar with him, though she'd never let anyone else see her smoke. She spoke out against smoking. He examined the cigar approvingly, a rare gift indeed.

He'd had his bath and Bridie had been playful giving it to him. Well, not really playful. Not taking pleasure for herself. Now that he thought about it, she had rushed him along, as if she'd wanted to get it over with. Not like her. Still... a smile formed on his lips. So, even with these small pleasures, he rumbled with discontent.

"Bridie," called Tim. "I think I'll take a walk over to see Colem."

No response from her.

Tim kicked a rock as he walked along, taking long, slow pulls on the cigar. Children shouted and laughed as they played their games. There was the low hum of conversation as he greeted neighbors sitting out, taking in the night air. Last time he spoke to the man whose leg he cut off, Colem had screamed at him, said Tim made him a cripple, said Tim should have let him die. Half a man is what he was, Colem had said. He'd be less than that once he started work as a breaker boy. A breaker boy again—that was worse than losing a leg, he'd said.

Sure 'n he'll be feelin' better by now, thought Tim. Colem will enjoy news of the mine. It'll keep him going to talk about mine politics. We'll grouse about the fire boss, chew about the price of coal being manipulated to keep the owner's pockets full and keep us in the poorhouse. He'll raise his voice, slam his fist on the table, and laugh when I tell Denny's dumb jokes. He'll want to hear about the lads, and the mischief, and the fun. Megan will see by the smile on his face when I leave, that the pain and gloom are gone, just by talking to me. He quickened his pace.

"Stay away from me house, Tim. Haven't ye done enough damage here? Is it more of Bridie's bad luck ye're bringing? I'll have no more of it in me house, ye hear?"

Megan slammed the door in Tim's face, but not before he heard "barbarian." He stood there thinking he'd hear Colem's voice telling Megan to shut up and for Tim to come in. He waited for a few minutes before he turned, but not in the direction of his house. He didn't feel like going home, just yet.

That woman is daft, he thought, but she's not the only one who is leery of Bridie. How does a man defend his wife when he's seen stranger things than anyone else has? 'Tisn't bad luck, he reminded himself, remembering a day when he'd wished he'd listened:

"Tim," Bridie had said that day when the weather had been warm enough for tulips to pop. "Bring your heavy coat to work with ye, today." He thought that was barmy. They left warm, humid darkness behind them in the morning as they entered the pit. Came out of the mine to an evening of freezing rain. He wished he'd brought his coat.

"How did ye know?" he'd asked.

"Just a guess, or maybe 'twas me Ma," said she, swatting the question away with her hand as if it were a pesky gnat.

Tim didn't press for an explanation; her Ma had been dead for years. Bridie didn't talk about how she knew what she knew or how she healed, apart from talking about her weeds: the ones growing in the garden, the ones browning and curling in the jars.

He remembered the winter evening Bridie had grabbed a coat and said she'd be goin' to see the Mahoneys. No great friends of theirs were they, but off she went on a night when the north wind could slice a body in half with the cold.

"What are ye going there for, woman?" Tim yelled as she ran down the road.

"Don't know," the wind carried back.

He'd slammed the door against the push of that night. Well, I'm not coming with ye, he thought. 'Tis for sure I'd know why I'd be goin' out on a night like this.

By the time she came back, the house rattled with the force of the wind and hail cracked against the roof, pellets hurled by the nor'easter. When she opened the door the cloth blew off the table she'd set for breakfast. 'Twas unusual she paid no mind to the articles that hit the floor.

"Good thing I got there when I did. Little Frankie Mahoney was chokin'. Anna, struck by fear, couldn't move to help him. I walked in on that, Tim."

She threw her coat onto the table instead of the hook by the door. It slid inch by inch to the floor, unseen.

"He was choked?" Tim asked. "How did ye know he was choked and not having a fit?"

"I picked him up by the feet and thumped him on his little back. 'What's in there Anna?' I asked her. I knew he'd put anything in his mouth—two-years-old, they do that.

"Anna, her mouth open, just shook her head. I thumped the child again. Nothing. His face turning blue, he flailed and kicked so that it was near impossible to hold him so his head was hangin' down.

"'Get over here,' I called to Big Frankie, who was snoozing on the chair. Snoozing through it all. But how would he know. The boy couldn't make any sound and neither could his mother. 'Take hold of your boy... his feet... or he'll choke to death.'"

Bridie had been talkin' so fast her words mushed together, spillin' out like overflow, spit scattered, hands worked her apron, tellin' what happened.

"'Anna, for God's sake, help me. Keep his arms still.' I knew he'd pass out soon. 'For God's sake, what's in there?' I yelled.

"Anna screamed when Big Frankie yanked the boy up and down

like he was dumping potatoes out of a sack. Out came three marbles. From the boy's *pocket*."

Bridie nodded her head. She looked me in the eye as if I'd put them there. "Marbles choking the boy."

Tim watched her face, as clear in his mind now as it was then, while she told how she put her finger in the boy's gullet, and without pushin' the marble in further, tried to hook the slippery, rollin' thing. She fell silent. Absolute determination pressed her lips and turned them inward; she closed her eyes as if she were still diggin' in there. One hand held an imaginary head whilst the other fished in the air that, in her mind, was his throat. Tim felt in his bones that she was thinkin' of Johnny.

Tim walked past the breaker, past the culm pile, sucking on his cigar, though it was no longer lit, thinking. How did she know to go to Mahoney's in the first place? I've asked meself the same sort of thing many times, he thought. She'd washed up the dishes and pots and was stoking ash off the coal in the stove when she upped and went to fish a red marble out of little Frankie's gullet.

Tim wandered about until at last he found himself at the bench in front of his house, not so much because of a need to be home, as out of habit. He finished the last of his beer—warm and flat with a few gnats floating in it—and flicked off the end of the cigar to save it for tomorrow. Through the window, he saw his wife mending someone else's clothes, probably the superintendent's.

I've seen the hardness forming around her, Tim thought. Yesterday, Maureen came to collect the weeds Bridie's been giving to her to give to Sheila, ever since some big scene at the oven or well.

"Not today, Maureen."

"Bridie? Ye know Sheila needs the herbs. Keeps her calm." Maureen tilted her head to one side, the expression on her face saying:

Come on, Bridie. Have a heart.

"There's no reason in the world she can't get it from me."

"She won't."

"Well then, she'll do without."

"She thinks you're cursed. That she'll be cursed."

"Then let her suffer."

I've never, in all me life, heard me wife say such a thing, Tim thought. Never! She didn't invite Maureen, her best friend, in out of the rain. Bridie just closed the door on her. Not slammin' it, but the goodbye-I'm-busy kind of closin' the door, mutterin' under her breath, not too quietly, that the curse Sheila was afraid of came from her own head.

Tim stood outside the window for a long while, feeling both pulled toward Bridie and pushed from her, wanting things to be as they used to be, when they didn't rush through love making, when they had their little Johnny with them.

Another child, that's what she needs, he decided.

"Tim," she said when he hauled himself into the stifling heat of the house, her face drawn, dark circles under her eyes. When did she get those? She usually looked happy, with a ready smile. There was no smile in her eyes or on her lips. When did she lose that? She's a good woman, a hard worker, he thought. I wouldn't want her lot in life. I'd much rather set a charge and risk gettin' me face blown off, than empty that slop pot every morning, or scrub a stranger's shitty underwear.

"Tim, I saw Frankie Mahoney playin' with his dog today. Running around as if he hadn't nearly choked to death last year."

'Twas as if she'd read his mind, her mentioning the Mahoney boy.

"Tim, I was there to save Little Frankie. It was like I was sent. Why is it that no one was there to save Johnny? No one was sent?" She let the mending drop to the floor.

"Who takes care of me? Who helped Johnny when he was hurt? Who listened when his young soul called out for help? Which of them that was there saw his torn body as more than another piece of slag to be thrown out of the way of making a profit?"

Tim was hoping she'd be softer today. It had been months since the boy died, still she grieved him as if it were yesterday. He told her there was nothing to do but let him go, that he was in a place of peace, smiling down on them. But she just looked at Tim like he didn't try to understand.

"You know what me mum would do when she was feeling sad?" Tim asked her, but she didn't let on that she'd heard him. "She'd get the beads out of her pocket and say the rosary."

"The rosary! The rosary!"

She was on her feet as if something had bit her arse. She threw her hands in the air.

"And when, tell me, did your mum ever make the blind see? How many lame walked? Tell me that. She didn't stop mine accidents with her rosary and neither did the Blessed Virgin or her Son. Tell me how many times you've prayed and how many answers to prayers came your way?"

"I thought it'd make you feel better, is all," Tim said. Good thing I didn't mention having another child.

"Feel better to pray to a God who gives so generously to some and withholds... no... *takes away* from those that have next to nothing?"

Her face got redder and redder and seemed to puff up with her anger.

"Maybe there is no Catholic God, only a Protestant God. If there were a Catholic God, would he allow the Irish to be denied the better jobs in or out of the mine?"

The woman was dangerous with the knife. She'd left the sewing in a heap on the floor, the needles and pins stuck into the front of her apron, and was now cutting the cabbage at the table. Tim wondered if she was beheading Gowen.

"I'd go to the Episcopal Church if I thought they'd let my Irish bones in. Must be only that *English* God who hands out the jobs and money."

Tim moved away from her, but he knew if she had a mind to, she could throw that knife a distance. Why was she cutting the cabbage in the evening?

"Frank Gowen! I bet he doesn't pray to anything but money. He's got lots of it. Look around here, if you can bear it. See any piles of money lying around? See the larder full? Meals sufficient to quiet hunger? How many rosaries does it take to get the stink out of this shit hole?"

Tim knew what was on her mind. 'Twasn't only Johnny that was grieving her. Gowen's wife and his sister, Mrs. Lansdale, were there yesterday.

"Did you see that bonnet on Esther Gowen, Tim? High fashion for a visit to the coal mine patch town to do her charity work! Do you like being a charity case, Tim?"

"Little Frankie was first in line for candy. He was happy, Bridie. A little candy, what's the harm?"

"Candy! Couldn't she see a piece of beef or a hunk of fruit was what the children needed? And shoes, for God's sake! Didn't she notice the rags some were wearing? That most ran around with no shoes? How skinny some were?"

Bridie chopped the cabbage till it seemed there'd be nothing left of it.

"Did you notice she lifted her skirts high and was ever so careful where she put her dainty feet, all laced in those fancy shoes?

She put the cabbage in a bucket and poured something on top of it, shook some seasonings in. Wiped her hands on her apron and screeched and swore. "I forgot about the pins," she said with the tiniest trace of a laugh.

She was a piece of work when she got going.

TWENTY-TWO

A Wedding

Ave Maria,
Gratia plena,
Dominus tecum.
Benedicta tu in mulieribus,
Et benedictus fructus ventris
Tui, Iesus.
Sancta Maria,
Mater Dei,
Ora pro nobis peccatoribus,
Nunc, et in hora mortis nostrae.
Amen.

Summer 1888

Kathleen and Sean, flanked by Bridie and Tim and the Slatterys, led
the procession from the O'Doyle house past the Episcopal Church to
The Church of the Immaculate Conception. The pure white building
gleamed inside its matching picket fence. It looked as if the Supreme
Being had shone a spotlight through the dreary patch town to the
church as a signal of His presence. A cross perched on the peak of the
church roof, but no bell tower announced the happy occasion.

The folks of Number Six mine patch town marched along the muddy road two by two, each making up a line of a ballad dedicated to the wedding couple. The long march allowed plenty of time for arguing over verses, shouting over the off-beat meter, rhyming, changing the words, laughing, and singing. Megan and Colem, with his new peg leg, processed with McGheehan and Marie, Sharon and Ryan Garrighan, Maureen and Martin McGonigal, Yolanda and Miklos. Those with no spouses paired up with each other. Children followed. Ed Foley, the minstrel, played the fiddle. No one was invited; everyone joined in.

Father O'Shea waited at the church entrance where he asked all to scrape the mud off their feet before entering. He'd dipped a brush in the bucket of whitewash and splashed one last touch-up on the fence before he stowed the stuff beneath the front steps.

Folks, dressed in their best clothes and Sunday shoes, filed into the sweet, spicy-smelling church. The good Father ushered only the Catholics up front for the wedding mass. The rest, not knowing when to stand or when to kneel, willingly sat back several rows. No one understood the Latin spoken during the mass.

Christ welcomed all with outstretched arms from a pedestal to the right of the consecrated marble altar, His sacred heart showing on the breast of flowing garments. The blessed Mother and other motionless saints watched the wedding party settle in.

In a room at the back of sacristy, Kathleen put on a too-snug dress. A woman who lived in Pottsville had given the fabric to Maureen, a seamstress as well as laundress, and paid her to make a party dress for her society-minded daughter. Seams can be adjusted easily, Maureen had said. It was a simple dress: white, with tiny embroidered pale pink flowers and lace trim. Kathleen would wear it for the wedding mass only, lest she soil it.

Yolanda adjusted the veil she'd worn at her long-ago wedding in Hungary. The beautiful not-quite-white handmade lace piled high atop Kathleen's head and flowed over her shoulders to the floor. Bridie had brushed her daughter's hair and fingered in waves like she'd seen in magazines. Kathleen didn't particularly like it but there was no time to change it. The veil covered most of it anyway.

Bridie had searched the box at the back of the church for weeks before she discovered the white shoes, a little too tight, but suitable for walking down the aisle.

An organ thundered out music as Tim escorted Kathleen down to the altar. As the nearly-empty collection plate passed from one to another, Sharon Garrighan sang "Ave Maria."

The bride's knees trembled as the priest pronounced them man and wife, but Kathleen and Sean had consummated their union already; the gathers of the homemade wedding dress didn't hide that fact at all.

Afterward Sean, his hair still slicked back, and Kathleen in her own plain dress and red hair brushed out and hanging loose, reigned, as if King and Queen, over a grand party that spilled out of Bridie and Tim's house into an open area. A dance floor—the usual sheet of iron borrowed from the mine—exploded with the color of swirling skirts, feet stomping out jigs and reels, laughter, and mayhem. An old door, formerly used below to control mine ventilation, accommodated more dancers and added a drumbeat sound to the fiddling.

Everyone—Irish, Hungarian, Polish, Welsh—brought food and drink. There were potato dishes of all kinds and golabki. Smells of fried bacon and cabbage, spiced beef, and homemade cheese filled the air. Chicken, pierogi and smoked sausage, rabbit, squirrel, fish, and beef tongue roasted over an open fire. Soda breads, cakes, cookies, and candies attracted stealing fingers before supper. Several women had baked a three-tiered wedding cake the likes of which had never been seen before. In it were more eggs than most people ate in a month.

For people whose lives were reined in by poverty, friends and neighbors put together a rich feast. For those few hours, it was as if they were not often hungry, did not live under the threat of the breaker whistle announcing an accident, or with the limitations of debt to the company store. Kathleen's wedding was an excuse for some much-needed fun.

Though there was still much disagreement about which verse should come first, and whether the mention of the bride's large commodiousness was appropriate, they finally agreed on this one.

You see before you Sean the lad,
A man both strong and hearty.
He's a ladies' pet with eyes sky blue,
An upright honest man.
Kathleen O'Doyle did snatch him up
Before the other girls him could snag.
To church we all did march this day
To tie the knot before 'twas too late,
And Sean the ladies' pet away did get.
A party then for us awaits.
With beer and food and music
We will celebrate.
　　　　　– A.M. Getty

Friends strummed banjos, blew horns, pounded drums, and even squeezed an accordion. Music filled the soot-dusted coal patch town and made it sparkle. Everyone danced till they could dance no more, sweat running down their faces and backs.

Yolanda and Miklos taught Bridie and Tim, who'd had his father-of-the-bride fill of beer and whiskey, how to do their favorite dances: the polka and mazurka. Young and old joined in, feuds and bigotries forgotten. They made plans for celebrating Midsummer Day next week and Foley promised to return for July 4th next month, all unaware of what the next few months would bring.

TWENTY-THREE

The Unthinkable

She'd heard the mid-afternoon colliery whistle—too late to signal lunch, too early for quitting—but didn't go with the other women as she usually would have.

She knew. In her bones, she knew. It was as if he'd whispered his final breath into her soul.

A scuffle of heavy boots on the porch, a gentle thump, the beat of feet jumping off, then no sounds from the porch, none apart from Bridie's breathing. The knock at the door finally came.

"Bridie," said Thomas Duffy. His eyes filled. Words caught in his throat.

"Mum," said another, swiping his cap from his head, eyes cast downward, pale wash streaks tracing their way down the cheeks of his soot black face.

"Miz O'Doyle, Ma'am," said a man who clenched to his chest a slouchy hat, thick with black grit, the kettle-shaped lamp half falling off it because of his grip.

Her eyes searched the clouds for signs of rain, anything to avoid what had been placed at her feet. Put off, for just another moment, what she'd known since the whistle. Snuff out the anguish threatening to break down the rock wall she'd been erecting since she'd married another coal miner. A coal miner with papers. Papers that gave him pride, purpose—evidence that he'd qualified to work the most dangerous job deep in the mine.

With gratitude in their hearts that their turn had not yet come, a parade of disheveled women, their aprons flapping, skirts sweeping across their shoe tops, strode out of step down the dirt roadway toward Bridie's house, dust flying in their wake. The priest followed.

She looked at her husband, laid out on the bare planks, his face black as miners' faces get. So black she couldn't see an expression, an attitude, his attitude, usually so feisty, full of vinegar and mirth, except when he made love to her. Then he was warm, gentle, rough, and passionate. There was none of that.

"A collapse?" she heard herself ask, even though she knew it couldn't have been. There was no blood; he had all his parts. Gowen, a man of riches, coal mines, and railroads, she thought. He has taken the last of my treasure.

"Choke damp, Ma'am."

"Must have been. We found him lying face down," said a different voice. "'Twere McGeehan that found him, Mum."

"Working alone, Bridie. Checking a new seam," said Duffy.

She glanced at the hook alongside the door. There hung his Davy lamp, for detecting gas. A peculiar looking thing, small, a couple of inches of brass that could have saved his life. He'd forgotten it. Forgotten to leave it behind last night at the mine office, as he usually did when he left the mine, forgotten it this morning.

"The fire boss refused to give him a lamp. Said go back and get what you left behind."

Duffy fidgeted. McGeehan looked anywhere but at Bridie, shuffling from one foot to another. Jamie McGee stepped toward Bridie, and then back, swiped his face with his hand.

"No need for the lamp neither, says the boss," said Finnighan.

"Fire boss checks before the mine opens. But the stickler he is, ma'am, Tim always checked again before he allowed his own crew to go down. But the boss, he had it out for Tim, he did, what with Tim speaking out about conditions not being fit for swine."

"And Tim," said Denny O'Reilly, "he'd not a mind to go home for a lamp and lose a couple tons of coal."

She'd thought to bring the lamp to him but knew he'd be deep under the earth by the time she got there. Ah well, she'd thought, there's sure to be extras.

"In here," she said, swinging her arm toward the door in what might have been a gesture of welcome on any other day.

The screen door screeched open, then slap-slapped behind the men who entered the front room. Tim had made the screen door as a surprise, a gift for no reason. It hadn't been her birthday or Christmas. A decadent luxury that had cost him nothing but time and a little ingenuity. They'd seen a screen door on a big house in town and she remarked how wonderful to be able to foil the mosquitoes on a warm summer night. The door was a patchwork of scrap wood and pieces of screen he sewed together. The first night it was up, the children asleep, they lay together, moonlight coming through the new door, and made love. When they moved to bigger house, after getting his papers, they brought it with them, making it fit.

The men heaved Tim onto the long wooden table that had been used for rolling dough, birthing babies, stitching cuts, mixing poultices, and feeding family, friends, and boarders. Dried herbs hung in bunches from the rafters. Jars of gray leaves and peeling brown roots lined up beside the stove.

Again, pounding on the porch, women's voices. Two came in, Maureen McGonigal and Sharon Garrighan, Sharon wiping her hands on her apron which she'd twisted into deep wrinkles. They approached the men one by one, nodding toward the front door, gently pressuring a shoulder in the direction of the road. Without a word they cleared the room, for this was woman's work.

Sunlight had the audacity to shine through a small window. Dogs barked as small boys at play squealed in glee. The smell of bread baking in the communal oven told a lie of abundant meals to come.

Bridie stood still as a pillar of stone. The only movement was invisible: the anguish that roiled inside her and her effort to keep it in check. She brushed off Maureen's attempt at an embrace, knowing that would unleash emotions she was not ready for, afraid of. Sharon patted her shoulder and picked up the water buckets and left, the screen door slapping behind her. Bridie stood, still on the outside, not even blinking, not even thinking, just holding back. That was all she could do.

Maureen moved about the house with the familiarity of a friend, gathering the lye soap, a brush, towels. "We need ice," she said to the men who lingered on the front porch.

Sharon returned with the water.

"Leave me," said Bridie.

Maureen squinted her eyes, tilted her head as if she hadn't understood.

"Leave me." Bridie, her voice small and weak, seemed on the verge of collapse.

"We'll help you wash him," said Sharon.

"Go... Please. I need to do this myself."

"He's so big, Bridie. Let us help you."

"I need to be alone with him. Just go."

The women left.

Bridie turned and moved to the table, as if in a trance. Her hand brushed lightly over Tim's hair then grabbed a handful as if trying to shake him awake, her whole being focused on him. It was as if the world ceased to exist, but for the two of them floating in silent emptiness. She pushed hair off his forehead. With her hands, because she didn't want anything else to touch him but her, she wiped the black from his face—first his forehead, which had relinquished the furrow she'd seen between his eyes this morning. She had seen in that scrunch that he'd expected trouble today. Then his eyes, closing the lids that had remained open, she guessed, so that he could see her one more time.

She scooped the black dust from the corners of his eyes and the wrinkled puffs under them. Gently she ran her thumbs across his eyelids, from the inside corners to the outside, again and again. He'd always loved her massaging his eyelids to sooth away a headache.

"You have the touch, Bridie," he'd say, as she could see the tension melt away and sense the pain dissolve beneath her touch.

"That's alright, Tim," she said without uttering a sound. "You can close your eyes now; I'm part of your soul and I'm never leaving you."

Grit rolling along her palm, she brushed off his cheeks usually bunched up in a smile, now flaccid, sagging in folds not there before. His nose next. He'd sniffed coal dust for so long he'd lost his sense of smell and grieved that he could no longer smell her cooking as he walked home at the end of the day. Even worse, he'd said, he couldn't smell her.

She passed over his mouth, not ready yet, and dusted his chin and neck, loosened his shirt that had gotten pulled beneath his shoulders. It was still just the two of them in a void of time and place. She even lost track of the clenching torment inside.

Her finger traced the indent that led from his nose to the center of his upper lip which was full and well defined. He'd wanted to grow a mustache but she'd objected to hiding his beautiful mouth.

She wiped his lips, moisture from just inside them making a sooty mud. She kissed them anyway, unable to hold back. Passionate at first, then forceful as if the kissing would breathe life into him. The unresponsiveness shocked her, broke down all defense. A long, guttural wail burst from her soul and filled the room. It would have filled the entire patch if it hadn't already been filled with grief.

She crawled up onto the table and lay on her side close to him. There was still a warmth to him, she noticed, as she closed her eyes and pictured him as he had looked on the day they met more than eight years ago.

Bridie took Tim's hand and touched it to her mouth. Cold. She placed his hand on his belly and slid her own beneath his body. There she could feel his warmth. She put her other hand on top of his. Bridie spoke to Tim as if she were telling a bedtime story about the olden days to a young child. "Tim O'Doyle, I remember the day you held a plate of food in this hand." She spoke to him quietly, regaining her composure as the vivid scene of this day unfolded in her mind, keeping it from the edge of despair.

Book Five

Fall 1888 – Spring 1890

TWENTY-FOUR

Dan's Place

I'm a celebrated workingman, My duties I don't shirk;
I can cut more coal than any man from Pittsburgh to New York,
It's a holy roaring terror, boys, how I get through my work,—
That's while I'm at my glory in the barroom.

I can stand a double timber, single post, a bar, or prop,
I can throw a chain on the bottom or I can throw it on the top,
Give me a pair of double engines and be damned I'll ne'er stop,
Till I land a couple of wagons in the barroom.

— From "A Celebrated Workingman" by Ed Foley

Fall 1888

"I will not leave my house," Bridie shouted at the Clerk of the company store, just two days after Tim died.

"You must, Ma'am. Them's the rules."

"He's here, my Tim... I can feel him, his spirit, smell his smell." She covered her mouth with her hand as if stifling a scream. Grief crumpled her face. "Johnny too, and Patrick, they're gone but still part of this house. How can you expect me to leave them?"

"'Tain't me, Bridie. 'Tis the Company. No wage earner with you, Bridie. 'Tis a rotten job, this, but it has fallen on me shoulders to tell ye to get out. If ye had a couple of boarders..."

"Boarders? No one will board here. Some are calling me a witch. They say I bring bad luck, curse the mine, cause accidents and death."

"I don' know anything about that, ma'am. I do know if ye don't get out on yer own the police will put ye out."

When the Coal and Iron Police arrived at Bridie's home, they didn't force her to leave. They tied their horses to a tree and entered her front room without a word. They simply threw her belongings onto the road. Everything from furniture to undergarments. Frying pans, bowls, rolling pins, and pillows. Teapots crashed to the ground, hard with early frost. Glass shattered, chair legs broke off. Her only personal luxury, homemade liquid lavender-scented soap, froze to the ground.

Frank Gowen's flunkies wore dark military-style uniforms with lots of brass buttons and badges. A strap with bullets hung from one shoulder, crossed the chest, and held a holster and gun. Their hats, marked with official-looking police emblems, were tall with rounded crowns and peaks to shade their eyes.

"Stop!" screamed Bridie, torn between standing guard in front of her herb-filled shelves and running outside to get help. "Someone help me," she yelled from the kitchen window.

Maureen, not one to be intimidated, ran from her house straight up to one of the policemen and shoved him. "Get away from this place if ye know what's good fer ye." She shoved him again. The blow knocked his hat off.

The lawman raised his nightstick, but by that time a few more women had arrived. Armed with clubs of their own, they outnumbered the police. Among the women were Sharon, Maggie, and surprisingly

Megan, who had started all the rumors about Bridie casting the evil eye over the colliery.

"Till this time tomorrow, then," said one of the policemen. "We'll bring twenty men with guns to be sure you've finished the job," he said fingering his own weapon.

Maureen made room for Bridie in her home but refused to let her pay rent. "You've been our doctor for so many years," Maureen said. "You never charged me or anyone else. If you must do something, there's lots of work around here."

When Dan McMonagle offered her a job at the saloon, she accepted. Bridie did laundry and mending, helped in the garden, baked, and scrubbed floors for Maureen before going to the saloon for afternoons and evenings. She took in additional ironing and laundry. Still, she couldn't work long or hard enough to keep her mind off her loss.

The first afternoon Bridie went to Dan's place, he was outside replacing split clapboard on the side of the saloon. She had watched him from across the road. He loosened the board above the one that needed to be replaced, popping the nails and removing them. In the same manner, he removed the nails from the broken board and slid it out. Bridie could see he'd already replaced several. Paint that crackled and peeled from the old boards contrasted with the new unpainted boards.

The smell of the sawdust and the sound and rhythm of the crosscut hand saw stirred deep feelings in Bridie. She remembered her father building and repairing as he hummed old Irish tunes. She recalled Tim sawing old lumber scraps to piece together their screen door. The sound of the saw rolled a lump of grief in Bridie's chest while, at the same time, giving her a safe feeling. Dan was a good man.

Dan and Tim were not close friends, but they respected each other. Tim had said, "He runs a clean place, that Dan McMonagle does. Never takes advantage of the poor drunken louts that drool on his bar. Charges fair prices. Refuses to allow anyone to run up a tab more than he can pay. And if the poor sucker has a bunch of mouths to feed, he kicks him out after three drinks."

When Maureen's husband had objected to Bridie taking up room a boarder would pay for, Dan fixed a room off the kitchen for Bridie. There was a big sign on the door: *KEEP OUT*. Dan installed Yale locks she could bolt from both the inside and outside. There would be no mistaking the room's purpose. In exchange, Bridie often cooked.

Most nights, there were few women who drank in the saloon. The women who were there spent most of the time in two small rooms upstairs. Bridie cleaned those rooms early in the day, before the quitting whistle sounded. She mopped up split beer, swept the floor, chased cobwebs from the ceiling, put fresh sheets on the bed—the only piece of furniture—and pretended not to know what the rooms were used for. This was Bridie's first experience in a bar.

On a blustery night before Thanksgiving, snow blew in through the barroom door when two policemen strutted in and sat at the bar. Her stomach clenched with the sight of the same two who had come to her only days after Tim died.

Now they were here, the police, ordering whiskey in Dan McMonagle's Saloon. The same Daniel McMonagle who had offered her the job cleaning his saloon. Bridie ignored her bucket of soapy water and rags. Her mind wandered these days. Scenes replayed in her head. Those policemen and their foul deeds. Her uncle hanging from a rope, Tim laid out on her kitchen table. Her mind flew from one to the other every day.

The policemen downed their shots of whiskey and left without hearing a friendly word from anyone. Bridie, her bucket in hand, followed them out as if in a trace. McMonagle's Saloon, a narrow but deep clapboard building, had an unfortunate location directly across from The Church of the Immaculate Conception. Many an evening Father O'Shea could be seen sitting on the front steps of the church, smoking a cigarette and blessing and greeting men as they came and went from Dan's place, often giving some a place to sleep it off after a payday toot. Bridie wondered if Father O'Shea would give the policemen a blessing.

He ignored the policemen. "Good day to ye, Mrs. O'Doyle," Father O'Shea said. "May the blessings of God go with ye this evening."

"And with you, Father." Bridie dumped the bucket and went back into the saloon. She wondered if the priest thought she worked in the upper rooms.

Inside, the rough wood bar stretched across most of one long wall. Four legged, tall, backless stools were lined up in front of the bar. Tables and chairs filled the rest of the room and were sometimes pushed back to allow space for dancing. The room was without windows. Gas lamps provided light. The broad plank flooring led to the kitchen in the back, and a flight of stairs led to the rooms above. Bridie slumped in a kitchen chair, then went to her room to lie down. She hadn't finished cleaning.

Ed Roarity spent most evenings drinking and telling bad jokes. Usually, Dan ushered him out before he got too obnoxious. This particular night, he grabbed Eddie Roarity by the scruff of the neck and dragged him across the barroom floor.

"Oww," howled Roarity.

"'Twill be enough from you," said Dan.

Bridie lay on the floor shivering, wiping her mouth, gulping deep breaths. Tears rolled down her reddened cheeks.

"Le'go a me." Roarity punched the air, kicked over a chair trying to get away.

"Lay a hand on Bridie again an ye'll pay fer it with yer life. Go home to your Mamie and children."

"No! Me Mamie? Me wife! 'Tis her that will kill me."

Dan opened the door and tossed him out into the cold rain, as he often did.

"Sorry, Bridie," Dan said. "The good Father will get him. He's really harmless. I try to get him out before he gets too drunk."

The saloon was dark despite the gas lamps. The aroma of beer that seeped through the cracks and crevices onto the road quickened the appetite of those passers-by inclined to indulge. The barroom air, rife with the scents of beer and whiskey, mixed the odor of sweaty clothes with wet wool.

Bridie nodded, shaken by the encounter with Roarity. She straightened her dress and retied her apron. A few stray hairs sprang from the bun at the nape of her neck. She could still feel Roarity's slimy lips and his rough whiskers, and smell his beer breath. She shuddered. Grief shot through her at the thought of her Tim, who would have broken Roarity into pieces.

Squaring her shoulders, Bridie tried to appear tough but could not look at anyone for fear they'd see the tears. I can put up with the likes of Eddie Roarity, she told herself. It's the empty hole in my gut that's killing me. I used to run a household. But now... now I'm a charwoman in a barroom that has rooms on the second floor. She shook that thought from her head. I'm a charwoman who'll soon be gone from this place. I hope Kathleen and Sean will come, too.

On his way from town to town, Ed Foley, Number Six's favorite minstrel, often visited Dan's place. "Beer and Whiskey," he said, "pump up the creative juices. I write me best songs when me mind is lubricated with a few drops." Eddie, most called him, as if he were still a little kid, stood nearly six feet tall, with a big smile and an empty purse. He sang for his drink and dinner. The size of his rotund belly was a testament to his success.

More than once, Bridie handed him a scrap of wrapping paper or a used envelope to scratch down the words he sang or suggestions offered by the barroom enthusiasts. On this night, Ed Roarity proved the inspiration for "A Celebrated Workingman," which became one of Foley's most popular ballads. Roarity couldn't hold his drink. After one beer he began to brag and boast about what a good hard worker he was. To listen to him, he could out-work any three men even on a bad day.

"I can drive a mule better'n any man here. Just try me out with the balkiest team ye got. I'll have em doin' me will in two minutes. I know mules, I do."

"Go on wit ye, Ed. Ye don't know a mule's arse from a hole in the ground, ye don't."

Roarity didn't care, or didn't hear, because he went on bragging. "And who do you think the fire boss comes to for advice? Can show them all how the steam should generate, I can. And how the air should circulate."

"You are so full of shite, man." Everyone laughed.

"He's the worst worker the mine has."

"Washout!" someone shouted.

"'Tis only when yer tipsy that yer such a star, ye old blowhard." Roarity laughed along with them.

Foley signaled for a new pencil, hailing Bridie with the broken one. "Another scrap of paper, too, my good woman." He got out his fiddle, mumbling a few words while trying out a tune. Soon Roarity was snoozing, head on a table, while the whole barroom sang the new verses.

On the few mild days in November, Dan opened the back porch where the men sat and gossiped about the mine, the foremen, and bosses. Welshmen and Hungarians, if none were present, provided fodder for their jokes. They shared quids of tobacco. Drank. Smoked clay pipes. Told tall tales, each trying to outdo the other.

McMonagle's kitchen, Bridie's favorite room in the saloon, produced Thanksgiving dinner for patrons. Bridie cooked on two modern stoves. A turkey, a goose, and all the fixings. The dinner was a McMonagle tradition. At Christmas, they'd roast a pig, beef, and potatoes, Dan said. Bridie could select vegetables, spices, trimmings of all sorts from the company store. Many patch town folks traveled to other towns to visit family, but those who remained were welcome to partake in the feast. She felt a tinge of happiness pierce her grief, but shoved it away, not trusting such feelings.

Dan hired Kathleen to help with the preparation and serving of Thanksgiving dinner. Sean helped by eating the biggest Thanksgiving turkey he'd ever seen. Kathleen, so large with the baby, was more obstacle than help in the kitchen and awkward at serving. Their baby surely was due soon.

TWENTY-FIVE

A Child Is Born

*...Naked came I out of my mother's womb, and naked shall I
return thither: the Lord gave, and the Lord hath taken away;
blessed be the name of the Lord.*

– Job 1:21 (KJV)

January 1889

Bridie folded the christening dress her grandson had worn. She
wrapped it in tissue paper and placed it in the trunk that locked.
She thought back to Kathleen's wedding day and wished she had
the wedding dress to preserve, too, but wishes were a waste of time
and hope.

Kathleen and Sean looked at each other as if they were the first
couple ever to make a baby together. When her labor began, he sent
for Bridie, then insisted that he stay to help with or at least watch
the birth.

"'Tis strange ideas you young people get," Bridie said as she
shooed him away. "This is for women only!" Bridie sent for Yolanda,
who also had experience birthing, though it included statues and
strange ideas from her Hungarian upbringing.

Bridie found it easier to allow for the possibility of a feminine kind of God, someone like the Blessed Virgin Mary who Yolanda and so many prayed to—easier than believing in a God The Father who treated his Irish children so poorly. Yolanda said the Blessed Mother rushed to the side of a woman in labor if her hair was not braided. Knots and locks increased a woman's labor pain, so Yolanda unlocked chests and doors while Bridie brushed the braids from Kathleen's hair and put it in a bun on the top of her head. Yolanda placed her holy pictures and small statues of the Blessed Mother and Baby Jesus around the bed that had been prepared for the birth.

Kathleen struggled all day and into the night. Sean paced and smoked, drank whiskey as the evening wore on. Every few minutes he asked about how things were moving on. A name had been picked for the baby, but it was bad luck to tell it before the christening. Bridie hoped it would be a boy and the name would be Timothy John. Then for confirmation, Daniel, after her father.

Tears filled her eyes with each labor pain as if it were her own. All she could do was to put cool cloths on her daughter's head and comfort her with soft words and Yolanda's sedating herbs. Kathleen squeezed her mother's hand so hard Bridie thought the bones would break. Yolanda was in charge of this birth; Bridie found herself to be too emotional, her hands too shaky to hold a slippery new baby.

"Labor pains," said Yolanda, "dey avaken de mother's love."

Kathleen smiled a weak smile. "Then it is more than enough love I'll have," she said.

The moans grew louder and the pushes stronger, beyond Kathleen's control. "How long?" she asked. "I can't push this baby out." With those words another pain brought a push and a squalling baby boy slid into Yolanda's hands, his arms and legs trembling with life. The first thing he did was pee.

"There's a fine boy for you," said Bridie, laughing with relief.

Yolanda placed the baby on Kathleen's chest while she took care of the cord and afterbirth. Bridie saw the mother love awaken in her daughter's eyes, and felt a grand surge of motherly love in her own heart. She helped Yolanda clean Kathleen, change the sheets, and put the bloody ones in the wash tub which had been filled with cold water.

It was Bridie who prepared the hazel water for the baby's first bath in the wooden bin she had used to make bread. She taped a coin on the baby's belly button. It was supposed to be a silver dollar but she didn't have one. After she wrapped him in a soft cloth, Bridie looked at the picture of the Blessed Mother. In her heart she said thank you, a natural, unplanned response, one of the few prayers she'd said since her father died.

"A few days you rest," Bridie heard Yolanda say. "You no leave da house and no take da bath for forty days. Den, you go church for dat special mother's blessing and have da baby christened."

None of that was important to Bridie, but she knew Sean's parents were strict Catholics and Kathleen would follow their wishes, especially since she lived in their house. In fact, she'd been going to mass every Sunday morning since the wedding. What *was* important to Bridie was that there didn't seem to be too much bleeding and that there would be no infection. She looked up to the holy picture again as if pleading for her daughter. Kathleen was not out of danger yet.

~

Bridie sat on the floor in her small room off the kitchen in McMonagle's saloon. She closed the lid of the trunk, securing the christening dress, locking away hope. She asked herself, what if all a person wanted to do was to live a better life? Not a grand life. Just a better life for her family and for herself. A better life for Bridie O'Doyle, a simple coal miner's wife.

I read in a magazine, a long time ago, she said to herself, when I could stand looking at magazines—when there was hope enough to wish for the life I saw the women in the pictures living, when I could bring myself to look at fashions for hair and clothes, when I could see pictures of beautiful, smiling women and handsome men and not wonder why I had to use a smelly latrine with a floor wet with pee and rain water and they didn't. A long time ago— when I didn't wonder why my Tim lies like a rock below the earth while fancy dressed people stroll down the avenue—I read that in a city called Chicago, a tall building reached high into the sky. It was the tallest in the world, I think. I wondered if the rain came through the roof, so close to the clouds. Do the people who live there plug holes in their walls to keep the sleet and snow out in the winter? But I guess people don't live there, just work there. Work at something different from shaking potato bugs off leaves into a can of kerosene. Go to work there every day and come home with money to buy food for their families. Actual money in their hands to exchange for what they need, maybe even what they want. Did their daughters die of infection after birthing a baby who dies, too?

She filled a bucket, collected rags. Scrubbing floors helps, she thought.

While she scrubbed and scrubbed she relived lifetimes in her head. Events and episodes replayed, recurred, repeated, past and present revolving. One moment, Kathleen scoured beside her. Next, Tim told her to rest. They were all on a picnic making baseballs and sledges. Johnny ran through the barroom and muddied the clean floor with his bare feet, Bridie laughing. Laughing at the muddied clean floor!

"What are you doing, woman?" Dan asked.

Bridie wrung the daylights out of the rag she'd pulled from the bucket of soapy water. She looked in Dan's direction with glazed eyes, moving her lips as if speaking to someone.

"Bridie!" Dan shouted.

Kneeling on the barroom floor, Bridie shook the rag, twisted it the opposite way, and wrung it again. She mumbled as if to an unseen person, but didn't respond to Dan.

"Bridie," Dan whispered, as he touched her shoulder.

She looked up at him but she didn't recognize him. "Tim's dead." She nodded. "He's dead, he is. Dead, dead, dead."

"What are you doing?"

"Johnny, too. Dead. Just like Tim. Dead," Bridie mumbled.

Bridie struggled to her feet. She shook the rag, smoothing the wrinkles. Her eyes focused on Dan's face.

"What does it look like I'm doing? Eejit! I'm washing the floor." Anger infected her voice.

Dan's eyebrows rose at the response but he was not surprised. Bridie had a temper for sure, but since Kathleen's death, she'd unleashed it on everyone. Maureen had tried to give Bridie the same herbal and laudanum mixture that had helped Sheila. Instead of finding the gesture kind, Bridie screamed for Maureen to get away. She accused her friend of trying to poison her.

"You've washed that floor twice this morning, Bridie."

Bridie dropped to the floor. She wrapped both arms around herself and rocked back and forth, keening. "Kathleen, too. Gone, gone, gone. My grandson. Little Timmy, dead!" She wailed. She howled.

"Is that you, Tim?" Bridie asked when Yolanda sat on the floor with her. "Have you seen Little Timmy yet?"

"It's me, Bridie. Yolanda. Get up, I need you fix me tea. We have a cupa together, den you rest."

Bridie abandoned her bucket, just left it in the middle of the floor. Groggy and glassy eyed, she shuffled to her room off the kitchen and removed her apron. She shrugged herself out of her dress and underwear. She pulled her nightgown over her head and flopped into bed. Then she sat up and shrieked "Kathleen, Kathleen! Come here girl. Yolanda, Kathleen's here. She's not dead."

Yolanda rushed in from the kitchen with a cup of tea she'd laced with laudanum and her own concoction of herbs.

"She's there, in the corner, with little Timmy sucking on her breast. Hear him? She has lots of milk for him."

"Ya. She came for da tea. Drink. Dis is your cup. I go get da cup for Kathleen."

Bridie slept all day. When she woke the moon shone through the window. Yolanda handed her another cup of tea. Bridie drank it without comment. Late the next day, she woke to find Maureen beside her with some soup. Tim stood beside Maureen as she lit the gas lamp. "Bridie, I'll open the widow, let in the fresh night air. Tell me if ye get too cold. Do ye need to go out to the latrine?"

"He's here, Tim is. Is he a ghost?" Bridie could hear her words slur. She felt the weakness of her knees as she stood. Her head spun. Her stomach lurched. "Johnny, Johnny, Johnny-boy. He's there, in the chair Kathleen usually sits in while she's here with Timmy."

When they returned from the latrine Bridie refused the soup. "They want you to eat, Bridie. Ye need nourishment. And more tea. Tim said 'Eat.'"

Then Sharon brought the sun and porridge.

"Dreaming," said Bridie. "Dreaming about Tim holding Timmy. About Yolanda with her tea. Was Maureen here? Dan?"

"Tim's the dream, Bridie. Your friends are real. You haven't been left alone all week."

"All week?" They've gone, thought Bridie. Tim, Johnny, Patrick, Kathleen, and her baby. Gone forever. Anger rose within her. They left me. I'm alone. She looked at Sharon with a sudden spark of clarity in her eyes. "I will not stay here in this town past spring."

TWENTY-SIX

A Wish Come True

March 1889

Bridie hadn't ever been on a train before, but like a seasoned traveler she swayed with the movement of the passenger car over the tracks, watching the new greening of the landscape go by. She wore her Sunday dress and the only shoes she owned. She guarded a large cloth travel bag that the superintendent's wife had given her and another smaller satchel she'd swapped some of her medicines with Yolanda for. These held all her belongings: two everyday dresses (one a gift hand-sewn by Maureen), undergarments and stockings, Johnny's green flannel shirt, and a gray shirt of Tim's that still smelled like him, Kathleen's apron, and the soft cloth Bridie had wrapped Timmy in after his first bath. She'd make a pillow from these articles and sleep in the presence of her family every night in this new place she'd be living, if she could ever bring herself to cut the fabric. She had nothing of Patrick's, only his letter.

One might expect a woman traveler to have toiletries, cosmetics, and perfumes, but Bridie had roots and herbs in packages, jars, and bottles. She'd wrapped roots in scraps of flowered oilcloth tied with strips of fabric from careworn clothes. The jars of dried, grayish-green leaves and berry jam Bridie had bedaubed with smudges of wax to seal and protect what looked almost like uncommon jewels. She'd nestled the larger leaves of dried herbs she used whole in long narrow boxes lined with a cushion of grass, wrapped with pages torn from magazines, and bound with old yarn. The most fragile were the bottles of tonic. Those she'd enfolded in layers of newspaper and sealed with wax.

Bridie hugged a handbag close to her—in it, money. Women whose husbands and children she'd nursed purchased her baking, cooking, and laundry tools with coins they could little spare. Tim's friends paid her for furniture he'd made, even the chairs with broken legs. Someone even purchased their screen door.

Miners all over the county contributed to a fund to be used for widows; she had been given a share of it. She still took in wash. All Kathleen's cleaning jobs became Bridie's after her daughter died. Bridie had saved money while living and working at McMonagle's Saloon—about three hundred dollars in all, the most money she'd ever had.

That money should have gone to the company store to pay off her debt, but she had no intention of doing that. Tim paid with his life; the company store would have to be satisfied with that.

The men who frequented the saloon held a Christmas raffle for her. The grand prize was a goat. Bridie won it and sold it to the highest bidder. A two-for-one, Dan had said.

The motion and rhythm of the wheels over the tracks and sounds of the engine soothed her. The landscape scenes moved rapidly past the train's window and mesmerized her so that she soon retreated into herself.

Not daring to think about what her life might be like in Washington, D.C., Bridie let herself go numb. Her feelings, her despair, strong as they were, seemed as if wrapped in thick cotton and stuffed away. To get out of the mine patch and somehow stay away were her only plans. She wanted to be excited about going to Washington, to be excited about the job Daniel McMonagle had gotten her through his acquaintance, James Thompson Wormley, who owned the hotel. But she blocked out excitement and hope, lest the enjoyment of these feelings extinguish them.

"Don't be put off by Wormley's brown skin, Bridie," Dan had said. "A good man, he is. I'd like to get to know him better, know how a man like him came to own a hotel. Well, 'twas his father, may he rest in peace, who came to own it. 'Tis in the most prestigious hotel in Washington you'll be working. Even presidents have stayed there."

"I wouldn't know a president if I bumped into one, Dan. Even if I did, I don't think I'd be inclined to be impressed by him. He's got two eyes, two ears, a nose, and a mouth just like me, does he?"

Dan laughed. "I'm so happy to see you feeling better, Bridie."

Bridie nodded, then shook her head as if uncertain how she felt.

"Here's something to impress you, Bridie. Frank Gowen himself stays there. Though if rumors are true, he'll soon be too poor for the Wormley Hotel."

Bridie, dumping a pail of dirty mop water out the back door, sloshed half of it on herself when she heard that. Somewhere in the deep quarry of her mind, just for an instant, she already knew what would happen if she ever met Gowen. Dan's mention of it triggered a flash of foreboding. She wanted to see Gowen, to tell him what he did to her, her father, about the suffering he caused miners everywhere. She wanted him to suffer, wanted to witness his suffering.

"Ah-hah! 'Tis impressed you are, woman. I can see that." Dan laughed.

No! Bridie did not want to see him suffer. She dismissed those thoughts. What foolish notions she's had since Tim died. She was not sure she wanted to be in the same building as Gowen.

"And how about this? There is a public telephone in the hotel. Are you impressed by that, Bridie?"

"I'd be more impressed with a toilet."

"You and Wormley have something in common, Lass. Maybe you'll be a maid for only a short time, if you can get on his good side."

"A rich, colored hotel owner has something in common with me?"

"He's a pharmacist, graduated university for that. Knows all about medicines, he does. Maybe even knows about your weeds, Bridie."

Tim always called them her weeds. Bridie's grief clenched at her heart. Images of Tim scouring the woods for herbs swamped her mind: Tim carving bark, scraping roots, snipping leaves and flowers, scurrying into crannies that hid morsels of fungus. Because he traipsed the woods with his rifle looking for game, he knew where to look, what season to harvest.

The train screeched and jerked to a stop in front of a bold sign. Finally, Washington D.C. Smartly dressed men and women walked along the train station platform. Some waited with stacks of trunks. Others sat on benches reading the newspaper. One headline read: "TODAY CONGRESS PASSED THE INDIAN APPROPRIATIONS BILL."

Bridie rose to her feet, stiff from sitting so long. She straightened her dress and hand-brushed her red hair back into a bun that had been messed up from the nap she'd taken. Just like in the pictures she'd seen, the women on the platform wore hats and carried muffs. Her mind had played so many tricks on her lately, Bridie wasn't sure if what she saw was real or another awake dream.

Even when she disembarked the train, she felt as if she were still moving. All around her people moved, getting off the train, boarding, greeting one another. Laughter, hugs, shouts for the porter to help with luggage swirled in the smoky air. Bridie had only the two bags. Maureen would send her trunk in a few days.

A young boy approached. "Where ya going?"

"Um... Well... The hotel. The Wormley Hotel."

"I'll give you a ride."

"How much?"

"Not much. Here, give me your bags."

"No. No thanks." I'm keeping my money, she thought, not giving it to this lad who looks no more than twelve. "I'll walk. Which way?"

The boy said, "Long walk, Ma'am."

Bridie looked up and down the cobblestone paved street, crowded with horse drawn carriages, people walking, dogs barking, children crying. A street peddler barked, "Roasted peanuts, here." Bridie decided to go right and began to walk with her bags, dodging a man galloping on a tall brown horse whose hooves ricocheted clickity-clacking sounds off the buildings. This late in the day, the smell of the evening meal cooking wafted through the air and stirred a hunger Bridie hadn't felt in a while.

"Yah-hoo," echoed down the street. A two-wheeled carriage harnessed to a black horse raced out from behind the train station. Standing on the foot rest, a skinny young girl twirled a whip in the air and snapped it just above the horse's rump. She pulled back on the reins, "Whoa, Midnight. Whoa, boy. Easy, easy."

Exactly beside Bridie, the carriage came to a halt, causing her to step back sharply and drop one bag. "Are you Bridie O'Doyle?"

"I am. And who might you be?"

The girl stood tall, head high. "I'm Caitlyn O'Reilly, Ma'am. Preston said you should walk but I thought it too far, especially since

you'd be carrying bags. And it's too cold, anyway. Not as cold as last
year. You know, just about a year ago we had forty inches of snow. In
March! The blizzard of '88. You'd never know it by today's weather.
Sure it's cold, but not that cold and thank God," she blessed herself,
"no snow."

"Who is Preston?"

"Oh, he's just the hotel clerk but to talk to him, you'd think he
owned the place."

"And you, what do you do besides running the horse into a
lather?"

"I'm a maid, Ma'am." Pride washed through her voice. "I work
for Mr. Wormley. He's the hotel owner and a lot nicer than Preston,
but I guess he's the boss of us maids, Preston is."

"I'm to be a maid too," said Bridie when she could get a word in.
She wished she felt the same enthusiasm Caitlyn did.

"Preston will tell you all the rules and regulations and how to act
around the guests and all. His last name is Wiltshire. If you write it,
don't forget the T or he'll get mad. Evan will help you too, show you
where things are. Evan McGee's been here years; he's the porter. So's
Preston, been at the hotel for years. Me, I'm new, only been here a
year, but now that Helen got fired for stealing, I'm head maid and I'm
only seventeen and a half. I'll show you what to do," she took a deep
breath, "and how to get a roll or a fresh pastry from the kitchen. We're
famous for our cooking, we are." Caitlyn rattled on and on, about the
turtle soup, and the Chesapeake Bay seafood folks came to the hotel
for.

The hotel was a large, five-story, square, tightly-cemented, brick
building with a solid looking roof. The women tied the horse and
carriage in the front but entered the building from the rear. Caitlyn
brought her straight up to their room on the top floor. Stale air

greeted Bridie in the long room with many windows and four beds lined up next to each other. It looked like the miner's hospital ward. Two beds had sheets and fresh towels.

"This is your bed, Bridie, and mine is here on the other end. I gave you that one so there could be two beds between us, now Helen's gone. I'll find sheets and a blanket for you." A colorful quilt covered Caitlyn's bed. Her bedside table held a small lamp, a book, and a rosary. An empty water pitcher and glass took the last remaining space. "Bridie, I'll try to find you a table and lamp from the storeroom. I didn't have time today. Maybe you'll want to buy one when you get paid. There's a used furniture shop, I'll show you."

"Who sleeps in the other beds?" Bridie pointed to the one next to Caitlyn's. It too had a bedspread and a side table.

"That's Hilda's. She works in the kitchen. The other one was Helen's. Stealing, can you believe that? I hope Mr. Wormley hires another maid because we really need one. Only you and me now to do all the work."

Weary from travel and Caitlyn's constant prattle, Bridie removed her nearly threadbare coat and lay down on the bed. "I'd like to rest now, Caitlyn." She closed her eyes. *I didn't realize I'd be sleeping in a ward*, she thought, *with a chatterbox—a nice girl, but too talkative.*

Early morning of her first day Bridie met Preston, the hotel clerk. Lanky and tall, he held his neck as if stretching upward while he tilted his chin up and head back. He cast his eyes down toward Bridie. He looked at her as if she was worthy only of his scorn. No how-do-you-dos or handshakes. "Are those the shoes you will wear with your Wormley Hotel uniform?" he asked in a snobby, I'm-such-an-important-person way. "Caitlyn, when I am finished with her, show her where she can find clean shoes." He backed away as if she still had *mine patch* dung-infested-mud on her shoes and he might step in it. Bridie appreciated the maid's uniform she wore, but her high-top, lace-up work-boots, even though she'd cleaned them, gave her away as they desecrated the fine carpets.

Preston told her all about the fine furnishings of this first-class hotel: mahogany, oak, walnut, some hand-carved by the best craftsmen, some imported. Many of the carpets were Belgian or Persian. The ornate gas lamps were works of art to be dusted carefully. "Some rooms have private bathrooms with all the modern fixtures. I require the utmost diligence in keeping all such facilities spotless.

"This hotel, the finest in the city, indeed the finest on the east coast, in my opinion, attracts important and wealthy people," he said. "We are privileged to serve Franklin Gowen, a very prominent citizen," the clerk told her, "and one of the nicest people who stay here," he said. "Generous, too." Bridie could see his eyes light up like silver in the sun. He fancies himself a butler like the ones in magazine pictures, thought Bridie, except I've never seen a real butler.

"We are so close to the White House that the government, even the President of the United States and Congress, have secret meetings here. It was my pleasure to be of service to those fine gentlemen in '76 when there was a great dispute over the Hayes-Tilden election. I wouldn't expect you to know..."

Bridie cut him off. "Tilden won the people's vote, but electoral votes went to Hayes after politicians battled with each other. Hayes became president even though the people wanted Tilden. That is clear in my mind, Mr. Preston. Father McDermott, at St. Patrick's Church in Pottsville discussed the dispute with anyone who would listen. That's how I learned about electoral votes, *Sir*. We did have newspapers, too, unbelievable as it might seem, and I could read and still can."

Caitlyn had a horrified look on her face. Evan, who had not yet been introduced, looked as if he might burst into laughter. Bridie was herself startled at her own impudence.

Preston turned on his heel. "Carry on, Caitlyn. Show the new maid her duties."

Once his boss was out of sight, Evan howled with laughter. "You are on his list now, lass." He held out his hand to Bridie. "Evan, Evan McGee. Welcome, Bridie. I'm officially the porter, but I do more cleaning than portering. Plumbing, too, and whatever else Preston asks of me. He's a pip, he is, but I've been working with him for five years. He's not so bad if you get your work done and stay out of trouble. I can see you'll not be scared of him, like this one." He hooked his thumb toward Caitlyn.

As if she'd walked through a photograph in the *Ladies' Home Journal*, Bridie entered a world as different from Number Six as different could be. Carved molding, woodwork, plush carpets, and upholstered furniture overwhelmed her, became too much to take in all at once. "Bridie, the lift is for guests only," Evan said. "This is the only hotel in the city that has an elevator, you know. Can't have maids carrying mops and pails in it now, can we?"

Caitlyn said, "There is a closet on the fifth floor. That's where we keep the brooms, pails, rags, and the carpet sweeper. Evan here will help carry them up and down stairs if he's not helping a guest or Preston. Those guest rooms with private bathrooms have to have maid service, sometimes twice a day. Most people don't lock their doors, except those who have suites. They usually keep the bathroom door locked. A key to the bathroom door hangs on a hook with other keys, in the hotel office." She pulled a key out of her pocket. When a knock at the door yielded no response, she opened the door.

Another universe opened before Bridie. Fixtures, Preston had called them, filled the room. The tub—copper, long, deep, and narrow.

"Difficult to clean," Caitlyn said. "The copper needs to be polished. You can only do that by climbing inside, dousing your skirts."

The sink, set atop a wooden cabinet, required polishing too, as its bowl and faucets for water were also copper. And finally, here stood the toilet—a bowl with a wooden seat, perched on a pedestal. A pipe went up from the back of the bowl to a wood box near the ceiling.

"Pull the chain," said Caitlyn. Bridie reached for the wood grip and pulled, but not hard enough. On the second try water gushed into the bowl and drained out somewhere, to the floor below? Nowhere that she could see when she looked into the bowl's hole.

She caught her own image in the oval mirror above the sink, and looked behind her to see who was there, so little did she seem like herself. This reflection cannot be Bridie O'Doyle, she thought. Not this woman wearing a black uniform with a white collar. Not this old woman whose face is drawn and her eyes sunken into dark shadows.

TWENTY-SEVEN

Cure For A Headache

Fall 1889

At Fifth and H Streets Bridie stood this morning, in front of the Wormley Hotel, looking up at five floors of brick and stone, her mind lurching from that sight alone. Behind her she heard the sounds of the city: the *clip-clop, clip-clop* of hooves on the street, the street sweeper whistling a tune in time with the *sht, sht, sht* of his broom, the call of a peddler selling his wares. She smelled bread baking and autumn's earthy scent. Last night's rain glistened on the paved streets, over which an elegant lady in a stylish hat swayed in the coach of a horse drawn carriage. Gas street lamps, still lit because daylight only hinted, rose from ornamental bases on the street, and tapered to an arched top that suspended the lamp, encased in a filigree cage.

The images looped through her head still, after months here. Her mind circled back as if her feet had never walked away, back to the home where walls let in the wind and snow, its patched and re-patched roof not always keeping out the rain, where streets ran with latrine overflow and mud, back to a place where candles burned for light, when she had candles to read or mend by. At one moment she felt as if she had awakened from a dream and the next like she dreamed it all and couldn't wake up.

Inside the hotel again. Careful, careful, she told herself, someone will think you're drunk. She stumbled down the hall, up the stairs to the small, ward-like room where she slept, unable to catch her breath, all of this too much to understand.

Caitlyn had told her she often called out in her sleep. "Most times I can't understand you. Who is Tim? That name is clear, loud sometimes and soft. And I wish I could hear what your angry voice says, who it is you're shouting at, I hope it's not me. Is it, Bridie? Are you mad at me?"

Bridie hadn't told anyone much about her life before she came to Wormley's Hotel. She wanted to keep her hell private, afraid if she began to talk about Tim, her corked hatred of Gowen would explode. If that happened, she'd be back in Number Six and never escape.

She rested for a few minutes, until time to start her job. She sat up too fast, her mind spinning at the notion of being one of those people working in a tall building. This can't be real, she still thought. Today her assignment would challenge her resolve to keep her job until she could find another.

Room 57, second floor, Franklin B. Gowen.

"Come in," Gowen called when she knocked.

The door opened when she turned the knob. Not locked!

When Evan helped her carry her cleaning tools down the stairs, Bridie wanted to ask him to take care of room 57. She believed he would have, if he hadn't told her he was already committed to drive a guest to the train station.

Gowen, a tall, handsome man with a pleasant square face, fair skin, and a warm hint of Irish in his deep voice, greeted her as if she were the most important person he'd seen that day. He looked directly at her, his eyes blue as hers, his smile as big as a hug.

This is the man I have hated for so long, Bridie thought. I

expected him to look evil, sound nasty, smile not at all, slither like the snake he is. I want him to be that way. I know under that smile is the man who is responsible for the way my Tim died. There he is, abuser of mine workers. To brace herself against the Gowen charm she'd heard about, she reminded herself that he allowed children to work in breakers where they were maimed and killed. If it weren't for him, my Tim and my babies would be alive. If he is as powerful and rich as Preston says he is, surely he has the power to make everything right: pay miners enough to feed their families, help widows and their wee ones, instead of turning them out of their miserable shelter with no money and nowhere to go. Yes, she thought, I see through that smile and your face looks scaly and your tongue forked.

"Sir, I'll come back later. I don't want to disturb you." Run, she said to herself, trembling with hatred inside, smiling outside.

"Come in, come in," Gowen said, sweet and syrupy, his eyes drawn back to the paper on his desk, pen in one hand while the other motioned her in.

"Yes sir." She held onto the door for a second. His voice sounded like it had moved through an echo as he became smaller, more distant. She blinked her eyes, focusing on his pen, and gritted her teeth. Heart thumping, she forced herself to be aware of her feet on the solid floor as she stepped into the room. She could clean this room as she had cleaned others for months now.

The massive marble fireplace and the huge mirror that hung above it seized her attention. The fire heated the whole room. How wasteful! One huge fire to heat this small room in a hotel protected from the cold. So many times, she thought, we slept in our clothes, huddled together, all of us. Still the cold nipped at us.

"Close the windows, will you," he asked. "So warm in here I opened them."

Heavy drapes hid the two windows, one on each side of the fireplace. Rage blazed in her belly.

Bridie's eyes drifted around the large, comfortable room. Gowen sat in a mahogany chair at a carved writing table in the middle of the room. A gas lamp lit his work. An ornate bed occupied one corner. Nearby, on the same side of the room, loomed a large oak wardrobe. Here, beneath her very own feet, expensive Belgian carpet awaited her sweeper. On the wall opposite the wardrobe, a heavy-looking bureau probably held many sets of folded, soft, white underwear washed by some poor woman with red-raw hands. On the same wall, the door to the bathroom.

Would Gowen's bathroom look like the others she'd scrubbed? Or would his be gold? By now, the idea that she found bathrooms astonishing provided much latrine humor among those who worked at the hotel. "Do you want us to build you an outhouse out in the woods, Lass?"

Gowen rubbed the back of his neck, then the side of his head.

"Headache," he said as she closed the door to his room. "Do you have a secret remedy for a headache?" he asked, half laughing.

"Yes, sir. Herbs from my garden and from the forest and fields."

He seemed surprised, as if he hadn't expected an answer. "You have a garden, then?"

"Not now, sir, Mr. Gowen, but when I lived in the Number Six mine patch in Schuylkill County." How has he done this, she thought, gotten me to give this away? "Would you like me to fix you a cup of herb tea? Sure to fix that headache." Why are helping him? Watch yourself, Bridie thought.

He looked up at her; she saw now his reddened eyes. Could this man have been crying? she wondered. Something on the paper on his desk? Or is it the headache?

"No," he shook his head. "No." He looked at her as if to judge her ability to make a cup of tea. "Well, yes. I'd like a cup of tea. Might as well be one that will fix this headache."

In the hotel kitchen, cooks flurried with the business of preparing lunch. Looking about for Hilda, Bridie pilfered a teapot, cup and saucer. Hilda wasn't to be trusted. Bridie learned that the hard way when a remark she'd made came back to her. "So, you think I'm like a hard-nosed butler, do you?" said Preston.

She placed the herbs that she'd carefully selected for a man his size from her satchel: Angelica, Echinacea, and Chamomile for pain, Catnip for a sense of well-being. Might make him feel like he's had too much beer. Just enough to ease the pain so he'll ask for more. Laudanum too, I'll add a few drops. There must be a place in this city where I can buy more.

The elevator is something like the cage that lowers miners into the pit, but much gentler with three sides and a gate that stretches across the front. Push the number two. Safer, too, she thought. Stop talking to yourself. No wonder Hilda thinks you're crazy. If Preston sees me, I'm in trouble, but if I walk up the stairs the tea will spill. Easing out of the elevator, Bridie looked to see if anyone walked along the hall.

This time, Gowen opened the door when she knocked.

"Thought you forgot about me," he said.

"Had to be careful. If I get caught, my head will be chopped off."

"Like Alice in Wonderland?" His eyes laughed.

Bridie nodded. She wondered if the hole she has fallen into, the one that led the way to this new life, was up or down. She'd found the book in the parlor, probably left behind by one of the guests, and read it. First book she'd read in a while. The author's name triggered thoughts about James Carroll, a Molly Maguire hanged in 1877, her uncle. A hanging plotted by Gowen. She wanted to tell Gowen all about her uncle, Tim, her babies. She wanted to bash his face in, like Tim had done to Schmidt, the inside foreman, after Sweeney died.

"Sometimes I feel like Alice, that I'm dreaming I live in this strange place, a city, not a mine patch."

His forehead wrinkled and his eyebrows came together. He looked at her in a peculiar way, like she was the strange thing.

"Drink all the tea. I'll bring you more tomorrow. Don't tell Mr. Wormley. He won't like me, a maid, giving his guests medicine.

But Gowen did tell Wormley.

TWENTY-EIGHT

Encounter With Wormley

"Bridie! Get down to Mr. Wormley's office immediately. Now! Go!" Preston shook his head as if to say, what can you expect from a mine-patch woman? The hotel clerk, his nose in the air, his eyes looking down at Bridie, called to her sharply, "Be quick about it."

As she squeezed from the depths of the tiny fifth floor closet past mops, sweepers, brooms, and rags, Caitlyn gave her a pat on the back and Evan rolled his eyes. Being summoned to the boss-man-Wormley, as they called him, was cause for alarm.

I'm going to lose my job, Bridie thought. What will I do? I'll be stranded in D.C. not knowing anyone, my money almost gone, not enough to rent a room for very long, not enough to buy a ticket back to Number Six—oh God, not back to Number Six. I'd rather die first.

She flew down one flight of stairs, then another, her feet barely touching the steps, propelled by anger. Fifth floor to fourth to third. No windows whizzed by, only the whoosh of air stinking with stale cooking odors, dirty, not like the swept stairway used by the guests, but a tomb. It's, my tomb, she thought, nailed shut by Gowen.

She stopped.

Why are you in such a hurry? she asked herself. For sure, he'll say get out, you don't belong in a nice, clean, elegant place like my hotel. All 'cause of Gowen. Bridie sat on a stair, jabbed her elbows on knees, and flopped her face in hands. Once again Gowen is controlling my life. The deliverer of death, of poverty, he'll have me on the streets, that snake.

She stood, breathed, smoothed out her hair, straightened her apron. I should change this dirty thing before going to see *the* James T. Wormley. No, why should I? What will it matter?

Will Mr. Wormley be angry? Fire me immediately? What if Gowen had a bad reaction to the herbs? It's possible; I've seen it before. What if Wormley tells me Gowen died as a result? Bridie sat down. Dead. Gowen dead. Her mind went blank. She closed her eyes. Blinked trying to bring it back. He can't be dead. I'd feel it if he were. I'd feel free. She laughed and the sound echoed through the stairway back to her. Why, if he were dead I'd start to float up into the air, twirl around. She flung her arms out and laughed again. She sobbed, tears exploding from her eyes. I'm no better than Gowen is. Rejoicing in my freedom at the expense of his life.

Shoulders sagging, she edged her body off the step and upright, inch by inch. She leaned a shoulder against the wall and slowly stepped down, one foot drifting after the other until she faced the door to the hallway that led to Mr. Wormley's office.

Her mind raced. I've only been in that office to pick up keys for guestrooms which I rarely need—guests don't lock doors, only the bathroom doors, if their accommodations have private bathrooms— still, I usually don't need a key; I can get to the bathroom from the bedroom. There is no excuse for what I did. I'm not at Number Six; it isn't my job to make folks well. These aren't my neighbors we don't share everything here...

Bridie reached for the hallway door.

I mop and dust and clean, bring fresh linens and towels, make beds, scrub fixtures in the bathroom... that's my job now... sweep carpets, polish, plump pillows, wash windows... not heal... The flat of her hand touched the door.

This is where I've wanted to be: in a city in a building that was dry and clean, money for my work, control of my life...

She stopped.

But what does it all matter? Tim's not here, or Johnny or Kathleen or Patrick.

Push. The door opened.

She squared her shoulders, straightened her body inside the black uniform with the dirty apron she hadn't changed, tilted her head upward, and took long, slow strides down the dark, empty hallway toward Mr. Wormley's office.

She knocked. I'll not beg, she thought. No answer. Knocked again. Bridie turned to run and slammed into a minty-smelling blockade. A big man, light brown skin, broad shoulders, and a big moustache. She'd met him before but had not been able to read him. Usually Bridie had a feel for folks at the first meeting. After several encounters she knew some of their secrets. But Mr. Wormley, owner of this hotel, a public figure, seemed to hide himself. He stood there chewing on a sprig of spearmint.

He opened the office door and made a sweeping motion in the direction of the interior. Intense black eyes shifted toward an armchair in front of a book-filled wall of shelves.

"Have a seat."

Was he angry? Bridie wondered. She tried to appear relaxed as she sat on the edge, her spine straight, ankles crossed and tucked under the chair so she almost fell forward. She slid back just a little.

Mr. Wormley sat across from her. He held out the sprig. "Are you aware of the benefits of spearmint?"

Bridie nodded her head but didn't speak.

"Where do you get your herbs?"

"I brought some with me. Dried. From my own garden."

Mr. Wormley tilted his head and raised his eyebrows as if surprised, but said nothing. She resisted the urge to fidget with her apron, put her hands over a stain. Preston had instructed her to always have a clean apron, to be careful to keep it clean but to change it if needed.

"And I found some in the wooded areas around, roots too."

Wormley nodded.

"I met a woman who grows herbs. When she weeds and thins she saves some for me."

"Mr. Franklin Gowen, room 57, said you have the best headache remedy he's ever had."

Bridie heard her breath release. He's not dead, she thought, feeling her whole body melt into the chair.

"Did you go to school to learn about healing herbs?"

Making fun of me, she thought, that's what he's doing. She uncrossed her feet and planted them squarely in front of her. Her body followed, straightening itself to a full upright seated position.

"Yes, Sir."

His eyebrows raised in surprise again, notched his head forward as if to ask where.

"I learned from my mother and Mam Mary. They learned from their mothers and grandmothers. I learned what worked and what didn't from helping people who lived in Number Six."

He moved to his desk, large and square, made from some kind of dark, almost black wood. An oak roll-top desk occupied the space behind him. He waved her toward the chair beside it. His dark hand rummaged about in white papers until he found a small black book. He pulled a pen from a glass inkwell. "Will you tell me what you used to cure Gowen's headache?"

Bridie stopped herself from responding immediately. She stared at him in disbelief. There he is, sitting at his fancy mahogany desk in this office, and he's asking me about curing headaches. He smiled broadly, his white teeth crooked and stained, probably from coffee.

"I made a strong tea from Angelica, Echinacea, and Chamomile. I added Catnip for a sense of well-being." Should I tell him about the laudanum? she wondered.

"Catnip, too! Mrs. O'Doyle, you are full of surprises."

That's the first time he's addressed me as Mrs. O'Doyle, Bridie thought. And with a tone of respect. He calls all the staff by their Christian name, including Preston.

"I'm a pharmacist, graduated from Howard University Pharmaceutical School. I own a drugstore in the city, did you know that? We should stock more herbs. Do you think you'd like to work in a drugstore?"

Too stunned to speak, Bridie shook her head then nodded. She'd never been in a drugstore. She wondered if that was where she could buy laudanum.

"Oh, yes. I remember Dan McMonagle told me that. About Howard, I mean, not the drugstore."

"It's the only drugstore that colored folks like me can use. We have much in common, Mrs. O'Doyle."

Surprised by his remarks, the right words escaped her. She stammered. "I... I... Dan thought we had herbs in common."

"Ah Dan! A fine man. Runs a fine establishment, a little bawdy, but respectable. He's told me about you, your family. I'm sorry for all you've lost. Dan told me how you worked at his pub as a clerk, barmaid, custodian. Said you kept order in that place better than any man.

"Come in," Wormley responded to a knock at the door. Preston walked in with his head held high. He nodded at Wormley and looked down his nose at Bridie.

"Making sure Bridie came along to see you, Mr. Wormley. Can I help at all?"

"Mrs. O'Doyle and I are having a discussion, Preston. She's excused from her afternoon duties."

A look of satisfaction spread across his face as if to say, I knew she'd be gone before the day was out.

"Pay her as if she had worked a full day, Preston." He gestured his hand toward the door and escorted Preston out of the office with his eyes.

Preston's eyes grew big and his lips pressed together as if he were restraining a smile. He left, headed for the fifth floor mop closet where Caitlyn and Evan waited. They soon spread the word that Bridie had been fired.

Caitlyn screeched when Bridie returned to their room. "Yahoo! You're still here. Oh, I hope you are still here. Not fired. Preston said you were fired." She ran to Bridie and grabbed her in a wild celebratory dance.

"I'm to work at the drugstore," Bridie said. "Can you believe it? Here on some days. At the drugstore the other days. Soon every day at the drugstore."

"Take me with you. I want to work there, too," begged Caitlyn.

TWENTY-NINE

A Momentary Aberration

Friday, December 13, 1889

The blood surprised Bridie. Gowen sat at his desk, blood pouring out; his shirt and waistcoat and whatever he wore underneath had soaked it up like an old cleaning rag would. She stuffed her rags under his neck to keep the blood from getting on the carpet; that expensive Belgian carpet would be costly to replace.

That thought linked memory to the mine mules. Tim had said the owners were more concerned for their mules' safety then the miners'. Mules cost two hundred dollars to replace. Miners cost nothing, only someone to take the dead man's place. Operators sent sick mules to the animal doctor, fed and sheltered them while they recovered. She felt bad that Wormley might have to spend money to replace the carpet. Maybe it couldn't be replaced.

He's dead, thought Bridie, though Gowen still sat upright in his chair, his head at a strange angle, chin resting on his chest. She looked around to see who could have done this, shot him in the head, frightened she'd be shot, too.

No one else here. Bridie searched with her eyes, her feet rooted to the carpet. No one. Did she hear someone in the bathroom? Its door to the hall was locked. No one could have come into the room. Could

I have done it? That gun couldn't have gone off. But here it is, still in my hand. Her arm jerked; the hand released the gun. It clunked onto the desk near Gowen's hand.

Check the lock from the bedroom to the hall, she thought, just in case Caitlyn comes to make the bed. Locked. Her head was in a fog. She moved back to the desk. She could see the powerful man had slumped down into himself even though he sat there much the same as before she... she... what?

What had we been talking about? I can't remember.

The gun. He'd never owned one until he'd purchased this the previous evening. A Smith and Wesson .38 caliber pistol, he'd said.

The flow of blood from his head seemed to lessen. She did not try to stop Gowen's bleeding. She felt no inclination to help him, even if he were not dead.

Johnny. She thought of her son... how no one had tried to stop his bleeding. Why was that? Because he was only a boy? Because there were enough boys around to take his place on the breaker?

His head! We talked about his headaches. I'd been mixing herbs for headaches. The cup is right there, on the desk. Empty. I'd come into his room to get the cup.

I wasn't supposed to bring food or drink to a guest's room. That was someone else's job. He'd said he'd been feeling tired and heavyhearted lately. I'd mixed him tonic, too. Every day, each time making it stronger, warning him not to hurt himself, falling down the stairs or jumping off the train when he went back to Philadelphia. I knew the combination of herbs could make people behave strangely, even violently. His sadness could deepen.

I didn't exactly have a plan to poison him.

The bed looked as if it had been made up that morning. As she climbed onto it, she wondered if he'd spent the night at his desk, trying to put that gun to his head, and never did go to bed. She curled into a fetal position on Gowen's bed, exhausted. Cleaning the drugstore and working at the hotel took too much out of her.

A sound drifted in through a deep sleep—a knock at the door. Caitlyn's voice, distant, calling, "Mr. Gowen, sir." The door knob jiggled. Bridie heard the other maid's footsteps, then the bathroom door knob jiggle. "Mr. Gowen? Are you in there?" A sigh followed a long pause. "I'll come back then."

Bridie leaped off the bed, became lightheaded, felt faint. She sat on the Belgian carpet, lost in the deep colors, the intricate patterns. She followed the lines of the design. Examined the variety of flowers which looped and swirled across the carpet.

She stood in front of Gowen, expecting him to comment, tell her what to do.

He's still sitting there, she thought, both hands on the desk, one near the gun. His fingers of that hand looked odd, some curled under his palm, some straight out, his whole hand positioned in an unnatural way. She tried to straighten his fingers, but they resisted. Her own hand brushed against, what? The gun! It lay on the desk, its handle in a pool of blood, but she could feel the sensation of it in her hands, both hands. She remembered!

Bridie stood beside Gowen as he showed her a photograph of his three children, two boys and a girl. He cried, tears streaming down his cheeks, down his neck, onto his collar. "My boys, I lost them. Both of them when they were wee ones. Measles."

The weight of her own grief buckled her knees. She leaned on the desk for support. Her mind reeled through images as vivid as if she'd been transported in time. Her mam, the herbs she kept in the kitchen, the cough of her final days. Her Da, teaching her sums, his rotting leg and its pungent odor. She whipped around, hearing a baby cry, her first son sliding beneath a mountain of culm. Saw Ellen crumpled on the stairs and Charles's blood-clotted head. James Carroll and the other Molly Maguires swinging at the end of a rope. Patrick. Kathleen. Johnny in his flannel shirt, the smell of boy about him.

Bridie grasped her chest. Struggled for breath. Her feet rooted to the carpet. She picked up the gun that lay on the desk. Tim's smile rose in her mind. His big belly laugh seemed to shake her. I want to be with them, she thought. All of them.

She put the gun to her face.

"No!" Gowen grabbed her hand that held the gun and knocked her off balance so she staggered against him, still clutching the gun.

He pulled the gun away; put it to his own head. That he experienced the same grief she did showed in his twisted, wet face. They struggled, Gowen unable to rise from the chair with the weight of her on him, Bridie unable to regain her balance.

"How dare you grieve for your dead sons," she shouted. "You are not worthy of sorrow. You don't deserve to escape your grief so easily. I will not let you kill yourself, coward."

She inched the gun away from him. "You killed all that I have loved. You will have to live with it."

The hate she'd stored erupted. She struggled to free the gun from his grip. His hand pinned hers to the gun, forced the barrel to his head.

"No!" She pulled his hand to deflect his aim. Her feet slid beneath her.

The explosion of the gun jolted both of them before she even realized she'd picked up the weapon. Before she realized the impulse to put it to her own face. Done without thought.

Bridie stepped back from the memory, from Gowen, as if stepping away from a gleaming copper bathtub, the polishing of which had caused a deep ache. Her eyes surveyed the room. What's happened, she wondered, dazed. I'm supposed to clean up.

She wiped her hands on a towel after she removed her rags from Gowen's neck. Calmly, she collected her cleaning supplies, careful to leave nothing behind. Papers that had been stained she rolled up in her apron, shoved them in her bucket.

The sun had gone down. She drew the shades down fully and pulled the curtains closed. Bridie waited for her eyes to adjust to the dark room.

She wondered if the rumors were true that Gowen was bankrupt. Was that why he had bought the gun? Or was he filled with remorse for having sent twenty Irish to the gallows and more to their death in the mines?

It's late in the day; there shouldn't be anyone about, she thought. Everyone is at dinner. She listened at the bathroom door for traffic in the hallway. She inspected the room again. The lamp that had been knocked from the desk during their struggle was still on the floor. Leave it there, get out!

Bridie pulled the nib on the lock down and closed the bathroom door behind her. Anyone wanting to get into room 57 would need to get the key from the hotel office. She went to Wormley's office.

THIRTY

Assassination Or Suicide?

December 14, 1889

Caitlyn knocked on the glazed glass panel in Mr. Wormley's office door before she burst in. "Mr. Wormley, sir, it's Mr. Gowen. I'm worried about him sir. I didn't clean his room or make his bed yesterday. I mean, he wouldn't let me in. I mean, he opened the door, said he was busy working, come back later. I could see papers on the writing table and he had his pen in his hand. I really tried, sir. It's not like I wasn't doing my job. I went back again and he said come back later again. I did that, sir. You know Preston, sir, he'll say I wasn't doing my job but I was. I went back again at 4:30 or so but the door was locked. He never locks his door, so I started thinking he's getting tired of me bothering him while he's working. Or maybe he went out and didn't want anyone in his room disturbing his papers."

"Whoa," said Wormley. "Slow down, Caitlyn. I'm sure you've done your job. Is that the problem? Preston said you didn't?"

"No. No. I mean, yes, Preston will say that, but he didn't. Not yet."

"What is it then?" He put his hand up to stop her from speaking. "Think a minute, about what you want to say."

Caitlyn took a deep breath, rolling her eyes as if searching her mind. "I'm worried, sir. It's not right that Mr. Gowen didn't answer his door this morning, either. I knocked twice."

"He may not want to be disturbed. Probably working on something important."

"Maybe he's sick. He usually comes to the door or at least calls out. I think you should go up there, sir."

"The man's entitled to his privacy, Caitlyn."

"Something's wrong, if you don't mind me saying so. I think you should go, see if he answers for you."

The door was locked. Gowen did not respond to Wormley's knock. "Mr. Gowen, sir, we are concerned. Are you all right?" No reply. "Tell Preston to come to my office, will you, Caitlyn?"

Preston reported that Gowen had not checked out and that no one had seen him leave the hotel. Evan hadn't helped him with bags or taken him to the train. The key to Gowen's bathroom door was missing from the hotel office. Wormley picked up the phone and called the police. "Can't be too careful," he said to Patrolman Cross when he arrived at Wormley's office moments later. The New Jersey Avenue Police Station was close by.

They knocked and called to Gowen. When there was no answer, Cross, Wormley, and Preston set up a ladder outside room 57. Wormley climbed the ladder. Caitlyn, unable to stay away, and impatient, asked "What's in there? What do you see?" even before Wormley climbed high enough to look through the transom, a horizontal window across the width and above the door.

"Good God! Caitlyn, get up here. Crawl through, you're small enough. It's so dark in there I can't be sure but it looks like he's lying on the floor."

Stumbling up the ladder, Caitlyn said, "I knew it. God have mercy." She blessed herself. I had a feeling something wasn't right."

She pushed so hard she almost fell off the ladder. "I can't get it open. It's stuck."

Preston yelled, "Push, girl. It hasn't been open for years."

"This looks too small for me to fit through," Caitlyn called down. "Even if I do squeeze through, I'm going to fall on my head."

"O'Reilly, do as you're told," said Preston. With that the transom gave way and Caitlyn wiggled her way in, managing to get one leg then the other through the opening first. She fell to the floor. Unhurt, she unlocked the door from the inside.

"The key was still in the door," said Caitlyn.

They all rushed to help Gowen. "He's gone," said Wormley. "Even in this light, anyone can see that. Preston, I may need you in here later. For now, go out to the front desk and keep order. Do not say anything to anyone about this. Send Evan and Bridie here. Close the door on your way out."

One hand on either side of her head, Caitlyn breathed rapidly, jumping up and down. "Oh my God," she said. "Oh my God. I've never seen a dead body before." She made the sign of the cross.

"Quiet," ordered Wormley. "Caitlyn, open the curtain and shades."

Gowen, fully dressed, lay on his back on the floor in front of the fireplace with his feet facing the mantel. Patrolman Cross circled the body while Wormley searched to see if anyone else was in the room.

"Smith and Wesson .38 caliber, sir." Cross pointed to the gun that lay beside Gowen. "Blood covering the handle. See? Blood pooled under his head."

Wormley and Cross knelt beside the body.

"Cold. Stiff," said the patrolman. "See here? The bullet entered here, just above and behind the ear on the right. Came out the left, here. Blood's congealed in the left ear. Looks like his brains, too, sir.

Strange though."

"What?" asked the hotel owner.

"There's so much blood on his waistcoat and shirt. I'd expect to see less there and more pooled on the carpet, under his head. Hmm, curious. The handle of the gun is covered with blood, too."

Bridie knocked on the door. Wormley unlocked it. He gave her an intense look before he ushered her into the room. Bridie gasped, shocked to see Gowen on the floor.

"This is Patrolman Cross, Bridie. I called him this morning when Caitlyn said Mr. Gowen hadn't answered her knock this morning." His eyes bored into hers. "She'd tried to make his bed and clean the bathroom twice yesterday but he'd refused service."

Bridie nodded, her eyebrows knitted together. She shook her head as if to clear it.

"Officer, this is Bridie O'Doyle. She's one of the maids here. She also tried to clean Gowen's room yesterday."

Cross bowed his head in acknowledgment of the introduction. "Don't be scared, miss. I know it can be a shocker to see a dead body when you're expecting something different."

Bridie, eyes lowered, nodded again, rendered speechless by the sight of Gowen's body on the floor and not at his desk. She looked up at Wormley; his eyes said, no.

Caitlyn rushed to hug Bridie. "Oh it's awful, isn't it? I just knew something was off this morning. Yesterday I tried..."

"Caitlyn, quiet. We've been through that," said Wormley. "We have work to do now."

Caitlyn unlocked the door for Evan. "What... Is that Mr. Gowen, there, on the floor? Dead?"

"Looks like he shot himself sometime last night," said the hotel owner. "Cross, wouldn't you agree? This is Evan McGee, our porter."

"McGee," Cross nodded, distracted. "I'm not so sure, Mr. Wormley. Seems that way, but I've not had time to look around."

"Well, I have. The door was locked from the inside with the key still in the lock. You saw Caitlyn here climb through the transom to get in and open the door."

"Yes, yes," said Cross.

"There's the bathroom door, sir," said Caitlyn. "A murderer could have got out that way."

Wormley gave her a sharp look. "I checked that. It's locked. Come take a look, Officer."

Evan, Caitlyn, and Bridie looked at each other but didn't speak.

"The chair at the writing table is overturned. The table lamp is on the floor. Signs of a struggle," said Cross.

"Or of a distraught man."

"True," said Cross.

"Look, both doors were locked. You saw that we had to go in through the transom. The windows were locked from the inside. If there was a murderer, how would he get out of the room?"

"Through the transom," Cross said.

"I can tell you no one has been through that transom for years," said Caitlyn. "It was full of dust and dirt. And stuck. It was as if the grime up there glued it shut."

"True enough," said the officer after he checked the widows and the doors again. "True enough."

"It looks to me as if he stood in front of the mirror and watched himself take aim. Pulled the trigger. The position of the body tells you that. It was hours ago, he did it hours ago. You saw how cold and stiff it is."

The patrolman looked thoughtful. "I need to question your staff and the other quests on this floor. See if anyone saw or heard anything."

"I agree," said Wormley. "But first, you need to get the body out of here. It's not good for business. And it's bad luck having a body lying around here in the hotel. You understand. Guests get uneasy, knowing they're staying under the same roof as a dead man."

"Yes, certainly, sir. I'll request some men, immediately. Can I use the phone?"

"Preston's downstairs. He will show you to the phone. Caitlyn, please take Officer Cross to Preston. Then come back."

Within the hour Cross returned with several men. "A horse and carriage is outside. We'll do our best to avoid notice as we transport the body to the police station, Mr. Wormley." The hotel was on the police officer's beat. He had often stopped into the hotel for a conversation with Mr. Wormley. Cross knew guests who were residents and frequent visitors by name. "Folks around know I come in and out often, sir."

As soon as Gowen's remains had been removed, the hotel owner issued orders to remove the blood-stained carpet and wallpaper. Bridie attempted to take Wormley aside but he shook his head. "Not now." he said.

"Excuse me, sir. I'm a reporter from *The Star*. Can I ask you a few questions?"

"Where is Preston? Why didn't he stop this man?" Wormley said. "This is not a good time, young man. You can see we are in the middle of a tragedy. Come back later."

"Forgive the interruption. This is important news. I thought you might want to be sure it was reported accurately. If you like, I'll ask other people what they think happened."

"Come in, come in. You're right. No one else can tell you about these events." Wormley told the reporter about the locked doors and windows. He left out no details.

The reporter made a sketch of the death scene, the position of furniture, the body and gun, noting where the fireplace and exits were. It was he who noticed the blob of blood on the floor at the foot of the bureau and the two splatters of blood on the mantel.

"It is obvious this man committed suicide. He stood right there and watched himself in the mirror as he took aim and pulled the trigger," Wormley told the reporter.

While they spoke, Preston and some men came to move the furniture to facilitate the cleanup. The staff worked quickly.

"Who was the last person to see the victim alive?" the reporter asked.

Bridie shrank inside herself, feeling trapped. She did not dare look up.

Caitlyn piped up, "Me. It was me. I tried to make his bed twice yesterday. He came to the door and said he was busy, to come back later. This morning he didn't answer my knock, like he didn't last time I tried yesterday. That's when I told Mr. Wormley."

The reporter interviewed other staff members, but Bridie managed to avoid him. Wormley sent her off to get more cleaning supplies. She didn't return to room 57.

Within hours, *The Star* circulated the news of Gowen's death. The reporter said, based on Mr. Wormley's statements, the man had taken his own life.

Mr. Cassius Anstett, a resident of the hotel, burst into Wormley's office with a protesting Preston on his heels. "Wormley, do you know Gowen has been made a spectacle? Laid out in the floor of the police station like a commoner. People queuing up to see the show. How could you let that happen?"

Wormley gestured Preston off with a wave of his hand. "Mr. Anstett, please sit down. I have called the family and the undertaker will soon transport the body to a more suitable location. I must say, this is the very reason I asked Patrolman Cross to remove Mr. Gowen from the hotel. I wanted to avoid a scene such as you describe.

"Sir, may I remind you that I am the person who knew Frank Gowen best. We've been long-time friends."

"This is a great loss."

"I'm appalled at you, sir. Your remarks as stated in *The Star* are outrageous. I was among the prosecution staff, Sir, and I know full well of the coal region's Irish hatred for Gowen because of his involvement in the Molly Maguire hangings," Anstett said. "There have been death threats. Suicide? What a lot of bunk. Murder is more likely. Assassination is the cause of death."

Involvement! thought Wormley. Gowen *orchestrated* the whole thing from accusations, to the trials, to the prosecution, and hangings. But he said nothing aloud.

"You know, sir, I never lock my door, never and neither did Gowen. Nor do any of the guests. The exception is the bathroom door. Who else witnessed these locked doors?"

"Several, including Officer Cross, Mr. Anstett. I can assure you if you'd been there, seen Mr. Gowen's body, you would have come to the same conclusion."

"Let me assure you, Sir, under no circumstances would Frank Gowen have taken his life."

With each utterance, "Sir" became more and more snarl-like.

"It was the maid, according to the paper. The maid was the last to see Gowen alive at 3:30 yesterday. He opened his door and said he was working. What's to prevent a murderer from entering the room after the maid left?"

Wormley clenched his anger as tightly as he clamped his jaw and held his tongue.

"Get rid of the body, so no one can deduce what really happened. Was that your plan, Sir? If so, you certainly succeeded. I will discuss this with the police, you can be sure of that. There will be an investigation."

THIRTY-ONE

They Decline To Believe

GOWEN'S FRIENDS GREATLY SHOCKED
They Decline To Believe That The Famous Lawyer Committed
Suicide

   The intelligence of the tragic death of Franklin B. Gowen, at
Washington, was received with the greatest possible surprise in
this city. Mr. Gowen's many warm friends in railroad, financial
and legal circles were shocked beyond expression and most of
them refused to believe that the death was a result of suicide.
The theories of murder and accident were general, and those who
believed in the suicide theory were hopelessly in the minority.
Those who knew Mr. Gowen best declared it was out of the
question for him to take his own life. They said a man of his fine
mental abilities, robust constitution and rugged manhood could
not have committed suicide.

     – The Philadelphia Inquirer, December 15, 1889

Spring 1890

The front room smelled mildly musty, herbal, in need of an open
window. The morning sun, low in the sky, shone through the front
windows. Dust particles glittered in the sunbeam shafts that pierced

the glass of the front windows. Bridie stood in the hazy light of the drugstore.

The three-story brick building on Pennsylvania Avenue held a row of other shops and businesses. The drugstore was narrow but deep and occupied about half of the depth of the street-level floor. Gas lamps lit the interior.

Months ago, on the first day Mr. Wormley brought her here, Bridie had investigated the ceiling-to-floor cabinets that held many small drawers. She moved from one to another looking at the fine wood, the small brass pulls and label holders. Some labels had a name on them, some were blank. Most medication names were unfamiliar. Occasionally, she recognized the name of a root or a bark: mayapple root, snake root, cherry tree bark, boneset leaves, and pennyroyal. She opened several of these drawers, reached in, and took out the root or herb, put it to her nose. When she came to ginseng root, she sniffed it and said to Wormley, "This is old, has lost its essence. It needs to be replaced." Wormley took it from her, walked over to a counter along the side, and placed it there. She continued her investigation of unfamiliar medicines, asking questions.

Today with winter behind her it all seemed familiar, like home. The symmetry of the rows and columns of drawers relaxed Bridie— each tucked securely into its place, its contents defined, arranged in alphabetical order. Larger drawers on the right, long narrow ones across the bottom row. She flicked the scale, setting it in motion, clanging. Her hand slid across the cool, soothing, polished, dark-wood counter. Solitude engulfed her, pulling her shoulders down as they released some of the tension of the last months.

No more questions from that foul Captain Robert Linden, the very same person who investigated her uncle James Carroll. The same man who testified at his trial, and had him, an innocent man, hanged for the murder of Benjamin Yost. She'd had nightmares he'd hang her too. The police and reporters from as far away as Philadelphia had questioned her. Linden, Gowen's nephew, and Coroner Patterson interrogated all the hotel staff. Was she a Molly Maguire? Was anyone in her family a member of that secret order? When had she seen Gowen last? Did she think he committed suicide? Was he murdered?

Bridie would have liked to have been able to answer the last question. She'd asked herself over and over: who pulled the trigger— me or Gowen? When she thought about that moment she recalled the sensation of the gun in her hand. The struggle. Her hatred and grief blended with the desire for revenge and compassion for the one she hated, an unexpected flash of sympathy for the man.

But she couldn't feel her finger on the trigger. She could still feel Gowen's hand clenched over hers. But couldn't remember what happened next, the moment before the blast of the gun.

Still, though the case was settled, there was bitter debate among some. Grieving family and friends could not believe Gowen would take his own life. Others, sure someone slipped in, shot him, and escaped without being seen, speculated on the ways the murderer could have exited the locked room. Gowen was assassinated by a Molly McGuire, they proclaimed. The Mollies were back! There was even the cover-up conspiracy theory involving the hotel owner, the porter, and a maid—all they had was Wormley's word the doors were locked. Coroner Patterson concluded it was suicide. In the end, so did Linden and some of Gowen's family.

There were questions on Bridie's mind that no one else had asked. What happened after she went to Mr. Wormley the night of the shooting? How did the body get from the chair, where she left him, to the floor? Wormley had refused to discuss it with her.

She worked in the silence of her office at her own desk, in the back room of the drugstore, where for the first time she recorded the herbs she used for various treatments. This job raised feelings of both gratitude and guilt, as if attained shamefully. She reached for the books in which all the drugstore's transactions were recorded. She could almost imagine Tim laughing, as he did that day so long ago. "See, I told you you'd get the clerk job." Clerk and herbalist, she corrected him.

Because of her suggestions Bridie became more and more involved with customers. She collected herbs, made tonics and herbal blends. Wormley worked there part time and so did Peter Walters, the Howard pharmacy student.

Mr. Wormley will be here, soon, thought Bridie. I will insist he tell how Gowen was moved from the chair to the floor. And she needed to know why he'd been so kind to her.

Almost as if he'd read her thoughts, he burst into the drugstore. "I don't know why I didn't think of this before," Wormley said. "Come, come with me." He headed for the stairs without waiting for a reply. "The third floor may be more to your liking, but we'll look at the second too."

Bridie had never seen the upper floors or the basement. The second floor was one undivided space littered with boxes and crates. Along the street side wall, three floor-to-ceiling windows, with a graceful arch forming the top of each, let in much light. The third floor was divided into three small rooms and a tiny kitchen. Small square windows looked out onto the street in front and the street behind.

"If you like, you can live here. I should have thought of that sooner. The previous owner lived here with his wife."

Bridie's eyebrows raised and her mouth dropped open. "I don't understand," she stammered. "Why are you so kind to me? After what I did?"

"After what you did? What do you mean?"

"Gowen. His death. I caused that. I caused a lot of trouble for you. For everybody."

"It is my firm belief that Gowen intended to take his own life. No one could have stopped him. You did not kill him. Whatever caused the gun to go off, he intended to take his own life and he made it happen."

Bridie's eyes filled. "But I will never know for certain."

"No. You can't change it, either. You can only change how you think about it."

"Thank you for helping me."

"My father, also James, was famous for his cooking. It was only with help from some influential people who enjoyed good food that he was able to start this hotel. He did not do it alone. When he became successful, my father remembered his people. He helped build schools to provide education for freed slaves and other colored people."

Wormley moved to the front windows and opened one. The sound of horses' hooves clickety-clacking on the cobblestone street drifted in with a soft, cool breeze.

"Most folks my color have been slaves or born of slaves. Not me or my siblings." He looked directly at her.

She'd not connected the hotel owner with slaves even if his skin was the same color as theirs.

"You don't need to have dark skin to be a slave, Mrs. O'Doyle. Miners are slaves, too. So are their families. Slaves to the coal mine operators and owners. Slaves have no control of their lives. But you," he slowed his words, "you are free, now."

Bridie had no words to offer, no gestures of gratitude. She was stunned. I am Bridie O'Doyle, herbalist, she thought. With my own apartment. Her eyes traveled around the room. She'd pay a visit to Caitlyn's second-hand furniture shop. Make some curtains. She didn't hear Mr. Wormley leave.

THIRTY-TWO

Decisions

But she did hear the door jingle when it announced a customer. "Bridie," called a craggy voice.

"Mrs. Donahue," Bridie responded as she clopped down the stairs, "I thought you might be in today." The wizened old lady sought Bridie out whenever she had an ailment, but Bridie thought it was she herself who received healing from this wise, thoughtful woman.

"Mamie, I keep telling you to call me Mamie. Everyone does. How are you today, my girl?"

"I sure don't feel like a girl, Mamie. How can I help you?"

"How old are you, child? Twenty? You sound too weary for one so young, but, I must say, you do look better than the first day I saw you. More rested."

"Twenty three, no longer a child." Bridie smiled at the old woman as she led her to the rocking chair in a sunny corner. She hooked Mamie's cane over the arm of the chair.

"It's slow going, Bridie," Mamie said as she creaked into the chair. "My bones don't want to move. Compared to my seventy years, you are a child." She settled in. "What has made your young bones weary today?"

Bridie groaned as she lowered herself to sit on the floor. She felt uncomfortable standing over the woman. "I am old in my spirit,

Mamie. I've buried my parents, two husbands, and four children. I watched my uncle hang. I've seen cousins shot to death. My youth was spent on grief. I'm grieving still. That's wearisome."

Mamie took Bridie's hand into her own. "You have told me about them." She nodded. "Yes, you have." She stroked Bridie with her ancient, silk-soft, knotted fingers. "Look at me, child." Mamie tilted Bridie's chin up, forcing Bridie to look at her. "When you decide to stop reliving these losses, your grief will lessen and your youth will return." The old lady nodded again. "Yes, you have to *decide* to let go of your Tim and your children. With love in your heart, free them. They don't belong to you anymore. They belong to the world of souls. Your grief is as much for your loss of them as it is for their letting go of you."

Bridie cried for the first time since Gowen died. When she could speak, she agreed, "It is true. I have lost them but they have left me, too. I can't feel them holding on to me anymore. There is nothing of them that remains but a big emptiness. My bones don't want to move either."

Mamie sang softly:

"Oh, the days of the Kerry dancing
Oh, the ring of the piper's tune
Oh, for one of those hours of gladness
Gone, alas, like our youth, too soon!"

"That's my mother's favorite song," Bridie said, humming along.

The last of the afternoon sun set on the old woman in a rocking chair and the young woman resting her head in the other's lap.

"In time, Tim will keep you company in your memories," Mamie said. "The memory of your children will be a comfort forever."

"Loving voices of old companions
Stealing out of the past once more
And the sound of the dear old music
Soft and sweet as in days of yore."

Epilogue

FRANKLIN B. GOWEN BURIED

A VERY SIMPLE FUNERAL, ATTENDED
ONLY BY INTIMATE FRIENDS

PHILADELPHIA, Dec. 17.– The body of the late Franklin B. Gowen, the lawyer and financier, whose tragic death in Washington so startled the community, was deposited in the grave at Ivy Cemetery this morning. As requested by the family, the funeral was strictly private, only relatives, a few intimate friends of the family, and the clergyman being present.

The simple but impressive funeral service of the Protestant Episcopal Church was performed at the residence by the Rev. H. C. Hill, rector of the church at which Mr. Gowen worshiped during the later years of his life. At the conclusion of the services a dozen or more closed carriages drove up to the door and received those who were to follow the hearse to the burial grounds. None of the female members of the family accompanied the remains to the grave, where the ceremony was brief, and in a light drizzling rain the body was lowered to its final resting place.

Among the few close friends of the family at the house was

Postmaster General John Wanamaker, who came from Washington last evening to attend the funeral. Mr. Wanamaker did not accompany the cortége to the train. Mr. Wanamaker was asked as to his opinion regarding the death of Mr. Gowen.

"Well," said Mr. Wanamaker, "It's hard to say. Mr. Gowen was a great and strong man mentally and physically, and when I last saw him a short time ago there was nothing in his actions or conversation that would lead anyone to believe that he contemplated such an act. I can only account for it by supposing a momentary aberration—a something which at present is unaccountable, but which may be explained sometime."

"Then you do not believe in the assassination theory advanced by some?"

"No, no. The act was self-committed, no doubt and that is all that can be said of it at present."

The life policies held by Mr. Gowen were in the following companies: Equitable, $90,000; New-York Life Insurance, $80,000; New-York Mutual, $30,000.

— Reprinted from The New York Times.
Published December 18, 1889.
Copyright © The New York Times.

About the Author

Mickey Getty is an award-winning author, writing coach, speaker, and fine art photographer.

Mickey is the recipient of numerous awards, including the fiction award from The Pennsylvania Writers Conference for "The Birth of William," an excerpt from her novel The Junk Lottery. She graduated from Florida Atlantic University where she studied writing and health administration. She resides in southeastern Pennsylvania.

For ongoing extension and end notes visit Mickey's website at mickeygettyauthor.com.

CPSIA information can be obtained at www.ICGtesting.com
Printed in the USA
BVOW07s1833221214

380384BV00003BA/270/P